Slow

to

Speak

Mia Amalia Snowley

Library of Congress Control Number: 2019910849
Summary: A 12th grade, timid student competes in a
reality competition game that pits her against
classmates in a survival of the fittest adventure, filled
with complicated friendships and hints of romance.

ISBN: 978-1-086-16362-9

Book cover design by Ronnie Datta.

First printing edition 2019.

For my mom and Grandma Molly

Contents

What Happened Before

Let me just be straight with you. I'm a much better thinker and writer than I am an out-of-mouth blurter. I don't tell stories, but I can definitely write them. And, dang, do I ever have a story to share with y'all.

But, I gotta start at the beginning and not like when I was born beginning, but when Beholden came and all that. And in order to set you up, I have to go back to the night before, Sunday, Senior Awards Night, when I was in the car with Abuelita on our way to my high school, Oliver James High.

"What are you reading back there *mija*?"

I stuffed the comic book *Moon Girl* under my black, pencil skirt and looked straight into the rearview mirror where Abuelita's brown eyes hit mine.

"Nothing," I said quickly.

"You excited for the banquet?"

"Kind of."

"Kind of? You're about to graduate!"

"I know. Two more weeks," I muttered.

"You don't sound excited."

I shrugged and looked out the window as we passed a dilapidated Piggly Wiggly next to an equally run-down Bojangles. My stomach growled 'cause I could've gone for some chicken and biscuits right at that moment. The drive to my school was taking longer than I anticipated. Crossing town to pick up my stepdad meant enduring a bit of traffic which was unusual for my mid-sized community.

Surrounded by rolling hills and humps we liked to call mountains, Normal, Alabama boasted of two major things: a popular space and rocket center and numerous hidden caves. Now, it may not sound like much to you, but we've had many tourists who were into all that space stuff or got their kicks out of spelunking. Despite what society tells you, Alabama ain't full of just backwood hicks and country music. Some of us learned ones do pursue space and aeronautic engineering (I mean just to name a few).

But from where I live, in my small circumference of home, school and a part-time job at the daycare, I don't get to visit those places. I'm no tourist. So all I see are the parts of the city where tourists' wouldn't dare step foot 'cause I'm sure they'd think we'd shoot, rob, or kill them. None of that's true, of course, but I'm positive that's what they'd presume.

I live on the north side of town, in the rougher-looking suburbs, where it seemed a subtle invisible line had been drawn years and years before. An invisible line that said the north belonged to the broke and the south belonged to the abundant.

Walk my streets and you'll see no Estates or Country Clubs. What you'll find are a bunch of cash advance places and pawn shops that keep us owing.

Abuelita's voice pulled my eyes back to the front of the car. "You feel pressure, but you shouldn't. There's no rush to go off to college, *mija*. You're 18. You can make your own decisions—like to stay right here with me." She flashed me a smile.

I nodded, masking my uncertainty with a blank stare. I was aimless, like a fat chicken running 'round with its head cut off. And I wasn't quite sure how to say exactly what I was thinking, which was I know I can make my own decisions, but that's not all I'm worried about. There was a heavy burden on my shoulders.

And as if reading my mind, Abuelita added quietly, "And there's no rush to talk to him either."

I knew that. Didn't she think I knew that?

We pulled into the practically empty parking lot, shadowed because of the numerous broken street lights that littered our school grounds. The moon was a luminescent thumbnail that hung in the sky and even though it shone directly above us, it didn't give off much light. I looked out the window and loudly exhaled, hoping it would lessen my anxiety.

Now, I love my school and my friends, but there's just something about social gatherings that I can't stand. Going to events makes my palms sweaty, my stomach tight and my knees buckle.

I may act like I'm comfortable, but I'm really not. Crowds make me nervous, like if all eyes on me then I want to disappear and become one with the floor.

I don't want people staring at me or checking my dress or making sure my legs are shaved (because they probably ain't.) I just want to be like everybody else and blend in, say hi to a few, and then I'm cool. And please don't shout my name or call me on stage 'cause all that nonsense will give me a migraine.

"You ready, Sonora?" Abuelita had already gotten out of the car. I stepped out beside her and tugged at the fitted skirt my mama found at the thrift store last week. Abuelita smiled, probably sensing my fear. "You look beautiful, *mija*. Now, don't be nervous."

"Easy for you to say," I said and shoved a loose curl into the nape of my thick bun. "You don't have to worry about going on stage."

It was May and it already felt sultry outside. Although I was sweating, Abuelita looked like she stepped off a cruise ship. Her creamy skin looked flawless, even with all the wrinkles. Her silver hair was teased into a wispy layered 'do with the fluffy bangs and all. Her small lips had just a dab of pink to match her cheeks and she wore her favorite white dress that went down to her ankles, brushing right above her beige espadrilles. I know she knew she looked good 'cause she flipped her hair over her shoulder and struck a pose.

Y'all, my grandma was stylin'.

I shook my head and held back a laugh as Tony got out from the passenger's side and stretched his legs. The man was 6 foot 2, had a pale thin face that was flushed from the heat, and proceeded to smooth his sweeping comb-over and adjust his blandly gray tie. He hadn't said a word since we picked him up from work.

But that's my stepdad, Tony. He doesn't ever talk unless he feels he has something to say.

"It's 6:32 and we're late," he said. And that was important to Tony because he also hated being late.

As we rushed into my school and headed to the auditorium, I was impressed with the recently added graffiti on the wall and wished whoever did it would just paint the whole ugly brick building. We walked down an aisle and avoided chairs with ripped cushions. Abuelita asked me when was the last time they cleaned the carpet in here and I told her she'd get used to the moldy smell.

Oliver James High. A school that ran 700 students deep with the majority of them being black. Did we aim for diversity? Hell no. That's just the way it was. And that's just the way we accepted it, just like how we accepted that our books were ratty, our extracurriculars were inadequate, our teachers were dead-tired and our building was crumbling. We got what was given or what was leftover. And we made do.

No matter the hardships faced by my neighborhood, there were still peeps acing it on the Academic Decathlon team, athletes seemed to flourish from our streets and don't even get me started on our marching band. The musicians and dance team could throw down with the best. If I could, I'd replay you the band competition from last year. We came out on top.

Just saying.

When Tony found us some seats in the front row of the auditorium, I internally groaned. I hate sitting in the front row. I prefer sitting in the back as I did in every class. People who sit in the front are just asking to be called on, looked at, scrutinized or criticized.

"NORA!"

I stiffened at hearing someone yell my name, but relaxed as my best friend Talia Talis moved toward us. She strut into our row wearing the yellowest, tightest, tiniest dress she could probably find.

"I like your shoes," I said admiring her hot pink platforms.

"Ain't they TD?" She looked down at them and beamed.

"T what?" I asked.

"To Die, girl." She pursed her thick, glossed lips together and fluttered her long eyelashes. "What century you livin' in Nora?"

"This one."

"You sure? Cuz I think you're sleeping right through it. You need to wake up."

"Waking."

"N-E-waaaay." Talia flung her long curls behind her back.

"Your hair looks good too," I said admiringly. "How you always get your curls so defined?"

"Lots of conditioning moisturizer straight out the shower."

I nodded, knowing I'd tried that before, but still couldn't get my hair to look anything like hers.

"Where's your mom?" Talia asked as she sat down beside me and waved at Abuelita and Tony. "Hello Mrs. Ramirez, Mr. Piazza."

"Talia," Abuelita said as she leaned over with the most serious expression on her face. "Can I ask you a question?"

"Yes, ma'am?"

"How on earth did you fit into that dress?"

"Abuela!" I cried covering my mouth.

Talia burst out laughing, not at all offended, although I was horrified. My grandmother always said things I wasn't prepared for.

"I just slipped it over my head," Talia answered with a shrug. But we all know that had to be a lie. There was no slipping when it came to that dress. It must've been a tug of war and her voluptuous body won.

I moved on and answered Talia's question. "My mom had to work late and then she's got to pick up the twins from Uncle Dee's—"

"Ooo. You think you can get me some chicken this week?" she asked with bright eyes.

I did a double-take. "Whatchu mean get you some chicken? He don't make it on the fly. I gotta give him a heads up or—"

"I know you got me covered, Nora," she interrupted. "His chicken is so good and make sure you get the white sauce to go with it. Can't miss that. Now—" Talia picked up her phone. "I need to start documenting this for my platform. Did you see how many followers I got? And my updated site? I had Sleepy Tom do some smooth work on it." Talia knew how to ask for something and then move on like her request had been accepted.

"Where are your parents?" I asked.

"My mama's in the back, setting up. You know how she do."

Yea, everybody did.

Mrs. Talis was the den mother of every student at Oliver James High. Because she had no job, she made it her business to volunteer for every program or function and somehow always knew what was going on. Who was dating who? How did so-and-so get pregnant and who was the baby's daddy? It seemed school wasn't the only business she was interested in.

I was going to ask about Talia's dad, but I already knew the answer. Her daddy was working. Always. Not like my mama who worked late, but made an effort to run to whatever event I was at. Mr. Talis worked late and stayed working. I don't know why his job required so much of him.

And Talia didn't seem the least bit concerned. With eyes glued to her phone, she snapped, clicked, and swiped until the evening ceremony began which was, according to Tony, 24 minutes behind schedule. My mother arrived a few minutes later with my squirmy toddler twin brothers, Marcello and Miguel. My mother's short layered curls framed her round face and I could tell she did not have time to go home because she still wore her pink cleaning uniform.

We clapped as our Vice-Principal (VP) got up on stage and said some bland words, then introduced our Senior Class Valedictorian, Damien Green, which brought a few claps and yawns. He talked about how excited he was for graduation and about our last few weeks of school and how he'd miss blah blah blah and did he just talk about the yearbook?

I snapped to attention as he made a snide remark about his senior superlative. He said he understood why he got Most Likely to be President, but why did there need to be a Most Likely to Succeed as well? Wasn't that redundant?

I wanted to slap the microphone out his hand, that sniveling know it all. Of course, there needed to be Most Likely to Succeed. As part of the yearbook staff, I was one of many who fought for that. Those were obviously two totally different categories. What, did he think he deserved both? Knowing Damien, I'm sure he would've loved to see his name listed for every award out there. I just wish we would've made Most Arrogant superlative 'cause Damien would've taken the cake.

After he went on for a few more minutes, the VP came and told him to wrap it up, but when he didn't, she snatched the mic and summoned our Senior Class President. The room erupted in whistles as Talia stood up, went to the stage and curtsied, which brought on more hollering and whistles.

Talia smiled big, waved at the audience and kept sayin' in a high-pitched voice, "Oh no, please don't. Just stop. Stop!" and then finally began her lengthy speech about how much she'd miss us and how great a year it's been, but once she gave her shameless platform plugs of, Tantalizing Talia, the VP politely took the mic and continued with the evening.

Each of our teachers stood and the awards began. I cringed in my seat, waiting for the grenade to fall in my lap. When it didn't, I was thrilled to see I hadn't received a single award.

My mother, on the other hand, looked down at me with sad, brown eyes and mouthed, *Lo siento*—I'm sorry. I shrugged and pretended to look a little down, even though inside I was thrilled. I didn't want an award. I didn't need anything telling me how appreciated or best at this or that I was…did I?

And just when I thought the evening was over and had already planned my plea bargain to Abuelita on why we should stop for chicken and biscuits instead of stay for the dry dessert and stale appetizers, our Principal stepped out onto the stage.

A hush fell over the crowd.

Now, Principal Weathers has been at Oliver James from like, birth. He graduated from the school, went off and got his degrees and came back to be the VP and then Principal. He was so focused on his work, I heard he'd never married or had children.

And the man looked like his name. His face was weathered as if time had beat down on him, turning his brown face hard and wrinkled, forcing specks of gray from his stubbled chin and mustache. And I know they used to call him Mayne Weather-Vane 'cause back in the day when he played football, he spun round them other players like, you guessed it, a weather vane.

But we all had mad respect for Principal Weathers 'cause he loved this school and wasn't like some teachers who took one look at you and judged by appearance. Even those who were dubbed "bad" or "troublemaker" were given a second chance by Principal Weathers. So we knew if he ever showed up in our class or called us out in the hall, we were in some serious trouble.

And that's why I got real nervous. Not because I was afraid of being called out, but because I knew if Principal Weathers was on stage at our little Senior Awards Night, something was foul.

He cleared his throat and opened the top button of his shirt. He looked tense even though I think it's impossible for somebody as big as him to be nervous about anything. After mumbling congratulations to the seniors, Principal Weathers dropped an unexpected bomb.

"They're closing us down."

I heard everyone rustling and shushing each other and I just stared in shock and confusion as he looked at us with droopy, mahogany eyes. What did he mean 'they're closing us down?' Who are they and why are they doing it to us?

And as if to answer my unspoken questions, he continued, "The district has decided to shut down our school. This will be our last year."

And then the whole room exploded.

Crying, shouting, questions and no answers. Principal Weathers had to get loud and then the room got quiet again, but all he could give us were talks on finances, lack of money, lack of students and more mumbo jumbo I didn't quite get.

"Not enough attendance. Too many transfers" were his words. Attendance? Transfers?

"It's 'cause we black!" someone shouted.

"The system has failed us!"

"We need better teachers!"

Principal Weathers had to get loud again and once the storm calmed, he explained they were thinking of rebuilding the school in another location. This new information brought on more confusion. Rebuild? What was wrong with our current building? Why not remodel? Why start something new?

"Well, it's 'bout time," a woman behind me mumbled. I was so mad, I wanted to turn around and ask her where she lived so I could drop by later tonight, but my fear won over my anger.

"Let's be positive," Principal Weathers went on. "Let's look to the future for our students and for our community."

His speech ended, ensuring us that we would finish the year well and that more information would be given during the summer approaching the fall year. But we weren't stupid. This news wasn't positive, no matter how hard the district tried to spin it.

I could see Mrs. Talis' face behind the curtain as Principal Weathers walked off stage. She looked like she just heard her baby had died. Apart of me felt bad for her, because there would be no more Oliver James campus for her to strut like a mama duck, no bleachers for her to cheer on "her" dance team, no pep rally's for her to attend all painted up in the blue and gold colors.

I looked at Talia who's head was ducked down, texting on her phone. She didn't seem too upset by the whole announcement. I guess she might've figured since this was the last year we didn't need to care that much.

But none of us knew that Beholden would come the next day.

What is Beholden? I assumed you already knew. But I'll go ahead and clarify.

Beholden is a live reality TV series where contestants compete in phases for one week. But these aren't normal contestants that go through interviews to be on TV. These are regular high school students that have no idea when Beholden is showing up because the game travels from state to state. And honestly, its probably the reason why most theaters are vacant these days. Why would people want to go to movies to watch actors pretend to fall off a cliff or run from a bear or fall in love or be overexposed to constant CGI when they can watch actual friends and classmates do the exact same thing (sans the overexposed CGI)?

You see, the thing about Beholden isn't that it's just a high-octane joyride, it's that you get to watch contestants walk through every one of your favorite television shows. I mean, really walkthrough. One year there was a murder, a car chase, and a drug bust all in one phase and real people (that you may even know) are the star, hero or villain.

I liked the show. I mean, I'd much rather read a good book or comic any day, but if the show had something supernatural in it, I'd tune in. I was always impressed by the outrageous costumes, like one year they reenacted the story of Frankenstein and had the monster with the lightning and everything. The dude who played the monster must've been a basketball player because he was a giant. Homeboy towered over every person in the game and the contestants were truly scared. He even made some blonde 9th grader wet her pants.

Abuelita, however, was cautious about Beholden. She said whoever ended up winning had to lose themselves to get there. Most folks hurt, lied and cheated in order to be the winner of all that money. So, I suppose Abuelita was right about that. Although my grandmother didn't have much schooling, she did have good sense, the type of sense that always knew what people's true intentions were. Like the time my mom met Tony.

Since my mama got pregnant at 16 (and my daddy had vanished), Abuelita stepped in to raise me while my mama finished school and worked odd jobs. But my abuela was no daddy, so my mother went on a hunt for a good one. She brought in all sorts of characters and Abuelita always knew which were decent and which weren't. She had a particular dislike of this guy named Terence which I am grateful to this day for—just typing that man's name makes my stomach clench into a thousand iron knots.

After many duds came and went, my mom met Antony Piazza, a quiet Italian who worked at Lowe's. I was in Mexico that summer with Abuelita and my mom was trying to surprise me with a room makeover by doing some DIY projects before I returned. (And my mother is not DIY so the effort was sweet but didn't turn out at all like the blog she read.) Tony was the one who helped her find the paint thinner.

After we returned, we were surprised my mom had been dating him the whole summer and when she invited him for dinner that evening, I didn't think much of him. With such a serious face and short answers, I didn't know what she could possibly see in the man. Even though he had a nice smell and helped with the dishes, I thought he was kind of boring. But Abuelita liked him.

"And he's got a job," my mother added cheerfully. That was enough for my mama.

Abuelita said, "He's a keeper." And winked at me. "Your mother chose well."

"How do you know?" I asked.

"You can't judge a book by its cover, *mija*," she said. "Trust me. That man is like an iceberg, doesn't look like much on top, but it's what's below the surface that's impressive."

And I don't know how she knew, but she was right. He was a keeper. Not only did Tony marry my mother in the end, but he turned out to be a pretty cool stepdad. Although he didn't smile very much, whenever he did flash one your way, it made your heart melt and feel as if you were sharing a marvelous secret.

He created Pancake Saturdays, was great at housework (which was good because my mother wasn't) and evened out my mother's erratic tendencies. Abuelita says when my mom's hot, he's cold and when they came together it made the warmest, most comfortable atmosphere. We were all thrilled when my mother became pregnant with Marcello and Miguel and I was pretty pumped to be a big sister.

But I'm way off track here, so back to Senior Awards night.

The news our school was closing made the appetizers sour and it was easy to skip out, but for some reason, I no longer wanted chicken and biscuits. I just wanted to get home. Talia, however, had other plans for me and asked my mama if I could sleepover at her house.

I looked at my mother and she firmly shook her head no. It was a school night, she said and I probably had to study for finals. Even though those were the words that she spoke, I could tell there was more behind her eyes. My mom and I had had a big talk ever since 10th grade Spring break. Me + Talia = Lots of Mistakes. After that, my mom made me promise to give our friendship space.

She was scared and I get why. She was afraid Talia had a big influence over me. And she was probably right. I did want to be like her. That's why I didn't argue when in fifth grade, Talia grabbed my hand on the playground and declared we were best friends. Since she moved to our neighborhood, Talia became the girl everyone wanted to be friends with, especially me.

She was like fireworks on the Fourth of July or the Christmas tree in Rockefeller Center. And you know what? I think I wanted to be the Christmas tree in Rockefeller Center. Maybe that's why I joined Beholden.

Look at me, going all deep.

But as Abuelita told me, a little bit of Talia in your life is good for you, but too much of her can turn you into a hurricane. I'm 100% sure that's why Abuelita took me to Mexico the past two summers. But that didn't kill our friendship. I've made an effort to keep our bond strong.

But I sensed a shift between us. One that I was unwilling to admit.

The Day Of

Beholden came to Normal, Alabama the very next day. But where was I? Walking to school because I didn't have a car. Abuelita went to work that day and yea, she's 73 years old and still mans the cash register at a lil' grocery store. So when you see an elderly Mexican lady scanning your produce, you best be nice.

I don't live far from the school, so I just popped in my earbuds and walked the couple blocks over. I used to get a ride from Talia, but I didn't mind walking, especially on nice days like that one. The morning air was cool before the heat settled in. Sky was baby blue and clouds looked like whipped marshmallow creme.

My mama hated leaving the windows open because her allergies always acted up around this time of the year, but not me. I loved the spring, the white and yellow dandelions that popped up on our small patch of lawn outside the apartment, the crisp smell of cut grass, the long days and the way you could tell when it was about to rain just by sniffing the air. I remembered one time I opened my window and watched it rain across the street for a few seconds before it hit me.

Nature so crazy.

Right at that moment, I was bobbing my head to a new artist Abuelita had introduced me to. I'm kind of an old soul, spent most of my childhood listening to my abuela's radio (and yea, she still had one of those big, gray boomboxes.) Recently I'd gotten hooked on everything by the Jackson Five, but today I was listening to a singer called Selena Quintanilla (who Abuelita highly recommended.) I was bobbing my head and swinging my hips to "Baila Esta Cumbia." I woulda' broke out and did the salsa in the middle of the street if I hadn't tripped over the Davidson's spilled garbage can. Knowing my surroundings, I prepared to be barked at by Roscoe, Ms. Childress' mangy mutt who sometimes chased you if he felt like it. But today he was distracted.

Barking feverishly, I halted to see a figure in a suit hop down the front steps of Ms. Childress' porch. The man was slipping on a shoe with one hand and trying to buckle his pants with the other.

Immediately I thought two things: whoever was coming out of Ms. Childress house this early in the morning was up to no good and I should turn away and mind my own business. But my curiosity was like a magnet and I zeroed in on the face of the escapee and wondered if this was the father of all Ms. Childress' children. She was currently well along in another pregnancy and had two other fatherless babes, both whom she stuck at the daycare I worked at. I often wondered what she did all day as she currently had no job and was always using it as an excuse for late payments. Ironically, she dressed like she had money, wearing expensive heels so tall I thought she'd fall over, big glasses so dark I could never see her true expression and clothes so tight you thought she'd bust out the seams if she took another breath.

I walked a bit closer to try to get a look at who I assumed was the provider of those expensive shoes. Roscoe jumped and snarled, his chain held tight as the man slipped past him and clicked the alarm off his car. My heart sank as I recognized the vehicle. A Lexus Talia had driven me around in many times.

"Mr. Talis?" I asked stupidly. I wanted to slap myself for not thinking before blurting.

Startled, he made the mistake of looking over, confirming my suspicion and creating the tensest moment that started my day.

"Uh—uh—good morning Sonora," he said. "I, uh, had a quick meeting this morning with Ms. Childress and I'm running late, so—"

He didn't even bother finishing his sentence as he got in and slammed the door, then pulled out of her driveway and sped down the road. My mind was an uncomfortable mess as I began to process what I had just seen. Forget it, Sonora, I told myself. Act like it never happened.

Losing myself again in the music, I continued my walk all the while avoiding eye contact with a group of freshmen boys across the street. They always tried to talk to me because they thought they had game. One of them in particular, Jerome, never quit. I took a deep breath of preparation as he ran up beside me. And just when I decided to be cordial this morning, that boy had the nerve to put his fingers on my hair.

"Don't touch," I said as I jerked my head and made sure my braided crown was still in place. Took me all morning to get it just right.

His mouth was moving, but I wasn't hearing. I guess I hoped he'd get the idea I wanted to be left alone, but he just kept staring at me so I pulled out my earbuds just as some lyrics about bidi and bom bom came on and asked in my most aggravated voice, "What?"

"Your hair feels soft," he said purposefully brushing his arm against mine. "When you get your hair done?"

I rolled my eyes.

"How long it take to do your hair?" he asked.

"How long does it take to do your hair?" I shot back.

"Dang, it's just a question," he smiled and tried to grab my hand. I quickly pulled away. "It probably takes all day, don't it? My sister stay at the salon on Saturdays and her hair don't look nothing like yours."

I sighed.

"Did you have Kiera's mom braid your hair?" a breathless voice said from behind.

Shanice Wilson walked briskly beside me and tried to fall in line with my steps. All I could think was *Oh Lord, here we go.*

"Don't go to her," she said in her I-know-everything voice. "Her mama still uses relaxers." I rolled my eyes inwardly because Shanice talked way too much. If she wasn't careful, her mouth would get her a beat down. I was surprised she had made it through her whole freshman year without a single fight.

But the year wasn't over yet.

She looked at me. "I can tell you don't get relaxers, though Nora. Your hair ain't that straight. I can give you some tips on how to keep them naps under control."

"I'm good," I said.

"Do you co-wash?" she continued. "You need to co-wash because I can see your ends look dry and your curls look frizzy. A deep moisturizer is what you need."

"Don't listen to her, Nora," Jerome cooed from the other side of me and tried to stroke my hair again. "You look good."

I slapped his hand. "Boy, quit!"

"Dang, them some reflexes!" he yelled shaking out his hand.

"My mama says relaxing your hair is going to make you go bald," Shanice said matter-of-factly. "She said, be black and be proud and embrace the way God made you. Look at me…" she said pulling one of her many thick coils. "I'm all na-choo-ral, baby."

"Mhmm," I murmured and stuck one earbud back in so I could still be apart of the conversation, yet look like I wasn't listening. Unfortunately not much was said. Those two just argued about what was the right way for a black girl to do her hair and all I could think was, who cares?

I know this doesn't have anything to do with anything, but just to paint you a picture, I don't have Abuelita's light skin or Talia's honey tone. You see I'm the color of copper and my hair is thick and curly. My mama has never taken me to a salon (too expensive) and she's never put a relaxer in my hair (no chemicals), but as soon as I'm allowed to ('cuz my mama is strict), I want to dye, straighten, relax, braid and weave it up and do you know why? Because it's my hair, ain't it? Can't I do what I want with it? Nobody else has to spend hours breaking combs trying to tame my tresses or be forced to stay home 'cause I'm at war with my hair and don't feel like bein' judged that day. All that to say, I really wanted to yell at Shanice and ask her and her mama what happened to black women having the freedom to do what they wanted with their hair and body? But instead, I was silent and tolerated Jerome's pestering.

"Is that a Spanish shirt, Nora? You get it from Mexico?" Jerome went on fingering my sleeve. "Is it your grandma's?"

I looked down at the black peasant top, embroidered with bright colored stitching. "No. I got it at Goodwill," I said.

"The blue and red look good with your chocolate skin."

Shanice gasped. "Boy, don't call her chocolate! She ain't your candy bar."

I pulled self-consciously at the shirt. "Did y'all hear about the school?" I asked, wanting to change the subject.

"What about it?" Jerome shrugged.

"Yea, I heard," Shanice answered. "They shutting us down."

"Yo, for real?" Jerome grabbed the straps of his backpack and bounced as he walked. "We get to pick the next school we going to?"

I looked at him. "You don't care that they shutting us down?"

"I don't," Shanice said. "I finally get to transfer."

"You want to leave?" I asked in shock.

"Girl, look around!" Shanice waved her hand around the block. "Don't nobody want to live over here! And don't nobody want to go to this crumbly-old-jacked-up school. Speaking of jacked-up, I'm surprised we hadn't run into Lil' P, yet."

As frustrated as I was, I understood where Shanice was coming from. Lil' P was the neighborhood supplier of all and everything you needed to get baked. I knew our neighborhood had taken a dive and folks were leaving the hood in droves.

They said it was getting too dangerous, but didn't we all know each other? I mean, Abuelita used to have Lil' P over for sweet tea and buñuelos on hot summer days after he mowed the neighbors' lawn. When did he decide to start selling and robbing houses?

And I still didn't get why people thought moving the school would help any of that. Wasn't that type of stuff everywhere? That just solved the outward problem, but not the inward. Deep in thought, I looked down at the loose strands on my imitation leather sandals and moved my feet faster so I could hurry up and get to homeroom.

At school, the hallways were crowded and everything was buzzing with excitement like it was a pep rally day. But I didn't think anything of it. I stopped at my locker, said hello to Theo Montgomery and Chloe Banks who were always smooching, then walked into my homeroom right as the bell rang. As soon as I sat down I felt a tap on my shoulder.

"Hey, Nora," said a tenor voice.

"Hey, Taj," I said trying to hide my smile. I didn't want to turn around, as it would draw attention to myself and him.

But it wasn't long before Talia burst into the room and yelled my name.

"NORA!"

"Miss Talis, you're late," said Ms. Rogers, my homeroom teacher who proudly sported her midsize afro. She put her hand on her hip.

"Not now, Ms. Rogers," Talia said flinging her long curls into a messy bun that plopped right on top of her round head.

"You must be crazy," I said quietly with my eyes glued to Ms. Rogers' glaring face.

"Miss Talis!" the teacher's voice boomed. "Your outfit is not in accordance with the school dress code and I have told you many times before I am not your friend and you will not talk to me like one. You think just 'cause you're graduating you can run your mouth? You're going straight to the principal's office young lady."

Talia held out her hand as if waiting for something and continued talking to me, her face contorted in excitement. "Nora, it's here!" she blurted.

"What is?" I said as I watched Ms. Rogers angrily scribble across a pad on her desk.

"Beholden!" she said in a low voice. "And I'm going to win," she squealed.

Now, at the time, I was more concerned about Ms. Rogers and her vengeance. Talia had been the thorn in her side all year. Constantly late, always talking back and never seemed to get any repercussions from the Vice-Principal. And this year had been rough for Ms. Rogers. She missed half the first semester because some relative died and when she came back she was meaner and would go off on you if you even looked at her the wrong way. Almost every student had been written up by the end of the year (and thank God I'd missed that bus.) Right now, she looked like she was ready to blow up at the whole world.

Out of the side of my mouth, I said, "You're getting written up again."

"Do I look like I care?" Talia answered. And why would she? This girl never got kicked off dance team or sent to In-School-Suspension no matter how short her skirts were or how high that crop top was. She wore a tie-dye one now under her black overalls.

Ms. Rogers walked over and slapped the slip of paper in Talia's extended hand.

"Thank ya!" Talia said without even looking at Ms. Rogers. "I'll see you in five minutes, Nora," she said with a wink and with her butt switching back and forth, walked out the door. I heard low murmurs of approval from most of the males in the room. I was sure all those eyes were on her rear as she sashayed out. Talia always welcomed the attention, even if she was making an exit.

I shook my head as I pulled a comic book out of my backpack. This was my way of subtracting myself from the situation. My escape from school until the first bell rang, that is.

"What are you reading?" Taj whispered from behind me as Ms. Rogers took attendance. I flinched. Not because I was annoyed, but because I was caught off guard. Taj Williams barely spoke to me in school. In church was another thing, but school had been unknown and very public territory.

"Uh, Spider-Man, the one with Miles Morales," I whispered back and instantly wondered why my hands were so sweaty and my armpits itched.

"You into comics?"

I shrugged, knowing good and well I loved comics to death but wasn't so sure what he thought about them.

"That's cool," Taj said. And I let out a huge sigh of relief.

"You like to read comics?" I asked eagerly, still not daring to turn around.

"Nah, not really."

I sucked in a quick breath. Too fast, Nora. Slow down, he doesn't have to like everything you do. But, I felt myself getting flustered. Taj Williams, the preacher's son, seemed to constantly stifle my words. I felt unsure around him and always cautious of what I said, probably because that boy was so confident it threw me off. Did he think reading comics was a sin? If so, he would've told me. He was blunt about his opinions and never shied from his beliefs. I liked that about him. But I also found it intimidating.

The bell rang for first period and I glanced at him nervously without allowing him to see me do it. Even if he occasionally unnerved me, no one could deny how cute Taj was. He had that boyish baby face, short wavy fade, and always dressed like his clothes were brand new. When he transferred to our school at the end of last year, girls were all on him like bees to honey. They couldn't resist those long eyelashes, those deep dimples, that cocoa skin.

"Hey, Taj!" A girl named Mercedes hooked her arm with his, making sure her substantial chest pressed up against his bicep. "Walk me to class?" And before he could answer, she dragged him out the door. Having no choice, I followed them out because we all were in the same next period.

I wasn't surprised to see Talia in our usual spot in the back row. She waved to me and as I headed back, I noticed our English teacher, Mr. Davis, was not in the room.

"Think we got a sub today?" I asked.

"No, I saw his nervous self in the office," Talia said. "Lots of teachers in there today."

"Lots of teachers?" I asked dropping my backpack on the floor next to my chair. "What for?"

"I told you. Beholden."

I rolled my eyes and plopped down in my seat. "Talia, why would Beholden come to Normal, Alabama? Nothing ever happens here, 'cept tornadoes."

She shrugged and stared at her phone. My encounter that morning with her father flashed through my mind. I didn't want to think about it. Instead, my eyes roamed our classroom, jammed with too many desks in too tiny of a room, popcorn ceiling looked like it was about to cave in, and faded khaki walls hadn't been painted in I don't know how long. Well, with all the names written on it saying so-and-so was here followed by the date, I guess I could do that math and figure out when the last paint job was. But Math is not my forte, so don't even ask.

When Talia finally tore her eyes away from her phone, she glanced down and used her pink platform to lift up my foot.

"Where you get those sandals?"

"My mama bought them at the thrift store on Pulaski."

"You need to stop letting your mama do your shopping. You see my new purse?"

I looked down as she used her other pink shoe to nudge a checkerboard-looking handbag.

"Gabrielle Union had the exact one," she said smiling proudly. "And J. Lo, my idol!" I lifted my eyebrows and tried to seem impressed.

I was reminded of our polar opposites again. Although we had been inseparable since fifth grade, I could see the strands beginning to loosen in our friendship like my gently-used sandals. We were so close, people assumed we were sisters even though I didn't think we looked anything alike. Talia was half black and half Samoan, and yet she looked more like my Mexican mama than I ever did. Everything about me must've come from my father's side.

I stiffened when Omri Jones bounced in. A goofball I'd known since the third grade who's A.D.D. made him impossible to be around. He jumped on Taj's back and wildly waved in my direction. I wanted to slink down in my chair.

"I can't believe you used to like him," Talia said still looking at her phone. "That boy has no brain."

"Sh!" I tried to hide my smile. "Somebody's gonna hear you."

"I mean look at him!" She put her phone down and stared across the room. I watched Omri shake and wiggle his rear around a desk. His dreads were high up in a ponytail and flopped around his ears. He then began to flex his biceps which forced me to look the other way. When had he gotten so built? I didn't remember him looking like that at the beginning of the year.

"Oh no," Talia hissed. "Here he comes!"

I heard chairs being pushed aside and then, "Sup, Nora…Talia."

"Hi, Omri," we said in unison. I looked up at him and he stared back at me and casually stroked the fuzz on his chin.

"What you girls over here whispering 'bout?" he asked.

"Nothing," I said quickly and looked away.

"You," Talia said and I shot her a hard look.

"Me?" Omri said and laughed excitedly, his white teeth shone in contrast to his dark complexion. "You talking 'bout how good I look, right? I've been working on my arms getting ready for the summer." He flexed again and I couldn't help but laugh at his loud outfit. Boy had on a black t-shirt with some rolled-up neon red pants, yellow socks, and army green Nikes. I forgot how proud Omri was last year when he found out his late mama was related to somebody in Ghana.

"It wasn't about that," Talia said.

"About my hair?" he asked tugging on his dreads. "Been trying to grow my locs out."

"Nope," Talia said. "But you need to cut that stuff off 'cause it's startin' to look dirty."

"Y'all checkin' out my butt? Or something else?" Ignoring Talia, Omri hopped up on a desk and started pelvic thrusting the air. I covered my eyes and shook my head. Sometimes just when I thought Omri was tolerable—he wasn't.

"Omri, sit your bony ass down!"

I recognized the brash voice of Lashonda Washington. She walked in and threw her bag across the room so it landed right next to me.

"Watch out!" Talia hissed. "She might have some cockroaches crawling out that thing!"

I shushed Talia as Lashonda sat on top of a desk close to ours. She was not the sort of girl you talked smack about. And she dressed just like her personality: girlishly gritty. Today she wore a sweatshirt with the words Strong. Black. Women. printed on the front, fishnet stockings and booty shorts. She shook her head as Omri kept dancing, then got up on her own desk with dirty combat boots, swung her long braids over her shoulder and started to gyrate too. Her big, hooped earrings slapped her cheeks as she shouted, "Naw, boy—you do it like this!" Lashonda dipped and popped like she was up in the stands with the rest of the dance team. I still didn't understand why she wasn't captain.

Well, that's not true. I knew why. Because Talia was captain and everybody knew Talia got what she wanted.

The room broke out in a loud uproar as the two of them danced side by side on the desks and soon Cordell Brown, our version of the young Biggie Smalls, struck up a beat. The room was whirling like a merry-go-round and I felt a bit out of place, like a silent observer that stands apart from the ride. Too timid to jump in, but feeling just as much a participant of the fun because of simply being there. But Damien Green, all too willing to fulfill his role as class valedictorian, shut down the ride as soon as he clapped his hands.

"Attention!" he yelled so loud his glasses slid down the bridge of his nose. "Hey!"

The room grew silent and Damien continued with his hands in the air. "Where is Mr. Davis?"

"Who cares!" someone yelled.

"I care!" Damien said. "I have a G.P.A. to maintain and I don't want his absence to reflect on my education! Come on people!" He clapped his hands again. "Y'all may be happy to attend the local college, but some of us are striving for Harvard or Yale! So, one of you needs to go down to the office and report that Mr. Davis is missing."

"Why don't you do it?" Omri said as he hopped down.

"Fine," Damien said as he tugged on his forest green polo shirt. "I will." He walked over to the door and turned the knob. The room began to bristle with voices again, but I watched as Damien continued to tug and tug at the door and the more he yanked, the more uneasy I became.

When I heard Taj ask Damien what was wrong, I got up, stepped through the crowded seats and approached just in time to hear Damien exclaim, "It's locked!" Both his hands were on the knob and his eyes were wide as he peered at us through his rectangular bifocals.

"Somebody locked us in!" he shouted.

A hush gradually fell over the room.

Then everyone erupted in chaos.

Startline

"Whatchu mean the door's locked?!"

"Get outta my way!"

"Yo, don't be playin' Damien," Omri said from behind me.

Bodies smashed against my back as folks desperately tried to open the door. I was shoved to the side while folks screamed and pounded against our only exit.

"Who locked it?"

"I'm getting the hell outta here!"

The noisy choir of voices rose like a pot of oatmeal on the stove, bubbling over and scalding the surface. My classmates elbowed each other, but there was nowhere else to go. No matter how hard they pulled, the door wouldn't open and as Dania Ford burst into tears, Lashonda yelled at her to shut up and soon a fight broke out between the two.

Thankfully it was only shoving and no hair pulling. Over the noise, I could barely hear anything else, but Taj stood up on a chair and yelled, "Everybody quiet!"

Cordell, like a giant bear, bristled at the command. "Who you think you talking to, new boy?" he asked in a gruff, deep voice. At his side, swung his large fists' balled up tight like sledgehammers and his chest puffed out like a gorilla ready for battle.

"Just hear me out," Taj said lowering his voice. "Something's going on with the intercom." He pointed to the old wooden box above the chalkboard. And as we listened there was a sort of static that gradually grew louder. The crackling cleared up and transformed to music that sounded like it came from a record player. The tune was low and mournful, rippling up and down. While a few of us stared at the intercom waiting for something to happen, the rest of the class was already on their phones.

"I just text my mama," Lashonda said.

"What did she say?" I asked not bothering to get my own phone out. My mother kept hers on silent during work, Tony would've been pissed if I was using my phone during school and Abuelita didn't have text messaging. Hell, she still didn't even get email.

"She ain't answering," Lashonda responded.

"What about you, Talia?" I asked.

Her eyes scanned her phone as a smile stretched across her face.

"What?" I asked hoping that grin meant something.

"I told you what this was, but you wouldn't listen."

"You still think its Beholden?" I scoffed.

"Ain't that what I said?"

"It can't be."

"It is!" Talia said shoving her screen in our faces. All I saw was a blurry picture. "Look. It says a caravan of blue trucks were spotted in town. That means they're here."

"I don't want to be on Beholden," Chloe Smith whined as she grabbed one of her long Senegalese twists and wrapped it around her finger. Chloe S. had been prom queen that year and I knew exactly why she didn't want to be on Beholden. Homegirl was dainty as a rose and sensitive as a baby. One time in 6th grade I accidentally bumped her in the hallway and she claimed I was a bully. Said I'd always ignored her in class and refused to sit by her at lunch.

When the counselor forced us to come into his office and settle the dispute I told her I never talked to anybody and I always sat with the same people at lunch, it was nothing against her. Talia thought the girl was crazy and actually told people that she was seeing a therapist. (Although I do believe Talia was jealous Chloe S. had won prom queen over her and so the rumor was started out of spite and not out of my benefit.)

"Are you stupid?" Talia looked at Chloe S. like she had just claimed she was the smartest woman on the planet. "You'll win $250,000!"

"Sh!" Omri hissed. "Everybody shut up and listen." The music had gotten louder and I recognized the song. An oldie my grandmother listened to. "The Great Pretender" by The Platters. But then the familiar tune skipped and the static returned to loud crackling. I clapped my hands over my ears until the noise abruptly ceased. A smooth voice, deep with a rhythmic resonance to it, belted out these words:

Beholden is here. Stand back. Be amazed!
Get in a tizzy, get pumped, get crazed
then do me a favor and just survey
As your friends rush past you down the hallway
You go to the right, they go to the gym
You make your exit, while they lookin' grim
Because to play, they first gotta sign
The paper on teach's desk, right on the dotted line
Now take the keys in the drawer and prepare to be dazed,
Beholden is here. Stand back. Be amazed!

If you've ever seen a classroom full of students scramble for one item, then you shouldn't be surprised at how quickly things escalated. I watched as folks fought to get to the desk, but Lashonda made her way there first. She pulled out a thick manilla folder and grabbed a pen. "Where do I sign?" she asked.

"On the dotted line," Talia said sarcastically.

"What do you think you're doing?" Damien asked as Chloe S. snatched the key.

"I'm leaving. I'm not playing this stupid game," she said heading for the door.

"If you leave before we sign the papers we'll be disqualified." He grabbed her shoulder.

"You better get your hands off me," she said eyeing his fingers as if her glare alone would snap them in two.

He removed his hand but still insisted, "We have to sign the papers first, then you can open the door."

"No, he never said anything about rules," Chloe S. said putting the key in the lock.

"I've seen other seasons where they were disqualified!" Damien shouted.

But Chloe S. already had the door open and walked out.

"Are y'all going too?" Damien asked as a few other people trailed behind her.

"I've read forums about this game," said Leticia Hayworth who was on the drumline. "People get hurt when they play. I'm not about to put my body on the line for $250,000."

"Girl, I'll step on some hot coals for $250,000!" Lashonda yelled gleefully and passed the pen around.

"Then step on some hot coals then!" Leticia shot back. "I'll see y'all if you make it through." She walked out of the room. After most of the girls and a few boys had left, I counted 15 still hanging on. The only girls that stayed behind were Chloe Banks (Chloe B.), Su-Min Johnson, Lashonda, Talia and me. The boys outnumbered us.

It was my turn to sign the paper and I was hesitant. But who could pass up an opportunity to win $250,000? I looked at Talia and Lashonda who chattered excitedly.

This was my chance to step out of my box and finally be something. And, after another nagging thought occurred to me, I knew this was an opportunity to put off some things I wasn't quite ready to think about. I looked at the contract and saw only a short paragraph.

"What's that supposed to mean?" I asked out loud after skimming it.

"That they can pretty much do anything, but kill you," Taj said.

"Oh," I said feeling a bit queasy. Was I the only one that felt like this might be a bad idea? The rest of the room was buzzing with voices and people were still waiting behind me to sign the form. Abuelita's warning words flew through my mind, but I brushed them away. There couldn't be anything shady about this. If my school had agreed to do it, then it must be okay, right? If anything, I'd get to be on TV. Maybe even famous.

I signed my name.

After everyone had finished, Damien yelled, "Okay! Let's get going!" with a look of authority and walked out the door.

"He said head to the gym," Lashonda said and ran so she was in front of him.

The hallway was filled with a sea of brown faces rushing alongside me. Following the crowd, we calmly made our way to the gym. I was surprised to see so many people had decided to stay and shocked students weren't running wild.

As we stood waiting, I observed there was a mix of grades from freshman to seniors and most of us stayed within our classes. I saw Jerome wave at me from across the gym on the bleachers and I gave him a half-wave back. Again, the intercom blasted The Platters' "The Great Pretender," then it softly faded and the voice from before began to belt out another melodic rhyme:

I could care less if you win or you lose
We got to thin the herd, get rid of the refuse
So you find a blue card
beat your friends by a yard
Heed my advice
And don't you dare think twice
They're hidden all over, listen to the clues
Some around the world,
Some evolved and curled,
Where greasy lunch is made
and music is played
Be quick to take one, then exit for your cruise
I could care less if you win or you lose

Before the speaker even finished, students ran out of the gym. My heart raced because I knew I had little time and wouldn't be able to compete with those who had stayed to search the bleachers, so I decided to run to the furthest place I could get to. Maybe I'd be the first one there.

Running through the halls I thought about the rhyme. This was it. I was actually playing Beholden. Would I find a clue? Would I make it to the next phase? I headed to the cafeteria but was annoyed to see a lot of people had the same idea. The lunchroom was more crowded than I liked. I brushed past others looking under tables on their hands and knees, ignored the squeals of excitement from some who found the prize and kept right on looking. Just as I saw something bright blue flapping beneath the salad bar, a girl snatched it before I could. At least I knew what it looked like.

"What's around the world supposed to mean?" I heard someone ask. Getting an idea, I retreated from the crowded cafeteria and made my way to the nearest History room. Thankfully, it was empty and I went straight to the chalkboard, pulled down a map and watched a blue envelope flutter down to the floor.

I scooped it up and heard someone behind me scream, "She found one!"

A throng of people crowded around me.

"Where did you find it?"

"What does it look like?"

"Let me see it!" A hand yanked the paper, but I clung to it tight and wedged my way through.

"Nora!" I heard Talia's shriek down the hall. She ran to me and looked with wide eyes at my hands. "You found one?"

I nodded and couldn't help but grin. "Yep."

"Where did you get it?"

"I found it in the maps."

"The maps?" She scratched her head.

"Yea, you know how he said, you can find some around the world."

"Oh!" Talia clapped her hands. "Thanks!" She took off down the hallway and I stood there staring at the mysterious envelope, noting the strange barcode at one end.

But I knew I was being watched and it made me nervous. I walked quickly to my locker hearing whispers from a group down the hall. While I pretended to search, I stuck the blue envelope inside my locker and carefully opened it.

But there was nothing inside. Frustrated, I tried to remember what the voice said. Then exit for your cruise. I slammed my locker shut and walked briskly to the nearest exit with the blue envelope in hand.

Walking up to the doors, I pushed but bounced right back. They didn't budge. I walked to the next set of doors and pushed, but they were locked as well. People looked at me curiously as they goofed off in the hallway, chasing one another or still looking and finding nothing.

"Whatchu doing?" someone hollered as I pushed the last set of doors that lead to the staff parking lot. "Them doors are locked!"

But I heard a click as the door swung freely open. The sun was bright compared to the dim hall lights and I walked out into the muggy air, hearing the door slam shut behind me. Pounding made me jump as I looked back to see faces pressed against the rectangular glass window. I lifted my hands in an innocent shrug, then walked down the steps happily because I had gotten to the next phase.

There, in the middle of the empty parking lot, stood a large blue charter bus. The words BEHOLDEN were printed across in bright gold letters. I saw some students had already gotten on. Walking up to the bus, I wondered where all the teachers were because there were no cars parked in the area. Did Beholden remove every single one just for this game? It made me wonder how far Beholden would go and what other tricks they had prepared for this season's show. If Beholden was good at one thing, it was toying with the minds' of the poor contestants like rats in a maze. Once on the bus, I was relieved to see some familiar faces. Damien stood at the front with his arms folded and a frown smeared across his face.

"Huh," he said eyeing me. "Surprised you're here alone. Usually, you and Talia are attached at the hip. Find a seat."

I laughed. "Are you in charge now?" I asked.

"Until somebody else wants to be."

I rolled my eyes and found an empty seat toward the back and waited with the rest. Damien's arrogance was sometimes infuriating, but in other situations, it was down-right humorous. I was just grateful I knew somebody else from my class was competing. It would make the game more interesting. As more people filed out of the school, I began to get a bit nervous. I'd made it to the first phase but wondered what would happen next. The people on my bus were my new competitors, but they were also my classmates, most I had grown up with from elementary days. And where was Talia? I wished she were in this with me. We'd make an amazing team.

I anxiously stared at the school doors. My eyes felt like lasers burning into the exit as I awaited the next contestant to depart. When Taj emerged my heart did a flip flop and squee, conflicted between excitement and worry. Taj Williams was going to be on Beholden? With me? How on earth would I react with him around? How could I compete with those brown eyes staring at me or that dimpled grin, smiling at me? My eyes glazed over as the next faces sprung out. All I could think was I had to race against Taj, the boy who sent my heart a-pounding and my mind a-numbing. And then I beamed and let out a sigh of relief when I saw Talia finally run out. And of course, she had to do a cartwheel toward the bus. When she got on she ran to sit next to me and we hugged. I was happier than ever to see my friend.

"Where's the driver?" Damien snapped. "How're we supposed to go anywhere?"

"Will you sit down and shut up?" Lashonda yelled three rows in front of me.

"So, this is my competition," Omri said as he waltzed down the aisle and looked all of us over. I couldn't believe he'd found a blue card. I was sure he'd gotten distracted by something bright and pretty halfway through the search. "Not bad…not bad," he said. "I bet I'll beat all y'all and win that money."

Lashonda turned around in her seat and pushed her braids over her shoulders. "How your stupid self find a card?" she yelled, reading my thoughts.

"You know," Brandon Heath, our prized quarterback said. "I'm surprised they trusted us not to drive off in the bus. The keys are still in the ignition."

I hadn't noticed that and as my classmates softly began to murmur, I don't think many others had either.

"So?" Damien said. "The driver must've gone out to use the bathroom or something."

Theo Montgomery spoke up and his light brown eyes peered around the bus. "I didn't see any grown folk in the school...where all the teachers at?" He suddenly stood up and started to shove his way to the door. "I changed my mind. I wanna get off!" And just as he pushed past Damien who still stood in the middle of the aisle, I saw a mist flowing through one of the air vents.

"Smoke!" I shouted and people began to scream.

"Are we on fire?"

"We all gonna die!"

People shoved their way to the front of the bus, and I joined them but realized my motions grew slower, my urgency lessened and I thought I heard someone say they felt high. And I had to agree. I hadn't ever gotten high before, but I felt my body relax, my head dizzy and suddenly I was overcome with exhaustion. Without even making it back to my seat, I slumped down on somebody's legs in the middle of the aisle and closed my eyes.

Personalities Emerge

I awoke to Talia shaking my shoulders and staring down at me.

"Nora's awake!" she called and then smiled. "We made it girl!" she squealed. "We've started Beholden!"

I groggily sat up. Someone had dragged me into a seat on the bus. Confused, I looked out the window and wondered if I was in a strange dream.

Our school parking lot was gone. In fact, our entire school had vanished and we were in the middle of what looked like the backwoods of 'Bama. Outside some of my classmates sat in lawn chairs while others unzipped duffel bags. There were piles of tubs, large coolers, and I noticed a picture of a tent on one of the long, bulky orange bags. But the piles were organized as if someone had dumped the contents of a huge storage unit and separated it into four heaps.

"Where are we?" I asked wiping the corners of my mouth. I felt like I had slept with it wide open. Oh, I'm sure the folks back home would be laughing at my Beholden-induced nap. I always hated when Abuelita took photos of me sleeping and now it was televised for everybody to see. Paranoid, I squinted at the ceiling corners of the bus. Where had they put them tiny hidden cameras?

"We don't know where we are!" Talia said with too much enthusiasm. "Isn't it great? They must've driven us here and when we woke up—"

"I was the first one awake," Damien informed me as he leaned over the back of the seat in front of mine.

"Anyway," Talia continued. "We woke up here. I think we're going camping or something because there's a bunch of tents and sleeping bags outside and a list of instructions on each pile."

"We're sleeping here tonight?" I asked grabbing my head.

"Yes! Now, come on before them fools claim our stuff! I've already established our group." Talia grabbed my arm and yanked me out into the woodsy air. I took in a deep breath and coughed as a bug flew up my nose.

"You okay?" Taj said as he slapped me on the back.

Covering my nose, I sneezed and turned away. I didn't want him to see bug snot dripping down my face. Frantically, I searched for a napkin or tissue, anything that could help remove this nightmarish embarrassment, but I had left my backpack in my locker at the school.

My backpack which also had my phone and anything else of value. And I was in the woods! A place I had never ventured because my family don't do camping. We don't spend our free time getting lost in the forest and bonding with nature or some crazy stuff like that. My life is already hard, why on earth would I try to make it harder in the wilderness?

"Come on Nora! We're over here!" Talia said waving me over. I had to use the back of my hand as a tissue 'cause there was nothing else. I noticed groups gathered around the other heaps of stuff and each was marked with its own distinct color. Talia had put herself right in the middle of a pile labeled green and held a Beholden blue card. She seemed to be reading the clue to herself, then informed us of what we needed to know.

"Okay, listen up!" she yelled. "Looks like we have to split up into groups of 20 and we're to follow our markers, make camp and then in the morning await further instructions."

"What markers?" Lashonda asked peering over Talia's shoulder at the paper.

"Some of y'all got to go!" shouted Damien as he clapped his hands at the crowd. "Come on. All y'all can't be in our group!" Some people muttered as they left, but I stayed. He then proceeded to count every person that surrounded our pile until he was satisfied, then looked to Talia and announced, "Alright. We got 20."

"These are the markers," Talia said as she pointed to a bright green flag on a tree. "All of our stuff is marked with green." She picked up a duffel bag with green duck tape that matched the flag on the tree. "Let's get going!" Talia heaved a bag onto her shoulder. We all obediently picked up equipment like burdened mules, except Damien who demanded people carry more.

"Let's make this one trip, people!" he shouted. "Take more stuff so when we get to our destination we don't have to come back! And stay together! No stragglers!"

"Why do you care?" a snippy voice asked.

I looked to see Shanice was on my team and thought, *Oh Lord, here we go.* Her mouth was going to make this game explosive. I could already see Lashonda giving her the look.

"Don't you watch the show?" Lashonda barked. "Everybody knows you got to keep your team together. That's 101 baby." She carried a heavy box on one end while Taj helped carry the other side.

"Yea," Shanice said in response. "And I know its a competition and you shouldn't trust nobody."

Damien breathlessly carried a large tub. "But in the beginning, everybody knows you got to stay together," he grunted through clenched teeth. "We got to make our team the strongest so we can beat the other three. After that, it's every man for himself."

Shanice walked off in a huff and I heard Lashonda mutter, "Can't stand dealing with stupid people."

I carried two sleeping bags and a heavy backpack with a large red cross patch on the front. I assumed it held medical supplies. When we got to our designated area, Talia and Damien were barking orders at anyone who would listen and I enjoyed watching the difference in personalities emerge. The extroverts walked around like roosters, crowing at the rest of us to take action, organize the food supplies, set up the other tent, dig a hole for the bathroom, find the first aid box, and the list went on. The introverts jumped to it or ignored them completely. For instance, Cordell was rapping with Ezekiel Thomas (who was also on the drumline) and both were making a contagious beat that even I couldn't help but bounce side to side to as I helped Su-Min put up the other tent.

Su-Min Johnson (last name used to be Zhao) was the only Chinese girl in our school, but since she grew up in our 'hood she acted just as black as everybody else. She had streaked ebony hair chopped at the waist, a serious face and a spirited, yet quiet demeanor. I didn't understand why she was in the game. She had money. But, then again, Su-Min was a bit unpredictable. There often was more to her than what you saw.

Like, you'd think by her calm voice she'd dress the same—you know, all dull tones like gray and taupe. But no. That was never the case with Su-Min. She always had on something bright. I stared at her cherry apple bulb earrings as they swung close to her chin and admired her multi-colored crochet top. Knowing Su-Min, she probably made everything herself, jewelry and all.

We'd known each other since kindergarten and were best friends until the fifth grade. We didn't hang out in middle school and I suppose that's my fault. Looking at her face, I thought, yea…she probably still blames me for it.

She frowned at me and sighed, "Nora, you can't put it like that."

"Does it matter?" I asked, smoothing the orange flap down.

"Yes, it matters," she said coming over to my side and taking the flap, hooking it onto some pole I didn't realize was there, and made the fabric come perfectly straight out. She instantly created a sort of mini roof over the already roof of our tent. "It needs to look like the picture," she said tightly.

"What do we even need this thing for?" I asked looking at the directions and searching for the name of the extra complicated piece. "The…rainfly? What the heck is a rainfly?"

"Whatever it is, it's probably important," Su-Min said as she went around checking every stake.

I forgot how tedious Su-Min was. This was why I couldn't stand being her lab partner, even though I knew she was smart. She was a well-known perfectionist.

"Now, we get the sleeping bags," she said.

"Can't everyone choose their own?" I asked.

"It should look like the picture!" Su-Min snapped tapping the paper. Our clue had also come with a list of instructions and a picture of the outside and inside of the tent. "They gave us this for a reason. They're probably watching us now…judging us…" She looked up into the trees and I followed her gaze.

A bird flew from treetop to treetop and I wondered what he was looking for. Then I thought maybe he was a mechanical bird put there by Beholden. They had been known to use robotics in past games for all sorts of things. I wouldn't put it past them to use a bird to film us. My growling stomach interrupted my suspicious thoughts.

"Alright," I said. "Let's hurry up and finish this so we can get something to eat."

After all the orange tents were set up, (was Beholden out of any other colors?) and food and supplies were taken stock, we learned Damien was the only one who knew how to start a fire. Talia and Chloe B. prepped the hot dogs and baked beans, while some of us gathered sticks to keep the flames going. There wasn't enough of those roasting forks for everybody, so we had to take turns cooking our hotdogs.

Shanice cried because she dropped hers in the fire and Ezekiel burned his hand trying to fish it out for her. Taj and I ended up using sticks to roast our dogs and even though I ate mine with a bag of chips and a bowl of beans, I was still hungry. And so was everyone else.

Soon the whining began. Lashonda was pissed we didn't save anything for breakfast even though Talia swore there were boxes of Pop-Tarts somewhere around camp. It was already getting dark and in the twilight, we searched and searched for that mysterious box and couldn't find it anywhere. Not to mention the mosquitos and gnats. Somebody asked for the bug spray and before it even got around to me the can was empty.

The complaints continued with Chloe B. whining she was still hungry and didn't want to pee outside. Shanice cried about how she needed a shower and Cordell asked if there was a second bag of marshmallows because we were already running low on the first.

Everyone looked at Cordell.

Omri jumped up. "Second bag? You sneakin' marshmallows?!" he shouted. "Man, I'm so hungry I'm over here eatin' leafs. Gimme that bag!" He walked over and snatched the sack from Cordell's thick hands, which he'd hidden beneath his jacket. The large boy stood and towered over Omri.

He bellowed, "Dawg, don't be grabbin' stuff outta my hands."

"I'll grab whatever the hell I please," Omri said stuffing his face. "You up here trying to cram your fat ass—"

Cordell moved to grab Omri, but he was too fast. Omri's limber legs took him across the camp area over by the tents, where he hopped from foot to foot as he downed the rest of the bag, crumpled it up and threw the plastic sack in the fire.

Yet, as entertaining as this moment was, the sky demanded an audience. My attention drifted up as the great stretch of navy blue roof mixed with a burnt orange sky. I stifled a yawn, knowing it must've been earlier than I thought. I did not want to be the first to go to bed and miss all the action.

To keep myself awake I looked around the group, noting who was on my team. I'm sure everyone else was doing the same as we had all grown quiet. We were on the same team for now, but later we'd be at each others' throats. The thoughts had to be similar: To succeed in the game of Beholden, you had to unite yourself with a few to get ahead. Who'd make a good alliance? Who to stay away from? Who could I trust? I knew Talia and I would be aligned, that was an unspoken loyalty, but who else could I see myself working with?

I barely knew Chloe B. She was a junior on the dance team, cute and was the type of girl who always had her hair, make-up, and nails on point. Even in the middle of a dirty campsite, her Bantu knots looked sassy. Each part of her thick black hair was equally sectioned off into tiny twisted balls.

She had carefully brushed her fine baby hair so they surrounded her hairline like a silky halo. Her full lips still had the rose matte lipstick and her long eyelashes stiff with perfect mascara. I knew she was popular in her class because she was voted on the homecoming court, she must've been smart because she was in the gifted program and I knew she would align herself with Theo because they were obviously a couple (even though they claimed no labels.)

I remember when they first started locking lips next to my locker and Talia had been all wound up. I asked her why she was sweatin' him and she said she hated that one of the cutest boys in our class was dating a junior. I think she was offended Theo had never been into her. I mean, what cute boy at our school hadn't dated Talia?

Taj and Theo were the only two I could think of. Now if you ask me, Taj is one thing, but Theo? I didn't think the boy was that cute. Light eyes ain't that big a deal.

My eyes roamed around the campsite and stopped on two lone boys leaned against a tree, so dark they almost blended in with the shadows. I was unsure about Akeem and Adrian Madaki. Twin brothers who always stuck together and alone. People (or should I say, just Talia) called them the Funk Brothers because they smelled like straight-up B.O.

I felt bad for them because they were so thin and looked like they never bathed. Sometimes they wore the same clothes twice in one week. I remember when we were in grade school, the brothers had ringworm and no one wanted to touch them. They were distant, but was that their fault? I couldn't remember a time I'd actually said hello to them.

My attention was drawn toward an uproarious laugh. Marcus Tate was surrounded by a couple of his basketball buddies. A tall, dark and thought-he-was-handsome boy who was the captain of the team. Marcus sweat testosterone, was cocky, a show-off, and had an ego so big I couldn't stand being around him. He always had a way of making everyone else feel small and I knew with him, Omri and Damien in the same group, there was bound to be war.

And then there were the strays not associated with anyone. I couldn't rely on Shanice because her loud mouth was going to get her accosted or abandoned. But there was Lashonda who with four older brothers was tough and fearless, Su-Min who was calm and level-headed, and Taj—I snuck a peek at him.

He sat quietly in a camping chair and laughed at Omri who was riding the ice chest like it was a wild bull. Taj seemed like the type of person I could trust and I knew he was smart. He'd make a good ally if only I could get over my own skittishness. But Omri? That boy was so obnoxious and immature I couldn't ever rely on him. He probably wouldn't even make it past this phase.

A puff of smoke snaked into the air and I saw Craig Wiley, a light-skinned brother leaned back with his eyes closed. He had a tiny-white-rolled-up piece of something, dangling between his fingers. I sighed. I wouldn't be able to get anywhere with him stoned the whole game and he'd run out of breath if we had to simply jog. Ezekiel and Cordell were chatting about music, distracted as usual, and that left Deshaun and Brandon, two football players who were strong and friendly enough. I could use their muscle on my team.

"Sizing everyone up?" Talia whispered with a smile as she sat down in a folding chair beside mine.

I tried to hide my sheepish grin. "I'll tell you about it later," I whispered.

"That's why I love you," she said poking the fire with her stick. "You're always thinking ahead."

DO-NOT-ADVANCE

I'd never been camping before and I'd never slept outdoors. I wasn't the only one uncomfortable with my surroundings, because everybody was acting stupid. If it wasn't Chloe B. crying because she wished she had her phone, it was one of the boys breaking something, throwing stuff in the fire, or getting hurt. And it was all because of Cordell. Said he had his own private stash that he brought. (Who knew he carried that many tiny bottles of vodka in his backpack?)

He claimed he planned on going over Craig's after school today so they could celebrate graduating, but said this occasion seemed even better. After sharing his alcohol with a select group, one of the basketball players hurt his ankle wrestling (I think his name was Jamal?), Quincy stupidly burned his hand on a metal pan by the fire and Craig passed out on the ground.

When I yawned so big I thought my jaw would pop, Talia announced we were going to get some sleep and head to our tent (which she loudly proclaimed as GIRLS ONLY), but once inside we could still hear the others being insanely loud. I was really tired, but Talia insisted I tell her everything I knew. She listened eagerly as I drowsily recounted my personal notes on our competition and then we laughed about how easy it would be to beat the people on our own team. None of them seemed like they'd be worthy competitors.

"You'd whoop them easy," Talia whispered. It was so dark I couldn't even see her face and I shivered inside my thin sleeping bag. The temperature had dropped more than I realized and the rocky ground was hard and cold.

"I don't think so," I whispered back. "You'd go far though. You're competitive."

"Nora, you're smarter than most of the people out there," Talia said. "And you're competitive when you want to be. Just stick with me and I'll always have your back."

"Promise?"

"Promise."

The later it got, the more footsteps shuffled into our tent, except Chloe B. I could hear her distance voice outside giggling near the dwindling fire. She came in briefly to grab her sleeping bag and whispered, "I'm sleeping next to the fire with my man, 'cause I mean, did y'all see the stars tonight? It's so romantic!" And then she was gone.

"Ho," Talia muttered. "She gonna end up getting transferred again. You know why she came here, right?" I knew Talia was about to go on her tangents and she didn't even wait for me to answer. "I heard she got pregnant 8th grade and had an abortion. That's why she got transferred here…mmhm. Her parents tried to cover it up."

"Fa real?" I said, my eyes burned with heaviness and I allowed them to close.

"Uh-huh. That skank been around town and if Theo ain't careful, she gonna make him her baby's daddy."

I used to believe all the stories Talia told me, thinking because her mama was always in folks' business she must've known things. But eventually, I realized Talia made a lot of stuff up, especially if she wasn't particularly fond of you.

I tried not to listen to Chloe B.'s giggles since they were obviously not stargazing and eventually Talia hollered for them to shut up before she came out there and chopped Theo's manhood off. I attempted to sleep after that, knowing it might be a while before I got any good rest, but it felt like only an hour had passed before I was startled awake by screams.

Lashonda, Talia and I jumped up, tumbled through the tent and ran out to see Theo standing with a knife in his hand, pointed at a gang of gold masks in the woods.

Yea, that's right. They looked like gold masks floating in some trees. The sight was downright eerie, especially when you'd just woken up. I couldn't control the pace of my heart as it quickened. I couldn't remind myself that this was all just a game that liked to play tricks on people in the middle of the night.

"What is this?" Theo yelled. "Get out of here!"

Chloe B. lay still on the ground, eyes closed, fainted I think. Some of the boys had already come out of their tent and Omri stood in the front and rubbed his eyes.

"Man, it's just them fools from the other team," he said squinting. "I see you, Chris! Quit playing!"

The masks silently and slowly backed up and by now my eyes had adjusted to the darkness and I could see an outline of figures attached to the golden faces. But as mysteriously as they came, they disappeared. Despite Omri claiming he knew somebody named Chris, there was still something off about the whole business. After Theo had roused Chloe B. from her fainting spell, I followed the others back to the tent and tried to sleep, but really laid listening to everyone else's heavy breathing, tossed and turned, then watched the tent turn from dark to light.

Even though I hadn't slept much, I was ready to begin the next day. Excited and pumped by Talia's pep talk the night before, I thought, I can do this. There was a chance I could beat everybody else. There was a slight percentage I could win this whole thing. But before I got ahead of myself, I needed to make it out of this wilderness. I needed to get out of this camping phase as soon as possible.

I slipped out followed by another person and looked behind to see Su-Min. We both grabbed some water bottles. I drank from mine, splashed some water on my face, picked a packaged toothbrush from a pile and brushed my teeth at the edge of the camp. Then, feeling a bit curious and brave, I got a good look at those footprints from the night before. Don't ask me why, as I'm sure they wouldn't tell me anything because I'm no tracker, but I was feeling a bit Holmesish. I peered at the prints like a detective. I noted how the prints were all over our camp. But there was one set that went off on its own. I followed the set until I caught sight of something familiar.

There was a blue envelope placed on top of a tub.

I picked it up, opened the flap and pulled out a piece of paper.

"What does it say?" Su-Min asked, looking over my shoulder. I read it aloud:

Make a beeline southeast and see a tree that cries,
Then head west and be careful of the buzzing nest,
Don't ignore the bear, look further with your eyes
you'll spot a cave beneath, go through for the test
your destination should be waiting at the end, like a prize.
But note the first team with all its members will rest
Comfortably and safely, while weeds are cut down to size.
And what remains is now called what is best.

"So, we've got to stay together," Su-Min mumbled to herself. "Guess it looks like you and Talia can't get rid of the rest of us yet."

I looked at her face and saw her eyes narrow accusingly.

"What are you talking about?" I asked, feeling my heart leap into my throat.

"I heard what you and Talia said last night," she said. "A tent has thin walls. You might as well been sitting right next to me." She crossed her arms.

A punch to the gut. Already I'd created an enemy. And just when I was about to say something to Su-Min, Talia and Shanice walked out of the tent and approached us.

"What's this?" Talia asked taking the clue from me and reading it quickly.

"I've got to pee," Shanice whined hopping up and down. I noticed her bouncy all-natural curls weren't all naturally hers. The girl's piece was starting to slide off. I pointed to my own head and nodded at her. Taking the hint, her eyes widened and she abruptly stopped her hopping and fixed her wig.

"Uh, I don't want to go in the woods by myself, can someone go with me?" she asked.

"I'll go," Su-Min sighed and they walked off together.

"Talia," I said grabbing my friend's arm. "Su-Min overheard us talking last night."

"So?" Talia said scrutinizing the paper. Her determined expression hadn't even changed. "We better get moving if we want to be the first ones there." She was focused. She picked up a pan and a stick and started to bang it near the boys' tents. "Wake up!" she yelled. Her banging brought the herd out like bees swarming from a hive.

Cordell was the first to grab the pan from her. He looked like he wanted to beat her with it.

Talia didn't even flinch. "We gotta get going now if we're going to make it to the next phase," she said. "So pack up the camp!"

"Says who?" Cordell asked gripping the pan.

"This clue!" She held the paper up and then put it in her pocket. "Now, let's go."

"Let me see it," Damien demanded and held out his hand.

"Why?" Talia asked.

"Because, I don't trust you," he said.

She pretended to be offended as she fished out the clue and gave him the paper. Then said with a wink, "You're smarter than I thought, Damien."

"Really?" he said snatching the clue. "I'm valedictorian and you didn't think I was smart? I didn't think you were that stupid."

"She's toying with you, man," Marcus said as he walked over and tried to take the slip from Damien.

"Anybody got a compass?" Damien asked, avoiding Marcus' long arms as the basketball player lunged again for the clue.

Talia ordered me to help her take down the tent, but my head was a storm of anxiety. I couldn't get over what had just happened. Was Su-Min going to work against me and Talia? Were we going to make it to the next phase in time? Maybe I had gotten too full of myself. I didn't actually think I could win this game, did I? Talia and I had gotten so far as removing the rainfly, when I was overcome with this strange sensation, like a pain in my gut that what I was doing was wrong. As if some little version of me were sitting on my shoulder and telling me not to do whatever I was planning on doing.

"Now ain't the time to daydream," Talia scolded me when I stopped. "Nora, help!"

But that feeling inside pressed harder in protest. I couldn't help it. This didn't feel right. And just as I opened my mouth to say exactly that, Damien's exclamation got everyone's attention.

"I found a compass!" he announced proudly.

"Give it to me," Marcus said. "I know how to read it."

"I found it first and I'm not giving it to anyone," Damien snapped. "especially somebody who can only find their way around a basketball court." He backed up and stuffed the compass in his pocket, which created an awkward bulge.

"Did you just call me stupid?" Marcus shouted. "You freakin—" He charged Damien and they were on the ground fighting before somebody could pull them apart. Cordell slowly strolled over and effortlessly separated the two. I always wondered why the big guy wasn't on the football team. Marcus' eyes bulged as Cordell gruffly held him by the collar of his shirt.

"Man, get off me!" Marcus yelled as he shook himself free. He looked embarrassed as he tried to fix his now stretched out neckline. It hung so low you could see the upper portion of his pecs.

Damien wiggled from Cordell's other grip and wiped the blood from his nose, then spat onto the ground and stalked off. Concerned, I began to follow him until I heard—

"Nora! Why aren't you helping?"

I snapped back to attention. Talia's eyes were fierce and I almost felt offended by the look she gave me. But, I calmly reminded myself we were in a game that made us all act a bit unhinged, so I opened my mouth and began explaining the reason why I had stopped. But the words that came out sounded odd. I mean, this was all new to me too. I probably sounded like a rambling idiot. I mumbled that what we were doing didn't feel right and tried to describe the DO-NOT-ADVANCE vibe, but you can imagine I had a pretty tough time putting it into words. And by the time I was through, she just gawked at me like I had worms falling out of my ears. Thankfully she was quickly distracted by what everybody else was doing.

"Where is everyone going?" she yelled, her eyes darted past me like a cat pounced its prey. Adrian and Akeem walked off into the woods, followed by Craig. Somebody's legs were hanging out of the boys' tent as if he were still passed out on the ground. Su-Min and Shanice were just walking up and I still hadn't seen Theo and Chloe B.

"We need to get packed up so we can leave!" Talia yelled frantically.

"I'm sure the other teams are struggling too," Omri said as he stretched, yawned and rubbed his belly. "I'm hungry, man. Where'd you say them Pop-Tarts were?"

"I got a headache," Lashonda moaned as she sat on the ground and rubbed her forehead. "Anybody got any coffee? Aspirin?"

"We need to get everything packed!" Talia shrieked and rapidly clapped her hands. She had lost her patience. With cheeks flushed, eyes wild and a look like she wanted to strangle everyone, Talia was through. But she still hadn't listened to a word I said. What I was trying to communicate would've helped her sanity. It would've prevented her from freaking out. And instead of graciously telling her what I had been trying to say, I stupidly blurted—

"But that's just it! We don't need to pack up anything."

The voice sounded like someone else.

"W-what?" she sputtered (and I didn't blame her, 'cause I was surprised at me too.) "Of course we need to pack. I'm not sleeping on the ground!"

"But it doesn't say we should pack, Talia," I said. "It just says to make a beeline there." Even though I wasn't looking at the clue, I remembered the strange phrasing.

Taj got up from beside the smoldering fire and walked over to Damien who had just returned. "Hey, can I read it?"

Damien handed him the paper and Taj's eyes flew over the clue and he frowned. "Nora's right," he said. "It doesn't say we need to bring anything with us. It just says to go." My heart melted and I had a sudden urge to kiss that boy.

"Well, of course, they're not going to tell us to take anything," Talia argued.

"Yea," Su-Min agreed. "That's understood. We don't want to get there and have nothing to sleep on."

"But does it make sense for us to carry everything there?" Taj asked. "We don't even know where we're going."

"Right," I said, feeling my heart flutter its wings. "Just think. If we skip packing and just go, we'll make it there first. We'll win. Then if we need to, we can come back and pick everything up."

"You can come back," Talia said crossing her arms.

Ooo. I did not like her tone. I felt my adrenaline kick up a notch as I tried to calm the angry voices in my head. What was her problem?

"It doesn't make any sense," Su-Min said. "I say we pack everything so we're prepared just in case. We can't leave things like first aid or water or supplies. What if someone gets hurt again?"

Lashonda groaned from the ground. "I'm not drinking another glass of liquor till the day I die," she said. "I hate alcohol! I hate what it does to my body!"

Talia now had her hands on her hips and frowned as she looked at her feet, deep in thought. It felt like a standoff until Omri's hand shot in the air.

"Alright, who votes we just go and come back for stuff later!" he said.

A bunch of hands went in the air including mine.

"Who votes we pack up all this crap and take it with us?" Omri put his hand down and Talia lifted hers and a few others.

"Deshaun you voted twice."

"Where's Theo and Chloe B.?" I asked. "They didn't vote."

"Probably tellin' each other about the birds and the bees," Omri said as he looked at me and winked. "You don't know nothing about that, do you, Nora?" He waltzed over and took my hand. "I'd be happy to give you a lesson…if you'd like."

I snatched my hand back. "Ugh. Get away." He chuckled in response.

"Let's get going," I said rubbing my hand, hoping to remove the disgust. "We need everyone together."

And I didn't think I had the nerve to motivate a group, but here I was, getting my Green Team to move forward in the game.

After Su-Min found Theo and Chloe B. (and her not giving us any of the dirty details, thank God) we were finally on our way. Everyone else seemed to fall in line, despite complaints from Talia and Su-Min. Talia grabbed a sleeping bag anyway and Su-Min brought the first aid backpack.

"Y'all can sleep on the ground if you want to," Talia grumbled.

Damien turned out to be a pretty good navigator, at least as far as I could tell. I didn't know anything about reading a compass and I didn't know certain details like you have to place the compass in the palm of your hand with the direction of the travel arrow pointed straight to your destination. It had to be in a particular position, Damien said, in line with your body or something like that. He talked on and on, giving us all a lesson on navigation, what berries we could and couldn't eat and how to tell which way was north.

We wove through trees with no particular path laid out in front of us. There was no dirt trail like you'd see in a park. This was just us and woods all around and the sight of it all was daunting. What if we got lost? What if we were going the wrong way? What if Damien was mistaken? When I asked him how he knew about compasses and starting fires, he said Boy Scouts and camping with his older brother, and just as I was about to ask him another question Lashonda told us to shut up and move. We walked pretty fast, except for that boy (Jamal?) who sprained his ankle, and Cordell's lazy behind who dragged slowly in the back, and for some reason, Deshaun and Brandon thought this was still a joke and goofed off climbing trees and chasing each other through bushes.

"My feet hurt!" Shanice groaned. "Let's take a break."

"Let's make it to the weeping willow tree first," I said.

"What about the bee's nest and the bear and all that?" Chloe B. asked. Even though she had let her Bantu knots loose (which produced full thick curls that framed her face) I was happy to see not all of her was perfect. Her eye makeup was smeared and her red matted lips had faded.

"They're just trying to scare you, baby," Theo said grabbing her hand. "We won't see any bears."

"Actually," Damien said. "There have been black bears spotted in North Alabama."

Chloe B.'s eyes widened.

"Get a move on, people!" Talia yelled at the front of the line. "We need to go faster so we can make it first!"

"There better be food," Cordell yelled from the back.

"How much farther?" Shanice whined.

"Girl, will you quit complaining?" Lashonda snapped. "My name is not Siri."

"I wish I had my phone," Shanice replied.

And then I heard it before I saw it. My heart sank at the sound of rushing water floating through the trees, blowing green leaves across the wooded ground, and the group in front had come to a sudden halt. Talia turned around with her hands on her hips and gave me an accusing look.

"Now what are we supposed to do, Nora?" she asked.

There was a river in front of us, not too wide to cross, but we'd definitely get wet. There were no visible rocks to hop on or fallen tree trunks to make us a bridge. We would have to go straight through.

"You took us the wrong way," Marcus said and shoved Damien. "Where's the crying tree?"

Damien looked shocked and stared at the contraption in his hand. "The compass said to go this way!"

I felt like all eyes were on me and the sudden attention caused me to break out in a sweat. I clutched my stomach, feeling a pang of guilt. I had gotten us into this mess. It was all my fault.

"This is on you, Nora!" Talia said. "I knew this was a bad idea! You just cost us all $250,000! And now we're lost and didn't bring any of our stuff. We're going to be wandering all night in the dark!"

"I ain't sleeping out here!" Shanice cried.

Everyone started shouting at once. Su-Min blamed me for convincing us to leave without our camping equipment, Marcus berated Damien for not knowing how to use a compass, and the others just complained about losing the money. Talia started to talk about going back and asked if anyone else knew how to get there and Chloe B. asked if we could just walk along the river and maybe we'd run into the other teams. My mind didn't have time to form a rebuttal, as Taj quickly got everyone's attention, but not by shouting. I watched as he took off his Chucks, rolled up his pant legs and plunged his feet right into the rushing water and walked across.

"Look at that crazy new boy!" Deshaun yelled.

"Yo! Taj!" Omri shouted. "Is it cold?"

But Taj didn't seem to hear him over the swift current. He reached the other side and disappeared into the woods.

"Where's he going?" Talia asked. Her grating voice was starting to irritate me, like sand in a wet bathing suit.

"We need to stick together," Su-Min complained. "We're going to lose because of him."

"Then let's go after him," I said starting down to the riverbank.

"Nora! What are you doing?" Talia asked.

"It's no use just standing here arguing." I took off my sandals, rolled up my skinny jeans as far as they would go (which wasn't very far) and held my shoes above my head as I walked through the river.

"Go Señora!" yelled Omri.

The cold water shocked me, like stinging needles pricking my feet and ankles. The bottoms of my jeans got soaked anyway, but I didn't care. I just wanted to make it to the other side quick. My feet slipped on the rocks and I had a hard time keeping my balance as the shallow water pushed against me. Wincing at the pain from stepping on something sharp, I made it to the other side and gingerly walked over the tiny pebbles on the muddy riverbank. I stuck my wet feet back in my sandals and took off after Taj, slipping along the way. It wasn't long until I saw him standing and looking up at a large tree with sagging limbs and green shaggy leaves.

"So Damien was right," I said excitedly. "The weeping willow is this way."

"Yea," Taj said with a smile.

Quickly I jogged back to the river and was frustrated to see most of the people already gone. To those who were left, I called out over the water, "We found the tree! Go get the others!"

Lashonda and Omri hopped into action, sprinting in two different directions. Soon, Lashonda jogged back with Chloe B., Theo, and the basketball players and Omri was trailed by Talia, Su-Min, and the rest. I could tell by the look on her face Talia was pissed and embarrassed. She had been wrong. Looking like she wanted to smack Damien, she shoved him into the water first and with a smug grin on his face, he splashed speedily across.

It was quite a sight to watch the rest of the group cross the river. Some waded through without care, while others tiptoed like squirmy kittens. Shanice and Craig were the most amusing, as she screamed about getting her hair wet and he shrieked like a lil' girl as soon as his feet touched the cold spring water.

But the journey wasn't over yet. We still had to find that cave. Damien pointed us in the right direction and soggy and tired, slapping mosquitos and breaking through newly spun cobwebs, we started off. The thrill was gone. Beholden had gotten real. Feeling the pressure, no one wanted to waste energy on talking. Well, no one but Omri.

"Hey Sonora, you bring any bug spray?" he asked as he stepped in line beside me.

"Nope."

"Fa' real? Not even one of them repellent bracelets? A hat? Some Raid?"

"No, Omri," I sighed.

"Dang. I'm getting bit up here!" He slapped his arm, then hopped on one foot as he scratched his ashy ankle. "Hey, Sonora?"

"Yea?"

"Remember freshmen year when we held hands in Mrs. Kay's class?"

I tripped over a jutting tree root and almost fell on my face.

"You okay?" Omri grabbed my arm and pulled me up. I could tell by the sound of his voice that he was smiling. "You didn't think I remembered that did you?" he continued as we walked side by side. "It was after school and you was trying out for something... what was it? Cheerleading?"

"Dance team," I mumbled. Yea, I remembered that horrible day filled with false hopes and rejection. How could I ever forget? I just wished Omri had.

"And you was crying in Mrs. Kay's because you didn't make the tea—"

"Omri, what's your point?" I asked, feeling my face grow warm. Perspiration was beading above my upper lip and collecting on the back of my neck. I swat at a sweat bee that began following me around.

"I got a lot of memories in that school," Omri muttered as he held up a low hanging branch so I could pass under. That was nice. I smiled thanks in reply and recognized an ancient attraction I thought had died long ago.

"You think they gonna keep the school?" he asked me. "Or still tear it down after Beholden gives them the money?"

"Oh, I think they'll keep the school," I said. "Why would they decide to get rid of it after we got Beholden?"

Omri shrugged and looked pretty thoughtful. "I don't know. I wouldn't be surprised if they found some other reason to still go 'head and shut us down. Money's not the only problem with Oliver James High."

I could tell by his face and the silence that followed, something was really bothering Omri. Sometimes I noticed, on rare occasions, he seemed like he wanted to say more. I waited, expecting his next words to be deep and heartfelt. And that nagging fondness that had grown on me since 7th grade resurfaced.

"It's a shame," he went on. "if we can't come back 10 years later, 'cause I'd love to show our kids where we first fell in love."

I squashed those affectionate thoughts as I pinched my lips together and quickly walked in front of him.

"Ay!" Omri yelled from behind me. "What I say?"

"Everything," I called back.

"Hold up!" I heard his feet pounding behind me and then he was past me, steadily jogging forward. "Anybody hear that?" He swatted the air and ducked fast. "Anybody see that?"

I saw another buzzing insect whip past my face.

"Bees!" Omri shouted.

The word alone set Chloe B. off.

"Bees?! Bees! Beeeeeeees!" she screamed as she ducked and whipped her head around. Theo protectively covered her with his arms and I dodged the flying insects that zipped past my head.

"They everywhere!" Lashonda screamed and sprinted through the bushes.

I followed, swatting my neck and trying not to get stung. Folks flew past me in a blur, brown bodies blending with green trees. I pumped my legs and ran like I was on track. What a sight we must've been to our audience. Black folks racing through the woods like we were runnin' from the cops.

By the time we stopped, the afternoon sun had slowly lowered and I was worried. How far had we run? Did we miss the cave?

"We're going the right way," Talia informed all of us once we got back together. She and Damien had been discussing our current direction. "Let's keep moving people!" she barked.

Nobody bothered to argue with her. We were all tired and didn't want to go back and investigate the bee-infested area. And it was a good thing we kept going because it wasn't long before we saw a large sculpture of a wooden bear. This got everyone excited.

"We're almost there!" Shanice said jumping up and down as she followed Talia who kept walking past the bear and deeper into the trees. Further and further we walked and the more we hiked, the stronger I felt something was off. My suspicions were confirmed when we came to a smaller river.

As Talia approached it, I yelled, "Stop!"

She looked back. "What now?"

"Something's not right," I said. I had that feeling again. You know, the DO-NOT-ADVANCE vibe. The kind of feeling Abuelita said never to ignore and I knew exactly what was bothering me. "The clue didn't talk about this water," I said.

"So? It didn't mention the other river either," Talia said.

"This isn't a river," Damien pointed out. "This is a creek."

"But the clue did mention the bear and the buzzing nest and the weeping willow," I said to Talia. "I feel like we're missing something. Who's got the clue?" I looked around at my classmates. Some looked irritated, others were confused.

"You wanted us to go through the water and we did," Talia snapped.

I could feel the heat in her voice, sense the impatience on her lips, and I squirmed beneath her irritated stare.

"And now you say we shouldn't?" Her face was red, even though she was shadowed by the trees. I could tell she had more on her mind than she wanted to say.

"Just hear me out," I said. "I feel like we missed something."

"She thinks we what?" Su-Min walked up.

"Nora's claiming this isn't right," Talia said and then looked at me squarely. "Is this one of your feelings again?"

"What do you mean?" Su-Min said pulling her hair away from her neck that was sticky with sweat. "We saw all the clues!"

"No, I think Nora's right," Taj said pulling the clue out of his pocket. "The first line talked about making a beeline."

"So?" Lashonda asked slapping her bare thigh. Her fishnet stockings were ripped and she'd removed her Strong. Black. Women. sweatshirt and tied it around her waist.

"A beeline means to go straight there," Damien said. "Whether it's through or over or under all obstacles including a river."

"Don't talk to me Poindexter," Lashonda snapped as she crossed her arms.

"Let's just hurry up and get there!" Cordell shouted impatiently. Sweat poured from his shiny forehead and his gray t-shirt had dark wet spots surrounding his armpits and chest.

"No, listen," Taj pointed at the paper. "The second part is specific. It tells us what we should expect to see: a buzzing nest, a bear, and something about looking beneath for a cave. It never mentions a river or a stream. We missed something. We should go back."

Something Taj said struck me. "Let me see the clue," I said taking the paper and rereading it again. My eyes flew over the words until I stopped and read the words aloud, "Don't ignore the bear, look further with your eyes and you'll spot a cave beneath…" I pointed to the phrase feeling my heart race.

"Who cares!" Cordell yelled, now sitting on the ground.

"Beneath what?" Damien asked slowly. "The bear?"

"There was no cave beneath the bear!" Talia snapped. "I passed right by it. I would've seen—"

"We have to go back!" I interrupted, sprinting toward the way we had come. And as I ran, I was glad I didn't need to explain, because Damien and Taj were running right beside me. We had ignored the wooden statue completely. And as I approached it, I heard voices ahead of me in the distance.

"Hurry up!" I yelled to my team as they approached. "The other teams are coming!" I looked all around that bear, but it wasn't me who saw it first.

"There. On the ground. What's that hole?" Taj asked.

I must've missed how much time had passed because the afternoon sun had turned to sunset, making the hole in the ground hard to see. After I insisted on leaving everything behind I hadn't even thought of bringing flashlights.

I'd been so consumed with being right and getting to our destination, I didn't think of how long it might take us to get there. Su-Min, however, reminded me that she and Talia hadn't forgotten. They put their headlamps on and shone the light down into the dark hole.

"It doesn't look deep," Talia said. "I'll go first."

I felt a twang of annoyance. Taj and I had discovered the hole and I selfishly wanted to be first, but she had already slipped down into the dark crevice with her headlamp shining the way. The rest of us slowly followed and Taj and Su-Min took the rear, making sure everyone got through the hole together.

Down below, the cave was damp but delightfully airy and breezy. Talia's light swept back and forth across the narrow, rocky cave that smelled of moist soil. She swatted at vines that hung from the cave's low ceiling and while most of the boys had to duck down to walk through, the rest of us easily made it to the other side of the cave without any problems. I chuckled as Shanice screamed when she thought she saw a bat and then screamed again when she felt something crawling on her arm.

"That was too easy," Talia said looking up at the hole above us. "But now, how are we supposed to get up there?"

"We'll need to boost each other up," I said with a bit of bravado. This whole wilderness thing wasn't as hard as I thought. I almost compared myself to that crazy outdoorsman named after a bear.

Almost.

Dull footsteps echoed through the cave as a bouncing headlamp ran up to us. It was Su-Min.

Breathlessly, she said, "The other team is coming! We've gotta hurry!"

Quickly, Cordell and Marcus took turns heaving us through the hole and above ground, Lashonda reached down to help pull folks the rest of the way up. I looked around and spotted what looked like the end of our journey. In the middle of an open field was a small log cabin with a brightly painted blue door.

"I'm going to check it out," Talia said running ahead.

"But what about the rest of us!" I yelled. Chloe B. went with her and so did Shanice, leaving me and Lashonda alone to help the others.

I wanted to run off to the cabin too, but the rest of our group hadn't made it through yet. And while we were trying to figure out how to squeeze Cordell's giant body through the tight hole, somebody from the other team poked his head up and yelled, "Get out the way!"

"You betta back the hell up!" Lashonda snapped and shoved his head back down.

Cordell and the other guy wrestled, but by the look of things, Cordell was the obvious winner.

"You two!" I yelled at Deshaun and Brandon, who were trying to catch lightning bugs. "Lift Cordell out of there."

They shrugged and Deshaun said, "We'll try."

After Taj, Omri and Marcus pushed Cordell from behind, the football players lifted him the rest of the way out. Once he was through, we ran to the cabin, pursued heavily by the other team. I could hear them shoutin' behind us even as we ran inside and Taj slammed the door.

Crowded by the windows, my group called out play by play of the other team behind us, noting how there were ten—no, fifteen people making their way to the cabin. And then how they suddenly stopped and were approached by strangers in masks.

"It's those guys from last night!" Theo yelled from the window.

"They're taking them away," Chloe B. said.

"Look at Tanisha fight! She don't wanna go home!" Omri laughed.

But my eyes were no longer behind me. I was taking in the sight before me.

What is Best

I expected the inside of the cabin to be rustic and small, but instead I was met with an air-conditioned, large open space. Thick rugs blanketed the left side of the room, where the twins, Adrian and Akeem, had already stationed themselves in front of the fireplace. And they were surrounded by comfy cream sofas and end tables that resembled wooden logs even though they looked expensive. Marcus pushed past me into the kitchen on the right, where Cordell was already rummaging through the dark cherry wood cabinets and laying snack food out on the granite kitchen counters. And directly in front of me, Su-Min disappeared down a long, narrow hallway that seemed endless. I noticed she was barefoot on the wooden floor and quickly removed my tattered sandals and felt the cold, smooth planks beneath my feet.

"I told y'all we'd win," Shanice said as she plopped down on a sofa.

"What you mean you told us?" Omri said. "It was Nora's idea to leave the camping gear."

"Yea, if we'd stayed to pack, we would've lost," said Chloe B. as she massaged Theo's shoulders from behind. He sat at a small round table by the kitchen.

I ran my hand over the soft couch and sat down across from Shanice. I sank into the squishy pillows and allowed them to envelop me. This felt like heaven.

"Where's Talia? I wanna see if she still thinks she needs her sleeping bag." Omri stalked down the hall.

Lashonda sat down next to me and put her dirty bare feet on a cream ottoman. "Girl, this place is nice! Did you see the kitchen?"

I closed my eyes and smiled. "Yea, I glanced."

"You glanced? It's full of food!"

"And there's pizza!" Cordell yelled and at the sound of the word, a horde stampeded across the room, cabinets flew open and slammed shut, and soon I was surrounded with classmates holding glass bottles of Coke, plates of pizza, chips, and stacks of Oreos.

"Aren't you hungry, Nora?" Taj asked as he sat down Indian style on the floor and began to eat.

"Yea," I said. "Just relaxing."

My family had been on vacation, but never to a place as nice as this. When Abuelita took me to Mexico, we always stayed with my tía abuela Isadora. Her stucco house was down a dusty road on the outskirts of a little town. I still had memories of sharing a squeaky bed with Abuelita on muggy nights and cruising the dirt roads with my cousins Andres and Nicolás during the long, hot days.

And then there was the time I went to Destin Beach with Talia's family for Spring Break, we stayed at their timeshare which was decent, but not swank. The worst place I vacationed was in a roach motel when Abuelita's oldest sister, tía abuela Francesca died and we went to her funeral down in Montgomery.

This cabin was on a whole 'nother level.

"This place ain't all that," Shanice said as she touched her head (probably making sure her hair was still in place.) She had a wine glass full of what I hoped was Coke and a bowl of fruit. "I've seen better."

"Where you seen better?" Chloe B. asked looking incredulous.

"Girl, have you seen what Queen Bey's house look like?"

Chloe B. rolled her eyes. "Yea, but you ain't ever stayed in it."

Just then Damien and Talia walked in together looking very pleased with themselves.

"Okay, listen up people," Damien said clapping his hands. "There are approximately four rooms with two sets of bunk beds. Now, if any of you can't do the math, that means only 16 people can sleep on a mattress tonight. Four of you will have to find other arrangements."

"I'm not sleeping on the floor," Lashonda said crossing her arms. She had pulled her braids free from the ponytail and they flowed over her shoulders beautifully. With her unblemished, dark skin and nose ring, she looked like an African goddess even in a dirty tank top and torn fishnet stockings.

"Well, somebody's gonna have to," Talia said. "Two people can use the sleeping bags Su-Min and I brought. Maybe the other two can sleep on the sofas."

"I'll take the couch," Cordell said with his mouth full.

The rest of the room was quiet as we all looked around to see who would volunteer next.

Suddenly an unfamiliar voice said gruffly, "We'll sleep on the floor...we're used to it." I looked over to see Akeem, one of the twins had spoken. A sting of guilt made me wish I had volunteered first.

"That means one more person left," Talia said looking around.

"I...uh," Chloe B. began with a giggle. "I have other arrangements so you won't have to worry about me." She sat on Theo's lap.

"Oh, hell naw," Omri said looking disgusted. "I ain't sleeping in a room with y'all."

"We promise we won't do...much," Theo said.

"Ugh," Lashonda got up and stomped down the hall. "I got this bed, right chere!" she shouted from one of the rooms.

Soon all of us had split up and were claiming bunks. I chose the bottom one in a room with Talia, Su-Min, and Shanice. I admired our sleeping quarters. The bunkbeds had fancy swirls engraved in the wood, the mattresses were thick and fluffy, and the pillows larger than I had ever seen. I laid down on the floral blankets and caressed the texture.

"Mmm. How do they make this so soft?" I asked.

"Haven't you ever felt a down comforter?" Su-Min asked.

Embarrassed, I shrugged. "Uh, yea."

Talia unhooked her overalls. "I'm going to take a shower," she said as she slipped her shirt over her head. I looked away. The girl had no shame. She didn't care who was around before she started stripping. "You think they have a pair of extra clothes in these drawers?" She opened the wooden bureau. "Nope," she said after pulling open the last drawer. She left the room in her bra with the overall straps dangling at her sides. I heard whistles down the hallway.

Su-Min and I were left in the room alone. The silence lingered between us until I knew there was something I needed to get off my chest.

"Su-Min, I didn't mean to hurt your feelings earlier," I said. "Talia and I were just playing the game, you know, trying to figure out our competition. No hard feelings?" I extended my hand and she hesitated…and left me hanging.

"I know it's just a game," she said. "But that doesn't mean things are going to change between us. As long as Talia's around, you'll keep doing exactly what she says." She sat down on her bunk and crossed her legs. Didn't even have the nerve to look me in the face.

Her words stung, so I did what any human person would do. I instinctively lashed back. "What do you mean, do what she says?"

"You know."

"I don't. Explain."

"If Talia says jump, you say how high. There's nothing to explain, Nora. She commands, you obey."

My face warmed and I wondered if my brown skin was turning red. "Is that what you think?"

"That's what everybody thinks," she said. "That's what I've known since you and Talia became besties."

"Jealous much?"

"Of what?"

"Our friendship."

She became tight-lipped and looked away. Was she crying? Oh, God, I hope I didn't make her cry. Here I was trying to get Su-Min to be friends with me again and I had to go and ruin it. Stupid, Nora. This was not the way I wanted to patch things up. I had ripped the chasm even wider.

"Look, I'm sorry I said that," I said. "I'm sorry about the whole thing. It's just that…we grew apart and, I guess we liked different things and…"

"Yea, you keep telling yourself that," Su-Min said. "I didn't change, Nora, you did." And she got up and left the room.

Dang. I thought I was bad about holding grudges, but Su-Min held onto one like a dog held onto a bone. I couldn't blame her though. I still felt pretty guilty about the way I'd treated her. After her nightmare of a sleepover in 5th grade, we went into middle school and stopped talking. But this year, I owned it. I knew what I did was wrong and I was motivated to rekindle our friendship.

You see, back in the day, I used to spend the night over Su-Min's house almost every weekend. It helped that our mamas were good friends. I had fond memories of sitting with her and her mama (before she became Mrs. Johnson) and having tea. They had those tiny cups without handles and her mom would always offer me cream and sugar with my drink even though they never used it in theirs.

But when her mama got remarried our friendship deteriorated and it was probably my fault. I felt I owed Su-Min after all these years and maybe, just maybe, she'd not hate me.

People were arguing in the living room. Even though it had only been one day, we'd all gotten angrier and more irritable. And I don't think Talia looked me in the eye once since we'd gotten into the cabin. Was she mad at me?

I went to go look for her, to straighten things out and make sure we were straight, but she was still in the shower singing off-key, so I walked into the kitchen to see if there was any pizza left. The once perfect and spotless kitchen was now cluttered with dirty dishes, empty boxes of pizza, and a sticky floor. I stepped over spilled soda and hunted through the empty boxes.

"They ate it all," Taj said from behind me. "Sorry, I should've saved you a slice, but they were vultures." His side grin revealed some of his shiny braces.

I smiled back and opened the cabinets. "That's okay, I'll find something else…Bingo." There was a shelf full of cereal boxes. I reached for one and grabbed a bowl.

"Cinnamon huh?" Taj said as he opened the refrigerator and pulled out a jug of milk.

I took it from him, awkwardly. "Thanks," I said. "Now to find a spoon." I sat everything down on the counter and began pulling open drawers, but was startled by the first one.

"What's this?" I asked as I reached inside and pulled out one, of many, keys. It was small, smaller than any normal key used for a door. Looked like it belonged to one of my childhood journals that had a tiny lock.

Taj looked in, must've mentally counted, then whispered aloud, "There's only twelve of them. What do you think they're for?"

"I don't know," I said slipping it into my pocket. "But you better take one too."

Taj grabbed one, then quickly closed the drawer and glanced around. The argument had ceased in the living room and a deck of cards had been brought out instead, inducing a relaxed atmosphere with few outbursts of objection. No one had noticed the two of us in the kitchen.

"Should we tell anybody?" I whispered.

Taj shook his head. "They can find it themselves. Plus, there's only ten, so you know everybody's going to fight over it."

I nodded in agreement and sat down at the empty round table as Marcus fumed about being cut. No, nobody had a knife. They were playing a game of Spades. Damien grinned across at him mischievously as Marcus shouted, "We on the same team, fool!" Taj sat down beside me and I instantly squirmed in my seat. What was he doing? Not only had we been alone in the kitchen together, but now he wanted to sit down with me at the table?

"You sure you wanna sit with me?" I asked as I filled my spoon with milky square cinnamon cereal.

He shrugged. "What?"

I sighed. "It's going to make us look like we're together or something." He smiled and my heart skipped a beat. That didn't come out right, so I hastily continued, "You know like we're a team?" I had to clarify because he kept on smiling and my heart was pitter-pattering so hard I wanted to crawl up the wall.

"Naw," Taj said with that lopsided grin. "Everybody knows you and Talia are."

I squirmed uncomfortably at his observation and decided to ignore his comment. Hungry, I ate so fast I finished my bowl and went back for more. The group in the living room had gotten rowdier. We didn't even need a television, because Lashonda and Omri were our entertainment. Both were up and stepping, trying to show Su-Min part of a routine. Lashonda's braids swung as she stomped, clapped, and snapped. A steady rhythm rose between them. Boom. Boom. Boom. Clap.Clap.Snap. Boom. Boom. Boom. Clap.Clap.Snap. And then Omri hopped from side to side and threw his arms up and down. His head popped to the left and right, hands clapped above and below, behind and in front. Boom. Boom. Boom. Clap.Clap.Snap. It was incredible to watch as both Omri and Lashonda took turns moving in quick, rhythmic sessions, a rhythm I loved to watch but didn't quite do well myself. I was transported back to our stuffy high school gym, on the bleachers, watching them keep a bodily beat on stage. And I was so enthralled by the show, I didn't even notice the silence between me and Taj.

But he did.

"So, did you talk to your dad yet?" he asked, grabbing my attention.

I swallowed hard and looked down at the little pool of milk at the bottom of my bowl. I did not want to talk about this. And when did he suddenly get so nosy? I shook my head slowly in answer to his question.

"You should."

"I know," I said, trying to be polite. "I'm just…"

"Afraid?" Taj finished for me.

I nodded. "It's been a long time and the whole situation is pretty messed up."

"That's what I heard."

His words struck a match and my cheeks grew warm. "Your dad talk about us when we're not around?" I asked heatedly. "Isn't that information confidential?" I glared at him, but his face was calm.

"Don't you remember your mom brought it up at dinner the other night?" he said. I felt my body tense up in frustration and embarrassment. I had forgotten about that whole evening. Put it out of my mind, is what I did. Instantly I regret my hasty judgment. And as if I didn't feel bad enough, Taj put his hands up in defense and those big brown eyes peered at me innocently.

"I'm not trying to start anything, Nora," he said. "I promise."

Embarrassed, I searched for some words to somehow save the conversation, but my words were cut short as Talia walked up.

"What are y'all talking about?" she asked. Her long, wet curls still dripped while she combed her fingers through her hair.

"Uh, nothing," I said quickly. I hadn't told Talia about my dad yet. She'd be pissed if she knew Taj found out about it first. Quickly, I needed a distraction. "Come on," I said taking her arm. "I've got to tell you something."

Shanice and Craig were talking quietly in our room and the only bathroom was full, so I took Talia to the far side of the hall where we could talk without prying ears. I wasn't in the mood to reveal all my personal tragedies at the moment, so instead, I told Talia about the keys.

Her eyes were wide in disbelief. "You think it's for the game?"

"It's got to be," I said. "You better get one because there's not that many left."

Without saying another word, she darted to the kitchen while I went to our room and squirmed with anticipation. She took a long time and I wondered if she had been caught rifling through the drawer. Thoughts bounced around my mind and I listened for hoots and hollers that would give me some sorta hint as to what had happened. So, when Talia returned and her face revealed nothing, I was stumped. She hopped onto the bunk above mine and began to hum to herself. I waited impatiently for Shanice and Craig to leave, then finally asked her if she got a key.

"Yea, I got one," she said. "But I made sure no one else did." I sat up and almost smacked my forehead on the top bunk.

"What do you mean?"

"I got rid of the rest."

"How?"

"Don't worry about that…wait—" Her head popped over the side and she looked at me upside down. "Did you tell anybody else about the keys?"

I hesitated.

"Nora!"

"What? Taj was right there when I found them."

"Ugh! Of course, you told Taj," Talia groaned and her head disappeared. She was quiet for a minute and I waited for the explosion. "Okay, we'll just have to make him a part of our alliance."

I didn't say anything.

"Just run everything by me next time, okay?"

"Okay," I said shortly. And how was I supposed to run everything by her when things happened so fast in this game? And why did she have to be the one who knew everything? Irritated with my own inner thoughts, I suddenly realized how difficult it might be playing on Talia's team. After another awkward period of silence, I asked, "Talia, are we cool?"

"Huh?" she asked, sounding distracted.

"I mean, are you mad at me or something?"

"No." Her answer was quick, but I felt like she wasn't being honest and I should've listened to my gut at that moment, but I didn't. I should've pressed her further even if she refused, because in the end that might've made a slight difference. In the end that might've changed the outcome. But I was too tired and ended up falling asleep without even taking a shower.

When my bladder woke me up, the room was pitch black. Heavy breathing and soft snores surrounded me and no matter how warm and comfy my bed was I had to get up. I stumbled to the door and barefoot, silently padded to the bathroom. After relieving myself, I went ahead and took a quick shower and wished I had a list of things like a watch, comb and clean underwear. Thankfully they provided new toothbrushes I found in the bathroom drawer.

When I walked out, the cabin was still silent, but I couldn't help but wonder if we'd received another clue. Curiosity plunged me into the dark hall, past my classmates closed doors. I tripped over a pair of dirty sneakers and somebody's jeans. Gross. I didn't want to run into any bare bodies. I peeked into the living room where two sleeping bags were sprawled across the floor, noisy exhaling filled the air, and Cordell's big, bare feet were propped over the side of the sofa. It smelled like a mixture of foul gas and sweaty bodies.

Covering my mouth, I walked over to the window and peeked out and saw the sky was turning a light shade of pink and purple. The sun was rising, so that meant it was morning. I jumped at seeing the bushes move in the distance. Was there someone out there? I walked over to make sure the door was locked and accidentally stepped on a piece of paper.

A clue.

The bright blue envelope was telling and I couldn't wait to tear it open. Again I was the first to stumble upon this secret that would get me closer to that $250,000.

"What you got there señora?"

I heard Omri's raspy voice from behind me. I turned around and winced.

"Will you put on some clothes?" I asked covering my eyes. Bare-chested and in only his loose boxers, he snatched the envelope from my hand.

"Let me see that." His eyes flew across the card and grew wider. "Hell yea!" He yelled and instantly Cordell popped up.

"Who there?!" the big guy sternly shouted.

"Our next clue, y'all!" Omri said as he slapped his bare chest. "We going to a party! I'm 'bout to be dressed to impress."

"What you yellin' bout now?" Adrian said with a yawn as he sat up and Akeem rubbed his eyes.

"Nora found the clue and it says we each need a key if we want to make it far," Omri said as he moved his feet in a little jig.

"A key?" Cordell asked and yawned. "What kind of key?"

I didn't hear the rest of the conversation because I walked quietly back to my room and jumped up to Talia's bed. She snored softly and I shook her.

"Talia!" I whispered. "We got another clue!"

Her eyes popped open at the last word and she sat up straight.

"And there's more," I said as she hopped down. "It says people need a key."

"It does?" she hissed as she pulled on her overalls.

"Where did you put them?"

"It doesn't matter and you better not say anything." She frowned and then looked behind me and instantly a smile masked the previous emotion. "Good morning! Did y'all hear we got our first clue?"

While Su-Min and Shanice rustled in their beds, I escaped into the hall where I could process my thoughts, but I didn't have any time because everyone was waking up and searching for the keys.

"Did anybody find one yet?" Damien demanded, slamming a cabinet.

"No, stupid, and even if we did, we wouldn't tell you," Marcus said from the living room. He had flipped over all the cushions and moved the couches back. I nervously looked at Taj who was pretending to look under the table.

"I'll look in the bathroom," I said.

"Already looked there," Chloe B. said from beside me. Theo was in his room singing as he pulled all the mattresses off the bunkbeds.

I looked behind a picture that hung on the wall.

"Good idea, Nora," Talia said in a loud voice. "They could be hiding back there."

I felt terrible as I pretended to search for keys that I knew Talia had sabotaged.

"Found them!" Akeem yelled. And I couldn't believe it. He'd found the keys in the bottom of the trash can. Talia didn't even look concerned.

"Hand them out," she said nonchalantly.

"Uh…" he said as he picked out two. "Y'all can get your own." And as soon as he walked away it was as if a gun had been shot. The rest of the group lunged at the bag of trash and tore through like raccoons.

Only a few of us stood back.

"There's no more left!" Chloe B. shrieked as she tried to shake the trash from her hands.

"That's not fair!" Shanice yelled and folded her arms.

"Yo' ass shoulda got down and dirty," Lashonda said gleaming as she held her key covered in pizza sauce.

"Ew, I don't think so," Chloe B. said.

"I didn't get one either," Talia said innocently. "Who all got one?"

"We ain't tellin' you," Lashonda said.

I looked around the room and had clearly seen Damien, Lashonda and the twins grab a key. Omri suspiciously had his hands tucked beneath his armpits. I stooped down to start cleaning up the mess.

"What's the point?" Omri asked standing over me. I was glad he had finally put on some clothes.

"We have to eat breakfast, don't we?" I said.

"We could leave in five minutes, you don't know."

"What did the clue say?" Taj asked. "Can I see it?"

"Yep, I had it—" Omri looked on the round table. "Ay! Who took the clue?"

We looked around and I noticed immediately Talia was gone.

"We didn't see the clue. Only you did, fool," Lashonda said.

"I had it right here," Omri said. "Somebody a klepto!" He glared around the room with clutched fists.

Chloe B. put her hand on her hip and said, "Really? We gonna play that game? Dang, y'all. I didn't get no key and now I can't even read the clue."

Still, no one came forward. I noticed Su-Min was missing too.

"Well, what did the clue say?" Taj asked.

"It talked about a party," Omri said scratching his head. "And uh…something about getting dressed up and the keys and…oh! A mystery—a murder mystery."

"A murder mystery dinner?" I asked.

"Yea! Sort of, but it wasn't a dinner," Omri said.

"What else?" I asked impatiently. "Anything specific, like time or place?"

Omri shrugged. "Uh…shoot, sorry y'all. I don't remember."

Groans resounded around the room. With no further information, I wanted to find out where those two girls were. I walked into our bedroom, but it was empty, so I grabbed my sandals and slipped them on as I checked the bathroom. It was empty too. After looking in the other bedrooms I noticed Deshaun, Brandon and the twins were missing as well.

"Where did the others go?" I asked, walking back into the living room.

"What are you talking 'bout?" Lashonda asked. "This ain't a big cabin and they didn't go through the front door. They around here somewhere."

Feeling my heart pound, I turned and walked back down the hall and then stopped short. There it was. Why hadn't I noticed it before? At the end of the hall was an opened door.

"Over here!" I yelled.

And without looking back I ran up to it, pushed the door wide and walked into another hallway. The door was probably there the whole time. I never thought to look behind it. I must've assumed it was a closet or a boiler room or something.

But I should've known not to take anything for granted in Beholden. The door led to a narrow hallway, so tight I could touch both sides of the bare white walls with my hands. There was one flickering bulb that hung from the ceiling. The string attached swung slightly. At the end of the hall was a closed door. I hastily approached it, turned the knob and opened the door to the next phase.

Rockefeller Christmas Tree

As I stepped into a room that resembled a private library, I wondered who was making breakfast because the air smelled like scrambled eggs and bacon. I thought about taking off my sandals because the fluffy rugs looked expensive.

To my left was a set of cushiony wingback chairs and behind them was a wall of bookshelves that went from ceiling to floor, flooded with beams of sunlight from the windows. Thick curtains hung on either side of the window seat and I leaned on the cushioned bench and looked out, but could only see a large bush that blocked my view.

I walked over to the bookshelves and ran my finger over the hardcovers. My mama always said you can tell a lot about a person by the books they displayed. From what I could see, the people who lived here loved poetry, investments, music, and money.

I heard yelling from behind and the silence of the room disappeared as Omri and Lashonda barged through the door behind me.

"What the——" Omri said as he knocked over a floor lamp and caught it.

"What just happened?" Lashonda asked. "Where are we?"

I couldn't tell her. But I was about to find out. I continued walking until I reached a flight of stairs going up and another empty hallway. There was a door with hooks beside it that hung an umbrella and a hat. I put my hand on the doorknob thinking it would take us outside, but the door was locked. I started down a hall until a voice spoke from above.

"Can I help you, Miss?"

It was a thin, older man, with skin as black as charcoal and hair speckled with gray. He wore a brown suit and his voice was deep as he asked, "Are you here for the O'Hare's brunch?" He descended slowly down the stairs, his gloved hand slid easily down the banister.

I hesitated but remembered this was all part of the game.

"Yes sir," I said. "Where is the brunch being held?"

"Well, you certainly can't go looking like that," he said walking down the stairs with his nose upturned. He pointed with his white glove at a clothing rack in the hall. "Please choose an appropriate garment for the meal. Master Sinclair and Mistress Gwendolyn are expecting you." He frowned at me which shot wrinkles across his forehead.

"Ah, shoot!" Omri yelled as he bounced in. "It's Alfred!" He slapped the man's hand and embraced him. "Ay! Where Bruce Wayne at?"

"My name is Keith," the man said tightly. His shoulders were stiff as he waited for Omri to let him go.

Yells from the library told me more people had figured out where we were and I had no time to waste. Game on. Quickly, I searched through the clothes on the rack and found a dress in my size.

"Where do I change?" I quickly asked Keith.

"There is a bathroom over there, Miss," he said and pointed to a door.

I wanted to get wherever Talia had disappeared to. I knew I was behind and didn't want to miss any clues she may have picked up.

As I slipped the apple red, slinky gown over my shoulders, I wondered why Talia hadn't included me on the secret door to this phase. And then, as I admired my shimmery dress in the mirror, lined up the dress straps so I was good and covered, I saw what I'd always wanted.

I looked as bright and beautiful as a Rockefeller Christmas tree. You know, I realize maybe I didn't know what I wanted. Part of me hated the stares and attention, but another part craved some admiration even though I knew I couldn't handle it. Was I selfish? Was I conceited? Was this Freud's ego rearing its ugly head? A knock told me I had run out of time.

"Hurry up!" Lashonda yelled.

After poking a few loose curls back into my now messy braided crown (and realizing I'd already lost a couple of bobby pins), I wiped the sleep out of my eyes, balled up my old clothes and walked out. People rushed past me as I set my clothes next to a pile that I recognized as Talia's overalls. I also took my key from my pocket and tucked it in my bra just in case.

"You still can't go looking like that," Keith said as I tried to walk past him. He cleared his throat and eyed my sandals.

I groaned, rushed back to take them off and found a pair of black, size eight heels beneath the clothing rack. Pushing them on I hopped over to him and said, "Now?"

"You may go. The others are waiting in the dining room."

Swiftly, I walked through the hallway while I straightened my dress. I smiled as I noted the faded, flowered wallpaper decorated with antique framed black and white photos. Beholden made sure every detail matched the theme. And when I walked into a large, but empty, living room that held a piano, a roaring fireplace, and an enormous chandelier, I couldn't help but gasp.

Beholden did too much. It's one thing to watch it on TV, but another to walk through it.

I couldn't get over the lushness of the entire room. So many questions flew through my mind. Was this a real home? How in the world did we go from a cabin to a mansion? It was like we were transported to another place entirely.

Hearing voices still further on, I pushed myself to move through this room to another hall that wound around. Peeking my head through the door to my left I saw the kitchen. Empty there as well. So I walked around the corner and into a long room filled with people at a dining table.

A table filled with familiar faces and strange ones.

"Don't you look stunning!" said the woman in front of me. She was adorned in a golden dress that touched the floor, glittering bangles on her tiny wrists, jewels dripped from her ears, neck and even surrounded her bare, coffee-brown scalp. And she was tall.

"Where are my manners? I am Mistress Gwendolyn," she said melodiously and extended her dainty hand. "Miss—?"

"Miss—uh, Nora," I said and took her hand, trying hard not to stare. I suddenly felt very small and so intimidated I wanted to go back to the cabin, shower and change again. Was I underdressed? Should I be here?

"Miss Nora, do please find a seat at our table. We were just about to begin."

I turned and walked past the staring eyes of Talia and Su-Min who sat beside Gwendolyn, past a dude with a thick curly mustache and a pipe dangling from his full lips, past the twins who looked pretty good in their suit jackets, all the way to an empty seat beside the man who sat at the opposite end of the table.

This dude looked very important. Where I thought the butler's suit was nice, this brother had garments that reeked expensive, like sparkling cufflinks, a silky midnight blue tie, and a navy blue suit.

And his face marveled me. Just gorgeous. His skin reminded me of maple syrup, smooth and rich brown. He even smelled pleasantly sweet. I averted my eyes nervously and wanted to giggle like a little school girl. Was he for real? I couldn't help but look back as he pulled out his silver pocket watch and lazily frowned, bringing his thick eyebrows together and pursed his lips.

"Well," he said in a baritone voice. "I'm ready to begin. Where is Keith?"

"I believe we have more guests that have arrived," Gwendolyn said as some of my classmates noisily poured into the room. There weren't enough chairs for them all, so a few were told to go back into the kitchen where they would be served. I was happy I had gotten a seat when I did.

In front of me sat Taj, who looked rather dapper in his suit and tie and whose eyes were round as saucers as he gawked at me. I shyly averted his gaze and instead looked at Lashonda who sat to his left in a green dress and Omri who winked at me as he adjusted his bright orange bow tie. As if I didn't get his first hint, he pursed his lips into a kiss and made loud smacking noises. I rolled my eyes and looked at the woman beside him.

She had caramel skin with visible brown freckles on her nose. Her sandy brown curls were twisted up into a high bun and she too was dressed very glamorous, but not nearly as fancy as Mistress Gwendolyn.

A little girl who looked around five or six sat between Brandon and Deshaun. She poked the two football players and giggled. She seemed to love the attention and her hazel eyes were large as she looked around the table. Her gapped teeth showed as she grinned up at the boys. I noticed her curly, sandy hair was identical to the other woman's, except her hair was pulled into two big puffs on either side of her head.

"Dang!" she blurted. "I ain't ever seen so many folks at breakfast before!"

"Brunch," the woman corrected her. "Put your napkin on your lap, Junie."

"It's Junebug!" the girl squeaked. Then she hopped up on her seat and pointed her butter knife across the table. "And HE did it!" she screamed and burst into giggles filled with snorts.

"Junebug, please sit in your seat like a lady," the man said who she'd pointed her knife at. He looked at the woman. "I thought we discussed this?"

"She's your child too," the woman muttered loud enough for everyone to hear.

Junebug preceded to stomp in her seat, slapping the heads of Deshaun and Brandon like she was keeping a beat in a marching band. Her white ruffled dress swung with every step and her eyes gleamed with excitement as she demanded the attention of the table.

"What y'all lookin' at?" she yelled.

"You," Omri said.

"Well, stop!" she ordered.

"Junebug, please sit down," Mistress Gwendolyn pleaded. "You know how this upsets your mother."

111

"I don't care." Junebug crossed her arms stubbornly and then stepped up and stomped across the white tablecloth, scattering the silverware everywhere with her shiny, patent leather Mary Jane's.

"Oh, you need to be whooped," Omri said grabbing his napkin and stuffing it in his lap.

"Who said that?" Junebug yelled and snapped her head around the table.

"I did," Omri said back. "Your mama need to get a switch and whoop your little a——"

"Enough!" said the man beside me and calmly stared at the little girl. "Junebug, if you do not sit in your seat, there will be no dessert."

"You can't do that! You ain't my daddy!" she shouted with her little hands balled up.

"No, I'm not," the man said. "But this is my house."

"So?"

"My house. My rules."

At that, Junebug's bottom lip quivered with anger as she glared across the table. It seemed as if the silence was so thin, no one wanted to breathe or else they'd break it.

"Fine," Junebug finally retorted as she walked back to her chair. "But I want brownies today, Uncle Sinclair."

As soon as she sat down, Keith rolled in a cart full of plates. My stomach grumbled as he began to set them in front of each of us.

"I'm allergic to nuts and I'm lactose intolerant," said Talia as she eyed her food. "Can I substitute this with something else?"

112

"I'm sorry, Miss, but Cook is on vacation this week," Keith said almost sounding like a recording. "and I've had to step in and take over. I am quite unfamiliar with the kitchen and all its contents. With all my duties it was impossible to prepare a separate menu. I do apologize."

He placed a plate in front of Lashonda.

"What the hell is this?" she asked and poked it with a fork.

"Eggs Benedict with spinach salad and a parfait."

"You got some hot sauce?" Lashonda had one eyebrow raised.

"No ma'am, I do not."

"What? Ain't y'all black?" she eyed the people around the table. "I can't believe there ain't no hot sauce in this house. You got some salt? I know y'all got some salt."

When Keith set the dish in front of me, my stomach growled. I didn't realize how hungry I'd been, but the unfamiliar dish in front of me didn't seem to satisfy my craving. The plate held a small round piece of crusty toast with a runny egg and mustard yellow sauce dribbled across. The spinach salad had a few waxy leaves and the watery yogurt looked like it could be eaten in one spoonful.

"Where's the Bloody Mary and Mimosas?" Deshaun asked holding up his glass. "I heard folks drink alcohol at brunch."

Keith straightened up at his comment and said, "Sir. This is an abstemious household."

"A what type of household?" Lashonda asked as her fork froze midway to her lips. She eyed her food warily.

"Abstemious, meaning we do not indulge in addictive behavior such as consuming spirits with every meal."

Deshaun looked depressed as he gulped his glass of water.

"Are there seconds?" Omri asked as he finished his plate.

"Sir?" Keith asked as he put the last plate on the table and sighed. "Do you mean, is there a second course? No, I'm sorry sir, this is the only course for the meal. Again, I do apologize as Cook has been away and I don't truly know my way around her area. She does keep the kitchen quite unorganized and—"

"Yes, yes, we know, Keith, you're excused," the man called Uncle Sinclair said from beside me.

The room grew quiet as everyone began to eat, except for Omri who was already finished and Junebug who was throwing her spinach leaves at Deshaun.

I looked down at my plate and warily put the eggs called Benedict on my fork. I had never eaten such a meal before, but I wasn't about to go hungry because of something unfamiliar. (Note- I will eat my own words later.) I took a bite and my taste buds searched for recognition. The cream had a tangy flavor that reminded me of lemon and butter, then there was the obvious salty bacon, the gooey egg and lastly the crunch of the crusty toast. After taking three more bites, I decided I loved me some Eggs Benedict. Wishing I had more, I sighed at the pile of greens that still sat on my plate and opted to indulge in the parfait instead.

"Quit," Brandon shouted from across the table. Junebug was now trying to push her runny eggs onto his plate. "I said, quit girl!"

She giggled uncontrollably and I wanted to laugh too. I had never seen beefy football player, Brandon look so unnerved.

"So, I didn't catch your name?" I heard Talia ask at the end of the table.

"Avery," Junebug yelled. "My daddy's name is Avery and that woman is my mama, Elisa." She looked proud as if she had answered a question correctly.

I knew what Talia was doing. She was trying to solve the mystery. But what mystery was there? Nothing seemed to be out of place. No one had been murdered. Unless it was the missing cook.

I heard Su-Min ask something and Gwendolyn answered, but their conversation was drowned out by Junebug's incessant laughter and her parents scolding her.

"Where do you hail from, young lady?" Sinclair asked from beside me.

Startled, I realized that I had someone of significance right here all along. He wasn't as interesting as Gwendolyn whom I wished I had gotten to sit next to, but I guess he'd have to do.

"I'm from Normal, Alabama," I said.

"Normal. How interesting. I've had investors from that little town."

"Investors?" Taj asked. "What sort of business do you have, Mr. Sinclair?"

"You haven't heard?" he asked with surprise and a bit of annoyance. He took a bite and swallowed his food. "I am the owner of Devilish Dish, the snack food that every pantry holds." He paused as if to wait for our reaction. "It's sinfully delicious by Sinclair O'Hare?" His eyebrows raised and he waited to see if perhaps now we had recognized his product.

"Oh!" I said pretending to know what he was talking about. "Yes, they're very good."

"Thank you," he said wiping his mouth with his napkin. "The key is hard work. If you have an impeccable work ethic, you will be successful. Doesn't matter where you come from. Just look at me," he said with a casual smile. "I grew up with a single mother who worked around the clock so I could have a good education. I started my own business and now I have a beautiful mansion, where my lovely wife, my sister-in-law and her husband may live. Not to mention their daughter who enjoys exploring all the secret passages."

My ears perked up. "Secret passages? In the house?"

"All over," he said. "This is an old home, used to belong to a family who hid runaway slaves in their very walls to sneak them up north."

"Wow," Taj said.

"But enough talk about that," Sinclair said. He then went on and on about how successful his business was and the dreams he had envisioned for his family. But as he talked, I couldn't help but let my mind wander. I wanted to take in the entire room, not just Sinclair's boring story about his success.

There was a cherry red hutch behind me with a portrait of an old woman beside it, fake trees in the corners of the room and a grandfather clock that read 10:05. That was odd. The first time I'd seen a clock in the game.

Suddenly a man's voice from the table snapped, "I'm sure our guests don't want to be bored about the details of your proficient business, Sinclair!"

It was the man Junebug had called Avery. His outburst silenced the table and all eyes were on him. His head was down, but I could see his curly mustache twitch, eyes fixed on his untouched plate, and he gripped his fork so hard his hand shook.

"If they don't want to hear about it, they are welcome to change the subject," Sinclair said calmly.

"But it's imperative, dear brother-in-law," Avery went on tight-lipped. "for a host to have some self-awareness so that he doesn't sound so pretentious."

Gwendolyn's voice rose at the end of the table. "Should we take this into the parlor?" she said shakily.

"Naw," Omri said with a grin on his face. "Let's watch how this plays out."

Sinclair tossed his napkin onto his empty plate. "I'd love to hear what else Avery thinks."

"Aw, shoot," Omri said as his eyes bounced from Avery to Sinclair and back to Avery. He leaned forward eagerly in his seat as if he were watching an NBA Finals game.

"Avery's so full of good ideas," Sinclair said sarcastically. "So many good ideas that I suppose he got that job? How did your interview go with the bank?"

"Dang! You gonna let him talk to you like that?" Omri asked.

"You know very well!" Avery roared as his head snapped up and he glared across the table at Sinclair.

"No, I don't," Sinclair said casually. "Only what my wife and Elisa tell me, which isn't much."

"Oh, we all know Elisa tells you everything." Avery's words were telling. The way he spoke Elisa's name made me look at her face. Her hand touched her cheek and I couldn't tell if that was blush or were her cheeks red with shame?

"Wait, what?" Omri shouted. "Whatchu not tellin' us Elisa? You got a thing for Sinclair behind your man's back?"

"Omri, shut up," Talia yelled.

Lashonda laughed. "Uh-uh. Let him do his thang. This is gettin' good."

"Well, the girls like to gossip," Sinclair went on. "Right, honey?"

Gwendolyn's smile had gotten tight. Her lips were stretched wide and thin and her eyes glistened.

"Why don't we retire to the parlor?" she said as she stood, her words coming out more of a command than a question.

"Fine. Lets," Sinclair said as he shoved back his chair. The residents followed, even Junebug, and so did the rest of us. To solve the mystery, we had to go where the clues lead.

Gwendolyn sat at the piano and played a melancholy tune, one I recognized from the year I sang in the school choir. "Summertime" was the name. Her alto voice was sultry like Ella Fitzgerald as she belted out:

"Summertime...and the livin' is easy..."

I saw Sinclair pour himself a drink by the bar and when he passed Elisa a glass, her stare seemed to linger a little too long. I wasn't the only one watching because Avery abruptly left the room.

Feeling out of place, I sat down in one of the overstuffed chairs by the fireplace and felt like something big was about to happen. There was a tremendous amount of tension in the room, stretched as tight as a string, so it's understandable that I jumped when Talia grabbed my hand.

"Dang, where'd you get that dress? I wish I found it," she said.

I almost smiled but remembered I was pissed at her. I didn't forget how she left me in the last phase. Especially after I had shared the hidden keys with her. What happened to sticking together and having each others' back?

I shrugged in answer to her question which lead to an uneasy silence between us. Finally, she cleared her throat. "Sorry I left you back there," she continued. "But I couldn't go back once we came through." I looked up at her. She sounded sincere. "You understand, right?"

I nodded, but still felt a little hurt. Was she serious or just saying it out of duty so she could move on? But I guess I sort of wanted to move on too. No point in holding grudges when you need your allies more than ever. After all, I wanted to win, didn't I? And to win, I needed to keep all communication lines open.

I looked around the room as groups of my classmates were huddled together. I was most interested in the group that surrounded Junebug. She seemed to be chatting endlessly and her audience was taking it all in. I got up to go over and see what the fuss was about, but Talia hooked her arm through mine.

"So, what did you learn?"

Slightly irritated, I shrugged and stared at Omri's face as he nodded rapidly while Junebug spoke. His eyes were lit like he had just won the $250,000 himself. I knew he was getting some good info.

"Come on," Talia said with a tug of my arm. "you sat next to Mr. Sinclair. I know he told you something."

I looked at Talia and lifted my eyebrows. "So? You sat next to Gwendolyn."

She put her hands up. "That's only fair. Alright, we'll trade information. You first."

I shook my head, feeling a knot form. "Oh, no," I said firmly.

"You don't trust me?" she asked.

I crossed my arms. Who did she think she was fooling? I knew her too well. "You've been here longer. I'm sure you found out more."

"I only know what you've heard," she insisted. "Gwendolyn talked about how the cook was gone and Keith filled in, then mentioned that she hadn't worked since she married Sinclair. But that was it."

"Really?"

"I promise."

"Okay," I said and hesitated. "Well, I did learn that Sinclair is the owner of a successful business."

"Doing what?"

"Snack food or something."

She nodded eagerly, expecting me to say more.

"That's it," I said with a shrug. "We should go see what Omri found out." Gwendolyn's song had changed to an unfamiliar one, but as we passed by her, I could see her eyes closed in a frustrated frown as she sorrowfully belted out her lyrics. There was a story behind her, more than glamour and glitz she had shown. As we approached the group, Junebug skittered off. I noticed Sinclair talking with Taj where Talia and I had just left and Elisa spoke with Marcus, Theo and Chloe B. Everybody was getting some information and I felt like I was missing out.

"What did you hear from the little girl?" Talia asked the group.

"Like we gonna tell you," Omri said and folded his arms, then looked at me and smiled. "Dang, Nora you rocking that dress."

"I'll tell you what I know," Talia said trying to get back his attention.

"It ain't much, I'm sure," Lashonda replied. "Su-Min already told us everything y'all heard."

"Su-Min!" Talia glared at her and Su-Min's response was priceless.

She smiled a little and said quietly, "They promised to include me in their group."

"Oh, so we're forming groups now?" Talia asked.

"Don't act like you and Nora ain't been a team from the start," Omri said. "Don't be mad Spicy Tuna on our side. And your shady self been lying to everybody. I know it was you who took that clue."

Talia looked furious, but not the least bit remorseful. She turned on her heel and commanded, "Come on Nora, we'll solve the mystery ourselves."

I looked from Omri to Talia.

"No offense, Señora, but we can't tell you either," Omri said.

"I understand," I said as I turned to follow Talia. But I wanted to kick myself and Talia.

Lines had been drawn. Sides had been chosen.

And we were the enemies.

Very Private Things

"Well, this has been enjoyable," Sinclair announced loudly. The handsome man of the house raised his glass, took one more sip and set it on top of the fireplace mantle. "But I have lots of work to do. I hope our guests enjoy the rest of their stay." He clapped his hands. "Keith! Prepare my afternoon cup of coffee and bring it to me in my study."

The butler seemed to appear from nowhere and said hastily, "Right away, sir."

Anxiously, I watched Sinclair leave the room. Was he out of the game already? How much time did we have left? The room now held only half of my classmates. I started to wonder if exploring the house was better than sitting in here trying to get information out of the others.

I grabbed Talia's arm and said, "We should start looking around and see where all the other suspects are."

"Suspects?" Talia raised her eyebrows. "Or should we say, victims?"

"Right," I said with a laugh. "Oh! I forgot to tell you about the house. Sinclair also said it has secret pass—"

A shrill scream cut off my words. It came from the hall and we all rushed out like the room was on fire. A thick crowd had formed a circle and I slipped through to see what everybody was staring at. Had the cook finally been found? Or had Avery met his demise? Did Sinclair keel over right as he walked out the door?

But all of my suspicions were incorrect. I looked at her little body, splayed motionless across the floor, and wondered who murdered Junebug.

Taj bent over the little girl and put his ear to her mouth.

"She ain't really dead, stupid," Lashonda muttered.

"Just trying to play along," Taj said sheepishly and stood.

"I knew it!" Omri said. "Didn't I tell you?" He looked around. "I told y'all she'd be the one to die! She said she would!"

Those of us not included in Omri's secret with Junebug were lost. And I had just begun to rack up all the clues that lead to Junebug's murder when the little girl jumped up and screeched, "Fooled y'all!" Then shoved past us and sprinted down the hall.

"That little liar," Su-Min said and shook her head.

"Dang!" Omri shouted. "And we was so close!"

I was carried with the crowd back to the living room. Mistress Gwendolyn was still there, but she now sat in one of the armchairs beside the fireplace, her body draped like a golden blanket over a recliner. The fire was out and the room felt a bit chillier.

I sat down on the chaise beneath the chandelier but jumped back up when I remembered what I was going to tell Talia. I looked around for her, but she wasn't in the room. I knew she had probably gone searching for more clues. What happened to us sticking together and being allies and all that?

Wanting to join her, I went to the door, but Gwendolyn clapped her hands and got everyone's attention, including mine.

"Let's play a game!" she suggested. "Have you ever heard of two truths and a lie?"

A game? And such a ridiculous one. I moved toward the door anyway but stopped when Gwendolyn called.

"Oh, girl in the red dress! Don't you want to join? I promise we'll have lots of fun." I turned around reluctantly and sat back down on the lounge. I couldn't deny her once she called me out.

"What kind of game is that?" Lashonda asked looking bored. She sat on a white love seat. Her body leaned forward, elbows on knees, legs sprawled out like she was taking a break on the bench during half time. Humorously, a stretch of green fabric flowed right between her legs, covering anything indecent in between.

"I've heard of it." Damien walked in, wearing baggy trousers. I assumed he couldn't find anything in his size. He had a piece of half-eaten fried chicken in his hand.

"Where you get that?" Omri asked. "I thought Alfred said there weren't no more food!"

"There's a bucket of drumsticks in the kitchen," Cordell said as he came out behind Damien. He had on a snug white jacket and in his hand, a plate piled with fudge brownies. They looked delicious.

"Gimme some!" Omri jumped up.

"In the kitchen," Damien said with his mouth full and Omri darted past him.

"Ah! Our famous Devilish snack cakes," Gwendolyn said looking at Cordell. "Sinfully gooey chocolate with a hint of crunch, yet a velvety texture." She looked at me and winked. "The crunch comes from the crushed pecans. My idea, not Sinclair's. It is my dear mama's recipe, intended for me to one day pass on to my children and their children and..." Her eyes turned sadly downward and she sighed, then brightened and looked up. "Who wants to go first?" she asked. "And no boring truths, like 'I have a pet dog.' Those won't count for me. I want to hear some outrageous truths. Truths that even your parents may not know." She lifted her eyebrows and looked around the room.

"Like we gon' tell you," Lashonda said and rolled her eyes. "I ain't airing my business with strangers."

Gwendolyn said in a sing-song voice, "If you don't play, you won't get the prize."

"Oh, I'm winning that money," Lashonda said. "Ain't no doubt about that." She sat up and smoothed her braids. "And why we playin' this game anyway? I thought there was supposed to be a murder?"

"A murder?" Gwendolyn gasped and put her hand to her chest. "Where?"

I had to roll my eyes at her corny performance, but Gwendolyn was not budging on revealing any information unless we played her game.

So play the game we did.

"I'll go first," Damien said. He threw his bone into the cold fireplace and wiped his greasy hands on his trousers. "Alright, so the game goes like this. You tell two truths and a lie and everybody has to guess which one is the lie." And as he started the game I found myself wishing I had joined Talia. Nothing was going on here, in fact, as I looked around the room, most of the people were slowly leaving. The only ones who stayed beside me were Damien, Cordell, Omri, Lashonda, Taj and the twins. I wanted to get up, but my turn was coming up next and it seemed too late to leave now that the game had started.

Some did a decent job hiding their lies. I learned some things I didn't know, like how Adrian had never gotten his license and Akeem had gone to the hospital with two broken arms. Even more interesting was when Taj revealed that he was adopted, a fact that I had never assumed because, well, his dad and mom were both black.

"So, you're not the preacher's son?" Omri asked in shock.

"Well, yea, he's my dad," Taj said. "But I was a foster kid for 12 years before they adopted me."

I would've never guessed.

But then some things didn't surprise me, like how Cordell could eat almost two large pizzas on his own, Damien took archery classes, and Omri lost his virginity at 13.

"Wow, Omri. I bet that was hard to share," Lashonda said rolling her eyes.

"Yea, it was," Omri said with a smirk. He looked at me and then looked away. I shook my head and wondered why he had to act so stupid sometimes.

"Your turn, Nora," Damien said.

"What about Lashonda?" I asked.

"I'm not playing," she said firmly.

I had already planned my two truths and a lie. And I knew it would be hard to get anything past this group. We'd all grown up together (except Taj) and they all knew my family. They'd seen my Mexican grandmother and mama (who some still thought was white). They knew about Tony. But I wanted to win this game. If Mistress Gwendolyn wanted me to play, then I was going to do my best to stump everybody else. But the scary part was, to do it, I had to reveal some very private things.

And it had to be recent.

"Now, don't worry, Nora," Omri said. "We won't judge you too hard."

"What you talkin' bout?" Lashonda asked as she grabbed a blanket and wrapped it around her shoulders. "Nora's got no secrets. Her life's as bland as that salad we had for brunch."

"Let her talk," Taj said and looked at me expectantly.

I hated moments like this when sweat migrated to my armpits and I felt like I would die if another eyeball looked in my direction. But I wanted to win this game. I wasn't ready to go home. So, I took a deep breath, looked around the room, and made my face serious so as not to reveal which was the lie and which was the truth.

"I was kidnapped," I began. "I've never been kissed and I've been to jail."

The room was silent and then erupted in laughter.

"You lie through your teeth," Lashonda said. "All of 'em lies."

"I know you ain't been kissed," Omri said thoughtfully and tapped his chin. "But what's the other truth?"

"She ain't been to no jail either," Cordell said with his mouth full. "She must've been kidnapped."

Lashonda looked at Omri. "How you know she ain't been kissed? Y'all think Nora so innocent, but I see how she do."

"Naw." Omri shook his head. "Mi Señora has been with no one but me." He thumped his chest.

Lashonda rolled her eyes so long I saw nothing but the whites of her eyes.

"Now, wait a minute!" Gwendolyn said lifting her hands. "This is a good one! It seems the young lady might have puzzled us all." She looked around the room. "Who wants to guess first?"

"I'll go," Damien said and scrunched up his nose in thought. He pushed his glasses back up and said confidently, "The obvious lie is been to jail."

"Next?" Gwendolyn said. One by one, different answers were given. Most people just blurted out the lie was either been to jail or kidnapped. Everybody, that is, but Lashonda. Her guess was never been kissed and she looked me right in the eye when she said it.

"Well?" Gwendolyn said, her eyes large as she stared across the room at me.

"The lie is…" I said with a dramatic pause. "I've never been kissed."

"I knew it!" Lashonda said punching her fist in the air.

"Who kissed you?" Omri asked jumping up like he was ready to fight.

"And when did you go to jail?" Damien asked.

"Naw, for real though," Omri said as he walked up to me. "Who defiled you, mi amor?"

"And you were kidnapped?" Damien exclaimed in disbelief. "That's a lie, I know it is."

I shook my head emphatically. "No, I promise, I'm telling the truth."

Omri grabbed my hand. "Tell me who this perpetrator is and I'll kill him."

I pulled my hand from Omri's clutch and tried not to laugh.

"Explain," Damien demanded with a frown.

"Wait, I haven't had a turn," Gwendolyn interrupted as she stood.

She walked around the room theatrically, running her hand over the piano as if deep in thought, then she slowly spoke each statement carefully.

"I am unable to have children…Junebug is my husband's child…and our company has gone bankrupt." Her smile didn't even twitch as she spoke those words. My stomach clenched as I knew this moment seemed important. Her command of the room was remarkable as we all consumed her performance. She stood with poise, one hand on her hip and one foot slightly forward.

"I'll go first," Damien said. "This'll be easy. The lie is you're unable to have children."

"And why would you say that?" Lashonda asked.

"Because I know something you don't," Damien said with a wink.

I hated when Damien did that. Somehow he was always ahead of the game and I wondered what he knew that I didn't. He had given that same wink to me countless times in class whenever he knew the answer to a question that had me stumped. The game continued as each person took their time guessing which of Gwendolyn's statements had been a lie.

"Your company is bankrupt," Omri said. "Easy."

Gwendolyn didn't say anything. Her eyes just gazed at us. I heard others murmur in agreement and I would've too if it hadn't been for the look on Taj's face. Even though we both had spoken with Sinclair and heard him brag about his successful snack food, Taj's face looked conflicted.

I assumed the obvious truth was Junebug had been the lovechild of Sinclair and Elise or did Gwendolyn actually have children and just hadn't told us? Or was the real truth Sinclair had lied to us about his business? I couldn't figure out which was the lie.

Taj spoke up next and said, "The lie is Junebug is your husband's child." I looked at his face. He was satisfied with his answer.

A few others answered and then it was my turn. Was Mistress Gwendolyn lying about Junebug or the business? I had to make a decision. I rubbed my bare arms and felt tiny goosebumps from the chill. "The lie is," I began hesitantly. "Junebug is your husband's child." I felt sure that Taj knew what he was talking about. He had talked to Sinclair alone and maybe he had some information that helped him come to his decision.

"The answer is…" Gwendolyn began, but before she could finish, another shrill scream pierced through the air.

"What is it this time?" Lashonda groaned as she grabbed the blanket. "And is the AC on? I'm frozen!"

Gwendolyn looked at the fire and frowned as if she hadn't noticed it. "Keith?" she called. "Where is Keith?"

I followed the others into the hall for the second time, expecting to see another dead body, but was met with the sight of Talia cradling a teary Junebug in her arms. The girl's parents, Elise and Avery, rushed down the stairs, followed by Chloe B., Theo, and Marcus.

"What happened?" Taj asked.

"She said she saw somebody," Su-Min said as she crossed her arms and frowned.

"She said someone went out the window," Talia corrected her.

"She lying," Omri said, waving her off.

"I'm not!" Junebug blubbered. "I promise, I saw someone!"

Questions flew around as everyone tried to interview Junebug on the mysterious stranger who exited the window. Some even ran to see which window he went through. I didn't know what to do. Junebug's character had been dark from the beginning. She loved attention and was known to lie, but her performance was very convincing. And what was up with her and Talia? She clung to my friend like she was her mother and Talia's face seemed to believe every word the girl said.

"He wore a purple suit," Junebug murmured as she wiped her runny nose on Talia's arm. "And he carried a rope."

"Professor Plum, in the kitchen, with the rope," Damien said and laughed.

"It's not funny!" Junebug shrieked.

"Who the hell is Professor Plum?" Lashonda asked.

"He's from the game Clue," Damien said knowingly.

"Well, where's the murder?" Su-Min asked with her hands on her hips. She looked at the clock. "We've been here for almost six hours."

"Sinclair?" I heard Gwendolyn's voice down the hall and rapping at a door. I walked toward her urgent voice and heard her call again. "Sinclair? Are you alright?"

The others still surrounded a sniffling Junebug as she had moved on to retell her story.

"Keith!" Gwendolyn called and looked back at me.

Keith pushed passed me. "Yes, Madame?"

"Do you have my keys to the study? Sinclair has locked himself in and isn't answering the door."

"No, ma'am. Master has never given me a key to the study."

"Well, I did have one…but it's missing. Please, Keith, can you try to force the door open? I feel something is wrong." Her eyes looked worried.

"Ma'am, I'll get us some help." He turned and looked past me.

"Is there a suitable person who can force open the door?" he called.

"I can do it," Taj volunteered. He smiled at me and whispered, "I've always wanted to do this." He walked over, fiddled with the knob first (probably to make sure it was actually locked) and with the help of Keith's assistance, rammed his body against the door.

It seemed to be made of something other than wood because the door broke easily. The room was dark with no windows to let in any light. Taj ran his hand along the side of the wall and flicked on the switch.

And then we saw what had become of Sinclair O'Hare.

He sat back, with eyes closed, and mouth slack.

Mistress Gwendolyn screamed.

I walked into the room and immediately covered my nose. The room smelt awful as if filled with rotten potatoes. The square office held a desk piled with papers, a cup of coffee on the table with a French Press beside it, and a bookshelf on the left. I peered into the trash can and saw a pile of slimy brown liquid. I could feel the contents of my belly gurgling as saliva rushed to my mouth. I covered my lips to prevent anything from coming out.

"What has happened to my love?" Gwendolyn wailed. She laid her head on his chest and cried. Her tears looked real and I was very impressed with her performance.

"What's going on?" Su-Min asked from behind me and instantly covered her nose. People were now rushing to squeeze into the room, so I was pushed against the bookshelf.

"What the hell is that smell?" Lashonda yelled.

I pointed to the trashcan. "Someone threw up."

Lashonda backed up and covered her mouth. "Okay, I'm gonna guess from back here," she said with a muffled voice. "I think it was Gwendolyn."

"What?" Gwendolyn shrieked. "How could I possibly have killed my husband? He was locked in the study!"

"It's true," Taj said with a frown. "I tried the door and it was locked." He looked serious but I think he was trying to not look disgusted like the rest of us.

"Well then he killed himself," Damien said using his sleeve to cover his nose and mouth. "That's simple. Now, how do we move on to the next phase?"

"Excuse me?" Gwendolyn shouted above the roar of voices. "Attention everyone!" Her black mascara was now streaked down her cheeks. "No one leaves my house until this murder is solved! The culprit must pay for his crime!"

"It was the man that went out the window!" Junebug said from Talia's arms.

"No, it was Avery," Marcus said with a cough. "He's the one who was jealous of his wife steppin' out with the dude." He coughed again and covered his face with the crook of his arm.

"It was definitely Elise," Chloe B. said pinching her nose. "'Cause we found a journal where she admits she was in love with him—"

"That's private information!" Elise yelled from down the hall.

"—and," Chloe B. continued. "she said she couldn't live without him. Where that journal at boo?" She looked at Theo, who picked up the cup of coffee on the desk and took a sip.

"Theo!" I yelled.

"Boy, what you doin?" Lashonda asked. "Thas' nasty."

"He got something else in there," Theo said. "Taste funny…too sweet."

"It's probably sugar, stupid," Lashonda said. "I can't stand the funk. I'm out." She threw up a peace sign and walked out the door.

"It's evidence," Damien snapped at Theo. "You shouldn't touch anything."

"I'll touch whatever I want," Theo said puffing out his chest. "You ain't the FBI."

"Everyone, please!" Gwendolyn shouted. She pushed Sinclair's head into her bosom and dabbed her eyes with a handkerchief. "You must solve this murder. I forbid anyone to leave until you can prove to me who killed my husband. And to do that…No, Junebug, put your hand down, you may not solve the case. I want—"

"But I told you, it was the man who jumped out the window!" Junebug blurted.

"As I was saying, I want four things from you. One: you must tell me who the murderer is. Two: you must tell me how he was murdered. Three: what was the motive? Why would this person kill my husband? And four: show me proof. Bring me hard evidence."

"And then?" Chloe B. asked.

"Then, I will give you a key to the front door, for that is your only way out."

"What?!" Feet pounded out of the room and I heard people shouting, "I got the key!" "Move out of my way!"

I didn't bother following. There was no way we were getting out that easy.

"When can we look for clues?" I asked. "I mean, we can't all fit into this room at the same time."

"She's right, Madame," Keith said. "We'll have to observe the room in groups of four. Does that sound alright?"

"I think that suffices," Gwendolyn said as she dramatically wiped her eyes, smudging more black mascara over her cheeks. "You, you and you two may stay," she said getting up. She had pointed to me and Taj, and I saw the twins had also stayed behind.

"Our keys don't work on the front door," Omri said from down the hall. There were muffled voices that followed. "What you mean we can't go in?" Omri shouted.

Keith's voice rose sternly, "I am sorry, but Mistress Gwendolyn only allows four in the room at a time. You must wait your turn."

"How long they get?"

"They have approximately fifteen more minutes."

There was a unified groan in the hall. I looked at Taj who was sniffing the coffee cup (although I don't see how he could sniff anything with that rancid smell in the air), then I started opening drawers. I didn't have any time to waste. The cold seemed to have increased in this tiny office and as my hands rubbed my arms, I quickly scanned the bookshelf, then pulled book after book.

Nothing seemed unusual until I noticed a bright blue book on a lower shelf. The color ignited something inside me. And it looked like the large book was out of place, like someone had shoved it in the wrong spot. All the other books on that shelf were black and small. Didn't Sinclair say something about secret passages?

I pulled the bright blue book, but it only came out halfway with a click, and my action must've caused a response because the entire bookcase made a creaking sound as it slid open like a pocket door. I jumped back and stared into the kitchen.

"A trap door!" Taj said from beside me.

"Hurry up and close it before somebody comes," Akeem hissed. I looked around frantically, but it was Taj who pushed a red button at the top and the door slid back into place.

"Anyone could've come in here," I said.

"It seems only from this side though," Taj remarked pointing at the blue book. That was a good point.

As Taj and I continued looking around the room, the twins observed Sinclair's body.

"He ain't cut up or shot up," Adrian said. "How'd he die?"

"Heart attack?" Akeem asked. "Poisoned?" He pointed to the coffee cup.

"We've got to have hard evidence," I said looking at them. It seemed although we were talking quietly amongst ourselves, an unlikely alliance had formed, at least for the sake of this phase. I knew we had an advantage that the others hadn't.

"Look," I said. "Why don't we work together? We could make use of the time and get ahead if we help each other."

The brothers looked at us and said nothing.

"I think he killed himself," Taj finally admitted out loud. "And I think it has to do with the coffee."

"Yea, Theo said it tasted too sweet," I added. Again, I observed the desk stacked with papers and files and as I perused through them. I noticed a lot of past-due bills and what drew my attention the most was the large hardcover book on pathology.

"Clinical Pathology?" I asked aloud.

"It focuses on diagnosing diseases," Adrian muttered as he peered over my shoulder at the book. Annoyed, I moved a little so the twin wasn't breathing down my neck. I saw Akeem look from the door where some of our classmates were crowded in the hall, back to Sinclair who was doing an impeccable job of playing dead.

"Didn't he ask Keith to bring him his coffee?" Akeem asked.

"He did," I said. "You think it was Keith?"

"He could've poisoned his coffee," Akeem said.

I opened up the book where a slip of paper was used as a bookmark. The paper was a scroll of old pictures taken in a photo booth. There were four silly photos of Sinclair and Gwendolyn. They were staged to look younger. Gwendolyn had hair and it was styled in a layered bob and Sinclair wore glasses and braces. On the back read, "Our first date. May we always put each other first," in feminine, swirly cursive. I assumed Gwendolyn had written the message to Sinclair.

"But wasn't the door locked?" Taj asked. "And Keith said he didn't have a key."

"He could be lying," Akeem said.

I looked down at the page that was bookmarked and sensed Adrian's stare on my back. I noticed a highlighted passage. "What's ethy—ethylene glycol toxicity?" I asked aloud. The room was silent until Adrian spoke up from beside me.

"It's a toxin…" he began slowly. I wasn't sure if he were thinking or just being extremely careful of his next statement. He watched us warily. "It's used in some household items."

"Like?" I asked as I got on my knees to rifle through Sinclair's drawers. My fingers stopped on something that felt hidden. I'm not sure if Adrian heard me because he never answered and at the moment my mind had moved on to something more pertinent. My heartbeat so loud in my ears I probably wouldn't have heard a train if it was coming right for me.

And do you know why?

Because I had stumbled upon a locked box in the bottom drawer.

I pulled it out and sat it on the floor, then feeling my hands shake with excitement and cold, I pulled my hidden key out, the one I had found in the kitchen at the cabin, the one I had stuffed into my bra and hidden for just a moment like this. I took that key and pushed it into the hole.

It was a perfect fit.

Quickly, I turned the key and threw open the box. It was filled with papers, all with the same information as if copies had been made. I read the top one and Taj took the rest and handed two more to Akeem and Adrian.

"They *are* going bankrupt," Taj whispered. "I knew it!"

"This is evidence," I said as I looked up. "This proves Sinclair killed himself. He couldn't live with the thought of going under."

"We solved it," Akeem said tucking the paper in his pocket.

"Times up!" Keith yelled from the hall.

"Quick! Lock the box and put it back where you found it!" Taj said. I did and made sure to shove it as far back in the drawer as I could. Then I stood and followed the others calmly out of the room, folding the paper into a little ball so it fit into the palm of my hand. The hall was crowded with eager faces, waiting to get in and hoping to hear what we knew.

"Spill it," Talia said as she grabbed my arm.

"I don't know everything yet," I said watching Akeem and Adrian approach Gwendolyn. "I didn't have much time. You need to go into the room and see, then we'll talk about what we know."

"But—"

I didn't let her finish as I pushed past the crowd and followed the brothers and Gwendolyn into the foyer. The woman's dangling earrings swung as she shook her head sadly and the twins turned and looked at each other in disbelief. Taj and I both went up to them.

"What happened?" he asked.

"She said we don't have enough evid—ow!" Akeem said and looked at his brother. Adrian gave him an ugly glare and I knew we were no longer sharing information. The two of them walked off, leaving us to figure things out on our own.

"Let's head to the kitchen," Taj said and I was fast behind him. The twins were there too opening all of the cabinets. They claimed the kitchen was their territory and made it impossible for us to even look around. Every time I went to open a door, Adrian positioned himself in my way.

"Come on!" I yelled. "Move!"

"Yo, we were here first," Adrian snapped.

I huffed and went to look beneath the sink instead, but found nothing out of the ordinary. I heard distant squeals of joy and jumped up to see if someone had gotten to the next phase. Taj grabbed my arm and whispered, "Look over there." I followed his eyes and saw the answer had been in front of us the entire time.

There was a clear bottle that looked like Gatorade on the counter. "Follow me," Taj said as he got a glass and filled the cup with water. As the cup filled he eyed the jug beside him and I read the label.

Antifreeze. I quickly scanned the ingredients and saw the words I had been searching for: ethylene glycol.

Taj casually drank from the glass and winked at me as the twins stopped what they were doing and watched us. I walked back into the hall and Taj followed.

"That's how he was poisoned," Taj murmured.

"How do you know?" I asked.

"Who leaves a jug of antifreeze on the kitchen counter? It's got to be it." We could hear footsteps behind us and rushed toward Gwendolyn. She was listening to Omri who loudly announced his findings.

"I think it was Alfred!"

"Who?" Gwendolyn asked.

"He killed him with the Cook and—and—" Omri continued.

"Who is this Alfred you speak of and how can you prove it?" Gwendolyn asked. "And what was his motive? You have nothing. Next!"

I looked at Taj and he put out his hand. "You first," he said.

I walked up to Gwendolyn and whispered in her ear, so no one would hear. "I believe Sinclair killed himself because he was depressed his business was going under. He put antifreeze in his coffee and drank it."

"And how do you know this?" Gwendolyn asked, her eyes shining and a smile crept across her lips. "He was locked in his study all afternoon."

"The bookcase is a secret passage into the kitchen," I said. "so he was able to get in and out without anyone seeing him." I pulled out the paper I had found. "And here's the proof and the antifreeze is on the counter, mostly empty."

She took the paper and studied it, as if she'd never seen it before, then called Elise over. The freckled face sister came carrying a small golden chest that she held with two hands.

Gwendolyn opened the box carefully and pulled out one large key. A hush fell over the foyer where a few people had gathered to watch.

"It seems you are our first winner," she said with a slight smile. "You may go on to phase three." The key looked antique and was heavy and cold in my hand, like steel. I clasped it in my palm, walked over to the door and started to put the key in the hole.

"NORA!" I heard Talia snap.

I stopped. I had been so excited to be the first one to solve the case, I forgot all about Talia. Guiltily, I turned around.

"Where do you think you're going?" she hissed.

"I figured it out."

"Dang, that's messed up," she said. Her face was cloudy and she jabbed her finger at me as she spoke. "So you were just going to leave me alone to figure this out on my own. I thought we were a team, Nora. We're supposed to be in this together."

"I know, I just got caught up and forgot—"

Her voice rose and turned shrill. "What? How you forget about your best friend? How you forget we promised to have each other's back?" Her eyes blazed right through me.

Embarrassed, I looked around the room. She was making a scene for no reason. I didn't go through the door, did I? I turned back to help her, right? But she didn't seem to remember that part. What was Talia so pissed for? It was just a game. Talia had left me in the last phase and hadn't even blinked an eye. She didn't have to go crazy on me. I took her arm and said, "Come on, I'll tell you everything."

Taj had already received his key and went through the door and the twins were reporting everything they knew to Gwendolyn, so I pulled Talia over toward the clothing rack and whispered the answer. I told her where to find the evidence and how the antifreeze was the poison. She nodded hastily and then kissed my cheek.

"Thanks, Nora, you're the best!" she said, her demeanor a complete one-eighty. I watched her skip down the hall like a kid in a candy store and wondered if I'd made a mistake.

Served on a Platter

Taking my key from Mistress Gwendolyn, I inserted it into the lock and hoped to chase Adrian and Akeem through the woods. My pursuit, however, was interrupted as I stepped outside the door, feeling a fresh breeze only for a second, and then darkness as a hood was thrown over my head. I shouldn't have been surprised, but I still let out a startled cry as someone lead me by the hand and then told me to 'get in.' This unknown individual directed me into a vehicle (as I could hear the running engine) where I was shoved onto a seat.

As soon as the door slammed behind me, my body jerked with the sudden movement of the car. I was told not to remove my hood or I would be eliminated and then the driver said nothing else for the rest of the ride. Don't remember how long I was in the car, nor did I ask any questions or make any responses. Just sat silent, waiting for the next phase.

When the car jerked to a stop, I heard the door open and felt my arm yanked. I was dragged out of the car, across what sounded like gravel and then inside a building. I could tell because the air changed from the smell of gasoline and burgers to a stuffy, cardboard scent like someone had just moved in and was unpacking boxes.

After I heard the click of the door close, I awkwardly stood alone for a few minutes before I realized it must've been safe for me to remove my hood. There was no need to even squint as I took the cloth off because the room was already dark, but a bit of light shone through a rectangular crack in front of me. Cautiously and with heart pounding in my ears, I nudged open the door and walked into the next room.

Box spring, adjustable, and the kind of mattresses that gave you a number were all lined up throughout the large, open space. There was a counter with a cash register to my left as I walked into the soft glowing room. A string of twinkly lights lined the edge of the ceiling and cast a warm radiance on the signs: BIG SALE, MATTRESS CLOSEOUT. And in the middle of the room, surrounded by mattresses stood Taj all by himself.

He was staring out the floor to ceiling glass windows where I saw night had already come. His arms lay limply at his sides when I approached him.

"Taj?" I whispered.

He turned, startled and smiled his half-smile. "Oh, hey. Didn't hear you back there."

"Is it night already?"

"Guess so."

"Man, the day went by so fast. Where are we?"

"Looks like a mattress store." I went to the front doors and pushed and pulled. "I already tried them," he said. "Locked."

Looking around at all the white, boxy beds, I spotted the twins, each curled up on a full-size bed and they looked fast asleep. Suddenly I realized how tired I was. The adrenaline had slowed and overcome with exhaustion, I was drawn toward the nearest mattress where I plopped down and bounced slightly. I had made it through the last phase and I felt I deserved a restful reward.

"What do you suppose this phase is?" I whispered in the dark. It felt strange to be in an empty store at night.

Taj didn't answer. Instead, he asked, "How long do you think until we see the rest?" He looked back the way we had come.

"Talia should be here soon…" I paused, about to say more, but faltered when he sat down on the mattress beside mine. My mouth grew dry. My thoughts a blur. This game was more challenging than I thought. Not only did I have to focus on the task and figure out how to win the money, but I had to do it with the boy that always seemed to make me forget who I was. My stomach growled and I clutched my stomach with both arms.

"Here," Taj said, taking off his suit coat. "You cold?"

"Oh, no," I half-heartedly protested, but he'd already draped it across my shoulders and sat back down.

I didn't mind pretending I was cold. I pushed my arms through the sleeves and wrapped myself in it, inhaling his crisp scent, then peeked up at him to see if he was watching me.

He was.

My heart leaped and just as he opened his mouth to speak, the door from the back burst open and I could hear Omri's loud voice yell, "Surprise!"

He threw up his arms. "Y'all thought I wouldn't make it." Then gyrated (with less vitality) and dove onto a mattress beside mine. "We having a sleepover Señora?"

"Omri, I'm too tired," I said and rolled onto my side away from him.

"No problemo," he said. "I got enough energy for the both of us. Yo, Taj! Did you know our keys unlocked the box in the desk? I thought the keys were for the door!"

Both Taj and Omri got into the details of the previous phase and as their voices droned on, my eyes grew heavy and my body relaxed. I don't know how long I slept for, but when I woke up, I heard Taj's voice say softly, "—didn't realize that man. I'm sorry."

"I'm good," Omri replied quietly. His voice wasn't its normal high-energy state. It sounded serious. "Don't know what my dad's going to do though. He'll have to find another job. He's worked at the school for like 15 years."

I slowly sat up and rubbed my eyes.

"Where do you think your dad will look?" Taj asked. He sat on the edge of his bed, hunched over with elbows on knees and hands clasped in front of his face. He was looking intently at Omri with a solemn expression.

"He'll probably apply somewhere else, but don't know if he wants to go to another high school and start over. You know he graduated from Oliver, then went straight into the Army." Omri sat at the end of my bed now. His legs were drawn up so his knees were practically at his chest. His head slumped forward and his eyes looked so sad. Any other moment I would've made some snippy remark, like go cry somewhere else or get that weeping off my bed, but the moment was too somber, too gloomy, which was so unlike Omri I didn't know what to do with myself.

"My dad don't like change," Omri muttered with a frown and rubbed his face. "Last time we went through that it was—well—" He glanced at me and our eyes met. I looked down as he finished his sentence. "When my mama passed…he didn't take that too well."

I remembered the day Omri lost his mother. It was the summer we went into 6th grade. He and I were one of the last to be picked up from Boys & Girl's Club that day. We'd gone on a field trip—bowling, I think. Abuelita was always late getting me so it was no big deal to wait and Omri didn't let the delay phase him either, even though I sensed he was nervous. His jittery self kept asking our counselor if his mom had come yet.

She stayed at home and as a military wife, was always on time, always made it her business to have everything in order from Omri's school supplies to homemade lunches. So it was no surprise that Omri was nervous about her being late. We found out the bad news when one of his aunties picked him up. I remember her face in tears, her body shaking hysterically, the way she knelt and threw herself around little Omri's skinny body.

After that Omri wasn't the same and neither was his daddy. He missed a lot of school and I heard his daddy almost lost his job. Omri had to stay with his aunt and uncle during middle school because home life had gotten worse. But then by our freshmen year, Omri was back with his father and back to his old over-hyperactive self.

"Your dad will find something," I said reassuringly.

Omri didn't respond. He looked deep in thought. Mr. Jones had been my teacher and I couldn't imagine what it would be like to have him as a father. He was stern, severe and had a face like granite. There was no playing in his class. No nonsense was ever accepted. I remember how he acted when Omri and I went to the Beautillion ball our junior year. Omri's aunts and uncles fussed over him with pictures and congratulations, but his dad only gave him a stern handshake.

I searched for something else encouraging to say but lost the effort once a stream of people poured through the door. Talia, Su-Min, Cordell, Damien and after a short break, Lashonda stumbled in with her blanket still wrapped around her. And she looked pissed.

"I'm done!" she shouted. "I don't want no more mysteries. Dang Junebug tellin' lies, Gwendolyn confusing the hell out of me and people being drugged. Don't give me no more mysteries!" She yelled up at the ceiling. "Ya hear? I had enough!"

She limped into the room on one high heel and the other in her hand. "And where the hell are we?"

"I'm hungry," Cordell announced. "What are we supposed to eat?"

"There's a box of food over there." Taj pointed and people were up in a flash, all over that cardboard box, like ants on a fallen lollipop stuck to the sidewalk.

"Move!"

"I was here first."

"Don't touch me!"

Taj, Su-Min and I stayed back and watched the grabby chaos, but then a familiar tune played throughout the store. "The Great Pretender" song played the chorus and we stopped to listen, except Cordell who busily unwrapped saran wrap from around a sandwich. Lashonda slapped his hand just as he was about to take a bite. The music skipped like a broken record and then the loud voice spoke:

Only ten of y'all remain,
the rest are out of the game.
Here you will stay,
till the break of day,
Then you're free to wander the lane.

But don't take your time, please hurry,
this town should make you worry,
in the arms of Morpheus,

search beside Scorpius,
And the answer will fill you with fury.

We stood in silence, waiting for more instructions, but none came.

"The arms of Morpheus," I muttered to myself. "Where have I heard that before?"

"It's an idiom," Damien said as he sat down beside me. He took a large bite out of a sub sandwich and the way he chewed with his mouth open made me almost lose my appetite. Almost. I wanted to get up and grab some food, but Damien's eyes gleamed like he wanted to say more.

"And?" I finally asked. "What does it mean?"

"I'm not telling you," he said with a wicked smile.

Frustrated, I got up and snagged a ham & cheese on white, bottle of water and cookie out of the box. My mouth watered as I thought of how good that sandwich would taste in my mouth. I caught a glimpse of Talia chatting with Su-Min and Omri on the other side of the room, but I didn't want to lose my mattress to Damien, who looked as if he were getting comfortable, so I went back and sat down on my bed.

"You better go get a sandwich before they're all gone," I whispered to Taj. He looked deep in thought, nodded and left.

I stretched out my legs and let my back rest against the wall. Damien had gone to join Talia, Omri, and Su-Min on the other side of the room and I tried my best to ignore my insecure thoughts. So what if they were together? What did I care if they were talking about the last phase, clues, or possibly even me?

I had to stop worrying about them. I chewed thoughtfully and wondered how I was going to make it through this next phase. I didn't even know how I'd made it this far. I figured by the time there were ten people left, I'd be on my way home having to make a tough decision I still didn't want to make. But now that I was still here, I entertained the idea of actually winning. What would it be like to bring home $250,000? Abuelita could quit her job, and it would take some pressure off Tony and my mom working so much. We could rent a house, even if it was a small one. Anything was better than our two-bedroom apartment.

"—least I got a daddy!" Talia shouted from across the room.

My thoughts immediately vanished.

"Yea, you do," Lashonda sneered. "And he laid up wit' everybody in town."

"Shut up!" Talia screamed, her eyes practically popping out of her head.

But Lashonda casually continued. "In fact, I know I saw him with my mama last week."

That was it.

Talia lunged her contorted body at Lashonda and the tension broke through the ceiling. Su-Min held Talia back as she glared at Lashonda. But that girl wasn't phased. She rigidly stood in a confrontational stance.

"I hear you talk shit behind my back again, I'll bust up that pretty face," Lashonda said. "And that ain't a warning. That's the word."

"Whoa—whoa!" Omri shouted and waved his arms. "Let's all calm down."

But Talia and Lashonda did not heed his words. Both girls looked ready to fight.

"Ay! Señora!" Omri looked at me. "What's this about you going to jail and being kidnapped?"

I knew what he was trying to do and his plan worked. The attention shifted from Talia and Lashonda's confrontation to me. Omri quickly took the group out of the frying pan and allowed them to cool on the paper towel. But, I didn't appreciate being the distraction. It gave them all a break, but it put me straight into the boiling oil.

"What?" Talia looked at me curiously and her shoulders went slack. "I never heard any of this." Su-Min dropped her hands from around Talia's arms and stood back. The oncoming battle had temporarily subsided.

"She didn't go to no jail," Cordell said with his mouth full.

"I didn't know you were such a good liar, Señora," Omri said with a grin.

"I didn't lie," I retorted. Why was everybody looking at me like that?

"Then, when did you go to jail?" Talia asked as her eyes narrowed. "You never told me."

I swallowed hard as I realized now I was in the hot seat. This was not the way I wanted to tell people, but Talia looked at me expectantly like this information should've been served to her on a platter.

"I went last week," I said.

Talia's eyes grew large.

"Why?" Omri asked.

"To visit my dad."

A murmur of understanding trickled through the room and then Omri piped, "But you said you went to jail. I thought you meant you was arrested—Ohhhh." He smiled and shook his head.

Damien pushed his glasses up his nose. "Very clever Nora."

"So, is Tony in jail?" Talia asked.

"No, my real dad."

Silence and then Cordell spoke, "Well, what about the kidnapping?"

"That's true too," I said.

"Explain."

"She don't have to tell nobody nothing," Lashonda said as she stood up. "Y'all nosy as hell. Go read a book or something."

"She the one who told us when she played the game!" Omri argued. "We just following up." He rubbed his hands together and grinned. "Come on, Nora, let's hear it."

I didn't want to, not with all nine people staring at me. "I don't have to say anything," I said with folded arms.

"Oh, come on!" Omri groaned. "You can't leave us hangin'!"

"And now we all know you cheated," Cordell said. "You a liar and a cheater."

"Nuff said," Su-Min muttered.

I shot Su-Min a nasty look. Dang, she was throwing me some shade. "I'm not a cheater," I snapped feeling the heat rise in the room. "And I didn't lie." I took a deep breath. I couldn't believe I was going to say this out loud. "My real dad stole me from my mother when I was three."

Not a word was spoken as my words hung in the air. For a minute I thought the conversation was over. The silence was uncomfortable, but at least people would move on to other topics.

"But that's not kidnapping," Su-Min objected. "if he's your dad."

My defense was up. Of all people, Su-Min shouldn't have been the one to egg me on. We had too much history for her to drag this out. "He left my mother after she had me and then just showed up one day and took me without her permission. And you don't call that kidnapping?" I could hear the strain in my voice. My anger was apparent and my vocals weren't doing a good job of hiding it.

"Still…he's your dad," Su-Min argued.

"But he ain't been there," Lashonda said and I could see her hands clenched in tight fists, her face twisted in aggravation. "He had no right to take her. That's kidnapping in my book." Her voice shook a little with passion. "If he can't commit and stick around to be a daddy, he don't deserve to come back into her life and take her as his. He wasn't the one to carry her for nine months. He wasn't the one to push her out his belly. He wasn't the one to nurse her, feed her, change her dirty diapers day after day—"

"Okay, Lashonda!" Omri shouted. "We get it! Dang."

Lashonda flinched at his words and then sat back down, unusually quiet. I was grateful for her defense and wish I had said the words myself.

"But still," Su-Min said softly. "He's technically her father."

"So, was he the one in jail last week?" Talia asked.

I'd forgotten about Talia. Su-Min's interrogation had shaken me so much I wanted to get at her throat. I sighed and nodded at Talia.

"Why is he coming back around?"

Really? Did she want to continue this in front of everybody? I was through and when I'm through, I shut down. I wish I was a fighter like Lashonda. I wish I was quick to the punch, but unfortunately, I stop responding physically and emotionally to my attacker. Like a turtle, I tuck into my shell. I looked down into my lap because I was done having my personal life on a tray for everyone to feast upon.

"Uh," Taj said and cleared his throat. "Why don't you guys tell me what happened after I left? Where's Chloe B. and Theo? What happened to the others?"

I was grateful for Taj because the room burst into excited chatter once they told us everything we had missed. Happy that the attention was now elsewhere, I felt my shoulders relax again and the tension slowly eased away. Talia sat beside me on the mattress and reassuringly took my hand and squeezed it. She said softly, "We'll talk later."

It was unnerving to hear what happened to the others. Theo collapsed and started convulsing on the floor. Lashonda was one of the last to get through and was there when the ambulance arrived. She said he'd been poisoned and that his hands and face were puffed up. At first, she thought it was because he had drunk that poisoned coffee, but then after the ambulance came, they said it was because he was allergic to the nuts in the brownies. But of course, that hadn't stopped her from solving the mystery.

"Is he okay?" I asked.

"As far as I know," Lashonda said with a shrug. She laid back on her mattress and closed her eyes. "Now, y'all shut up. I'm a light sleeper and I needs me to be beautiful for the cameras tomorrow."

Once Lashonda told people to shut up, most of us respected her wishes. The room was quiet again and I laid down on my mattress and closed my eyes, hoping to get a little bit of sleep before the sun rose and the phase began.

"Nora," Talia whispered from beside me. My eyes popped open and I rolled over to face my friend. "Yea?"

"Why didn't you tell me about your dad?" Her curls swirled around her head like a halo.

"I don't know," I whispered. "It all happened so fast…and you've been busy with—"

"Oh, this again?" Talia said as she propped up on her elbow. "You always have to bring up Matthias. I'm flattered, but you don't have to be jealous, Nora."

"I'm not jealous," I said exasperatedly. "I didn't tell you 'cause it didn't seem like that big of a deal…yet. My dad just came around last week!"

"It doesn't matter if it was yesterday, you should've told me!" Talia hissed. "What's wrong with you? You —you've changed."

I didn't answer her. I laid back and stared at the ceiling. Why was everybody saying that? First Su-Min and now Talia. But it wasn't just me. Talia had changed too. Once junior year hit, she started dating Matthias and in addition to being on the dance team and school functions, she didn't have much time to chill with me.

With so much free time, I gravitated to family and my after school job at the daycare. Then my mom started making everybody go to church more, per Abuelita's request. I didn't realize the church we started going to was also attended by Taj. That certainly was an incentive to get me in those church doors and attend every youth group event.

I turned back onto my side to face Taj who laid on the bed next to mine. I watched him sleep for a minute, then closed my eyes. Since Talia and I had been friends I had become known as her twin, but better understood as her tag-a-long. She led and I followed, that's how it had always been until recently. I enjoyed the friends I made in youth group, I enjoyed my after school job with the kids, I especially liked hanging out with Abuelita. So Talia was right, some things had changed about me.

But had I let the game change me? I didn't think so. And had it changed Talia? I wasn't sure. She was brasher, but wasn't that how she'd always been? I wondered if Beholden had bled out the true colors of us, like bringing what was tucked away in secret out into the blazing light.

"You sleep?" Talia whispered. I didn't answer. I didn't want to talk anymore. It wasn't that I was mad at her, it was just that I truly was exhausted. And within minutes, my mind turned off and I was out.

And as weary as I was, I still didn't sleep well. I had a terrible dream that I was on a deserted island with Talia. I was locked in a cramped, metal cage.

And she held the key.

Playin' Dirty

"You okay?" Talia asked as she shook me awake. "You cried out in your sleep."

I rubbed my eyes and sat up. "I'm fine," I said hugging Taj's jacket close to my body. I tried to shake the nightmare from my head as I frowned at Talia. I didn't realize how accusatory I looked.

"What?" she demanded.

"Nothing," I said and got up.

The others were starting to rouse as well and the soft pink sky could be seen through the glass windows. It took me a few seconds to recall where I was. Stuck in the middle of Beholden.

I quickly recapped the previous phase, reminding myself to stay alert and attentive during this oncoming one. I didn't know what Beholden would throw at me next, but I was learning to roll with the punches. I told my mind to accept and adapt to whatever came next.

If Beholden wanted to throw me into a new phase every few hours, then I would gladly walk through that door. Didn't matter if I couldn't explain it. I'd endure just about anything to keep from going home.

Taj stood ready at the door, first to go out, and called back to us, "It looks like we're on some main street in the middle of town." He looked both ways. "I don't see anyone yet. I wonder who's going to open the d—" And before he could finish, we all heard a loud beeping sound, like a car alarm going off. Taj hesitated, then pushed and the door swung open.

"It's time!" yelled Omri as he sprinted out the door behind Taj. I didn't even have time to use the bathroom as I ran behind Talia.

It was an eerie sight. A downtown street void of all people. Cars were parked on the road, some were lined up at the traffic light, which was still changing from yellow to red and back to green. There was construction going on at the end of the street, blocking the sidewalks and I looked back and saw the other end of the street looked the same. It seemed the game of Beholden had confined us to this particular area. I looked up at the sky, now a hazy pinkish orange as the sun rose on a new day.

My eyes drifted down and I wondered if this town was celebrating Christmas in the spring. As if frozen in time, green garland was wrapped around street lamps, banners with the words MERRY, JOY, and PEACE hung from poles and brightly wrapped presents were stuffed into the backseats of cars.

As my nine classmates scattered in different directions, I walked up to a car that looked like it had just picked up a tree for Christmas, because the plant was wrapped with rope on the roof. I looked inside and jumped back.

There was a blonde woman behind the wheel. Her head slumped forward as if she had fallen asleep driving. I touched her arm and it was warm.

"Hello!" I called shaking her, but she didn't wake. "Ma'am?" I said again, but nothing happened. I slowly backed up and walked into an old-fashioned ice cream parlor. Seeing a man leaning against a broom, I approached him.

"Sir—" I tapped his shoulder, but he didn't respond. I looked at his face. His eyes were closed, head leaned forward. It was as if they were all asleep. A man and young boy sat in a booth with pools of ice cream in their bowls, their heads rest on the table. A girl in a skirt lay on the floor beside a boy in front of a jukebox. A prickling sensation went up my spine as I rushed out of the shop and down to the next store and the next. It was the same in every shop. All the folks were sleeping.

"Why won't they wake up?" Su-Min asked. She tugged uncomfortably at her cream lace dress. We both looked at two women at a cafe table on the sidewalk. Their cups of cappuccino hadn't been touched and a stack of papers sat beside their snoozing heads.

"How are we supposed to solve this?" I asked.

"We should work together," Talia said as she appeared beside me. I looked at her uncertainly, my dream haunted me even during the day. I shook off the nightmare. We weren't on an island. I didn't have to worry about it coming true.

"You're probably right," I said. "Let's go over the riddle again."

"What was that about Morpheus?" Su-Min asked.

"Sounds Greek or something," Talia said.

"Damien knows," I said. "But he won't tell."

"What about the rest?" Su-Min continued. "What's a Scorpius? Sounds like scorpio...are all these people into cosmology?"

I sighed. We were getting nowhere. I watched Lashonda and Omri dash into another building and wondered what they had found.

"We've got to do something. We can't just stand here," Talia said. "Let's go find Damien."

"He won't tell us," I said.

"He won't tell you," she said with a wink. "I know how to make him talk."

But none of us knew where Damien was. Su-Min suggested we just go from store to store and search for him, but I argued that would take up too much precious time.

So Talia took command. "Let's split up and look for him. If one of us finds him first we'll let each other know—deal?" Su-Min and I looked at each other. The plan sounded alright. I still thought we were wasting time.

But I didn't have any better ideas, so I went along with it and decided to head over to the vintage record store. Lashonda and Omri were inside flipping through the albums. They were oddly quiet when I walked in and both glanced up at the same time.

"Whatchu want, Nora?" Lashonda asked saltily.

"Just looking," I said as I glanced through the records too, trying to appear as if I knew what I was doing.

"Señora, you got to do better than that," Omri said and I looked up just in time to see him flash a smile.

Lashonda snorted. "Girl, don't act like you 'jus lookin'. We ain't stupid. You spyin' on us?"

"Naw, just trying to get through this phase, that's all," I said.

"Whatchu looking for, then?"

"Morpheus," I said. I had no idea what I was talking about. I promise the words just slipped out of my mouth.

They were both silent and I suppose my answer had been acceptable.

"You in the wrong section," Lashonda commented. "The M's are over there."

I looked up and saw that I was.

"I'm looking for Scorpion," Omri said.

"It's Scorpius stupid and shut up!" Lashonda blurted.

"Anybody seen Damien?" I asked trying to sound like I didn't care.

"Oh yea," Omri said. "They over at the bookstore."

"They?" I asked.

"Yea, he and Taj over there looking for—ow!" I looked up to see Omri rubbing his head. Lashonda's heel lay on a pile of records in front of Omri.

"You threw yo' shoe at me!" Omri yelled angrily.

"To shut you up!" Lashonda snapped.

That was all I needed to hear. I raced into the street and found Talia and Su-Min. Together we headed into the bookstore, past the front desk where Cordell was trying to use the computer. We found the boys sitting at two long wooden tables. Books were piled around them as they flipped hastily through the pages.

"Hey, Damien," Talia said sweetly and he and Taj abruptly stopped working.

"What?" he asked.

"Just wanted to see what you guys knew so far."

"I ain't tellin' you jack," Damien said and narrowed his eyes. "I see how you play—dirty."

Talia threw up her hands. "I'm just trying to have a conversation. The girls and I were comparing notes —"

"Uh-huh."

"—about you."

"So?"

"We figured you should've known the answer by now. I mean, you act like you know everything."

"What do you mean?" Damien asked looking annoyed. "I do know everything."

"About literature?"

"Yea."

"Ancient mythology?"

"Of course."

"Cosmology?"

"…Yea."

"Well, Nora here thinks you don't know anything about cosmology. You don't even know who Morpheus is."

"I do too!" Damien said as he jumped up. "He's the god of dreams or sleep and--" He stopped and scowled, realizing his mistake. He slowly sat down.

"So," Talia said smugly as she crossed her arms in satisfaction. "that's what in the arms of Morpheus means."

"That they're all asleep," Su-Min said and slapped her forehead. "Of course."

"And Scorpius?" Talia asked.

"Uh-uh!" Damien shouted. "You won't get me to say another word!"

I looked at him and Taj who had open books all around them.

"It's because they haven't figured it out yet." I smiled. "You guys are still looking, aren't you?"

"I ain't sayin' jack," Damien muttered.

"Let's work together," Talia pleaded. "If we find the answer first, we'll let you in. Just think, we can go the rest of the way together. We'd make a great team."

I'd heard Talia use that phrase with almost everybody now. But Taj and Damien didn't know that. Damien hesitated, but Taj shrugged. "It's better to have more people looking anyway."

"Fine," Damien said and then whispered, "But we're not bringing in Cordell. That idiot still thinks he can get the computer going."

So, after finding out that Damien and Taj were searching for books on Scorpius, we hunted with them, trying to find the answer before anyone else.

It felt like hours as we settled down at the long wooden tables, bookshelves like a wall around us and no one said a word as we worked steadily. With a few potty breaks and bags of chips Taj bought with some loose change in his pocket, we were good. And as I frantically poured over each cosmology, astrology and mythology book, I couldn't help but wonder if we were going about this the wrong way.

A feeling inside kept reminding me to think about the riddle. I repeated the phrases over and over in my head until I had an idea. A thought that struck me like a drumstick hitting a snare. I looked over at Taj, who was flipping through a book titled, Scorpius.

"Where did you get that book?" I asked him. He looked up and pointed toward the back of the store.

"Show me," I said and we got up together and went to the dark corner. The lighting flickered as Taj pointed to the spot. I picked up the books on either side and flipped hastily through. The first one was filled with pages, so I dropped it, then flipped open the other book and saw it was exactly what I had been searching for. There were no pages. Only a large hole filled with bright blue envelopes.

I wanted to scream.

I squeezed my mouth tight and spun around to stare at Taj. He looked at me in shock and asked, "How did you know?"

"The riddle!" I exclaimed. "He said look beside Scorpius!"

"Of course!" Taj said. "Scorpius is the name of the book!"

I handed him an envelope and got out three more. Just then, Talia and Damien came running back.

"Quick! Lashonda and Omri are in the store."

"I found the clue!" I said and handed them each an envelope and turned to put the book back.

Talia looked at the clue and stuffed it into the top of her dress. "What are you doing?" she exclaimed. She grabbed the book from me and chucked it down the aisle. Blue envelopes fluttered out everywhere.

"What are you doing Talia?" I hissed.

"Winning," she snapped.

"But Talia—"

"We don't got time for this!" Damien hissed.

"And who cares?" Taj said. "I left the Scorpius book on the table."

"What should we do now?" Damien asked.

"Open our envelope," I said with a sigh.

But Lashonda and Omri were beside us with grins on their faces.

"Look like y'all figured it out," Lashonda said. "So where's Scorpius or Morpheus or whoever?"

Damien backed up and ran through the store, Taj shrugged and I looked up at the ceiling and slowly tucked the two envelopes behind my back.

"Saw it!" Omri shouted and pointed at me. "It's back here somewhere, Shonda. Let's find it." They scrambled behind us and began pulling books off the shelves.

"Way to go, Nora," Talia said curtly. We rushed through the bookstore and I shoved the envelope into Su-Min's shocked face. Don't say I never helped the girl, even if she hated me. I was trying to make up for my past stupid mistakes. I was trying to be her friend.

"Quick! Open it before the others see!" I said as I raced back out to the street where Talia was opening her clue. Still pissed about the way she blamed me, I couldn't help but give her a piece of my mind.

"You playin' dirty is going to hurt you in the end," I said to her as I tore open my envelope.

"It's not playing dirty if there are no rules," Talia retorted.

I shook my head, pulled out the card, and read four words:

Show me the clue.

I flipped the card over and on the back was a snapshot of the woman in the car, the woman I had seen at the traffic light. Yanking off my heels, I took off down the street, not needing to say anything more to Taj or Talia. They had already sprinted to their destinations and I assumed each card had its person. My bare feet slapped the cement as I sped to the car with the Christmas tree on the roof.

I found the woman and wasted no time pushing her head back and putting the paper in her face. There was no need for politeness now. Beholden had taken that out of me.

But she didn't open her eyes, so I said, "Look! I have the clue!" Her eyes slowly parted, so little that it was barely a slit, and then they opened and she smiled at me.

"Well done," she said. I stepped back as she opened the car door and got out. She fixed her midi skirt and slowly brushed off her pink sweater. I wanted to tell her skinny self to hurry it up and get going, but instead, I waited patiently as Taj ran with his woken man and Su-Min held hands with a little woken girl. Impatiently, I bounced on my toes as she reached in and grabbed her chain purse, then turned and said, "Please follow me." She walked briskly toward the sidewalk that was blocked.

"Congratulations," she said over her shoulder. "You've moved on to the next phase." She removed the wooden sign that said NO ENTRY and motioned me to pass through. Immediately I noticed a radiant blue van with Su-Min and Taj already in the front row. A man stood with the door open as I slipped in the back. Damien quickly came next and hopped in beside me without saying a word. He was out of breath and kept looking behind him. I thought we'd wait for the others, but the man got into the driver's seat and started the engine.

The last phase was over and another had already begun.

The Idea of

I had to pee so bad I thought if the car jerked around any more my bladder would release everything it held inside.

We wove through back streets that looked unfamiliar to me and just as I was about to ask the driver if he could stop, he said, "Alright, put on the hoods in the seat pocket in front of you." Obediently, we did as we were told and the blackness returned as I slid the cloth into place. I squirmed uncomfortably in my seat and tried to think about something other than my need to pee. The fight with Talia was still fresh on my mind.

I felt so mad at her, but also pissed at myself for letting it get to me. It's just a game, Nora. No need to get heated. Talia's always been competitive and always told me how she feels. And she was sort of right. There hadn't been any official rules that said you couldn't hide the clues from other people. I just felt like playing her way was…messy.

The car jerked around another corner and I winced. My ears perked at a tiny sneeze from Su-Min. Even after that tense night of camping and the cabin, Su-Min hadn't been awful toward me. Yea, she'd had some snarky remarks, but who wouldn't after playing a game like Beholden? I felt a tiny spark of hope inside. Maybe she was being decent because she wanted to be friends again? Maybe she wasn't being mean because perhaps she had gotten over what I'd done so long ago? I sat there mulling over our recent interactions and reflected back to that treacherous fifth-grade year.

The summer before, Su-Min's mother remarried. I should've been happy for her. I mean her dad had died when she was a baby. Her mother and mine struggled together as single moms, but at least I had family around to help. She had none. So when her mother met Mr. Johnson who worked for NASA as some highly esteemed engineer, I should've celebrated with Su-Min. I should have been happy for her when they got married and she moved into a big house. But I didn't. I'll admit it. I was jealous. She had a new dad and I didn't. She had a mansion and I still (pre-Tony) had a tiny one-bedroom apartment. She had all the toys we ever dreamed of and I still had my hand-me-down junk from cousins. Soon, I couldn't stand being around Su-Min because she reminded me of everything I never got. When Talia proclaimed we were best friends, I ended up spending a lot of time with her and less with Su-Min.

Su-Min made an effort however and invited me, along with most of the girls in our class, to her sleepover. It was during some boring movie that Talia and I found Su-Min's journal laying clumsily on her bed. (I mean, for real though, who has a sleepover and leaves their business out like that?) And it was Talia's idea to tear out pages and place a sheet on every girl's sleeping bag. The pages didn't say much. I mean I think she mentioned some crush she had at the time and might've talked about our class, but it didn't seem like that big of a deal. Ay Dios mío, was I wrong. I remember she was in tears the entire night and refused to come out of the bathroom. By the time she came to bed, the rest of us were already in our sleeping bags and practically asleep.

I know she knew it was me and we didn't speak after that.

The car slowed and the driver said, "Keep your hoods on. I'll get you out one by one." I heard the door slide open and the driver giving careful instructions to watch our step and turn here and stand there. I was the last to get out and I felt the cold cement beneath my bare feet. I couldn't believe I forgot my shoes. I took in a deep breath and smelled the fresh air. It reminded me of something sour. I could hear a familiar sound close by as the driver instructed us to hold the shoulders of the person in front of us. And as we were lead in a straight line, the familiar sound had a name. The distant swishing and sloshing told me we were near water.

My fear emerged like a rocket shot to the moon. I did not want to swim. If anything had to do with me getting in the water, I was sure to drown.

"Where are we?" Damien asked. But the driver didn't answer. We were told to carefully step up on something shaky and immediately my fears intensified.

"Are we getting into the water?" I shrieked. "Is this a boat?"

"Sit down," the driver instructed.

I slowly sat and knew instantly my guess was correct. And then we were coasting. Drifting with a steady pace toward an unknown location. The wind whipped along my body and I was glad for Taj's jacket and was happy my hood hid the sight of water. I said a silent prayer and hoped swimming wasn't included in any part of Beholden.

"I bet we're on Mastin Lake," Damien said.

"That's too small," Su-Min replied. "And we drove pretty far. I think we're further north. Maybe Tennessee?" Their voices were muffled beneath the hoods, but I could hear their entire conversation.

"Nah," Damien said. "They're trying to confuse us. Maybe we went south."

"What do you think we're going to do?" I asked unable to hide the worry in my voice. There was no answer, except for the swish, swish of the paddles as they cut in and out of the water.

"I guess we'll have to wait and see," Taj finally answered.

When the boat came to a stop, the driver helped each of us out and I felt I could finally breathe. My bare feet were on solid ground. Rocky, prickly, and dirty ground, but solid none the less.

But then, without a word he was gone and when we slowly took off our hoods to view our surroundings I stumbled backward and almost tripped over a large tree root. I stared at a mirror image of the murky water that reflected two sets of cloudy, gray sky. An outline of buildings could be seen in the distance. I watched the water ripple from the boat as it slid smoothly across the water. I squinted as I looked out at the driver. He was halfway to the mainland.

"Where are we?" Damien asked for a second time.

But my mind was focused on only one thing.

"Where's the bathroom?" I asked frantically searching the woods for any sign of a port-a-potty.

"Not sure," Taj said. "What are we supposed to do now?"

The sun was hidden behind billowed clouds and I knew it wouldn't be there for long. Where were we supposed to sleep? Eat? Pee?

Su-Min was the first to make the discovery. "Our clues are over here." Her voice came from where she had dared to walk into the dense trees. I winced as we followed, my bare feet carefully tiptoed around precarious rocks and weeds that could've been poison ivy. We found a pile of boxes labeled just like when we camped. She held a blue envelope in her hands.

Reading it to herself her face fell into a frown, then she handed it to Taj who began to read it aloud:

"Tonight you'll make camp—"

"Again?" I cried. I wanted to fall to my knees. "We're staying the night here?" My voice was shrill, my head was beginning to thump with pain.

"I'll help you find a place to go—you know," Su-Min said as she searched through a box and found a small shovel, roll of toilet paper and hand sanitizer. "We'll make a designated spot." She rifled through another box and pulled out two plastic bags with folded clothes inside. "And we've got something to wear besides these ridiculous dresses." She gave me a reassuring smile, but I had no heart to smile back.

After finding a bushy enough spot that was an adequate bathroom, I finally (and with great discomfort) relieved myself, then Su-Min and I changed our clothes. Our new outfits reminded me of cotton pajamas. Plain white and loose. The pain in my stomach lessened as I put on the slippers that came with the pajamas, but the pain in my head did not. It increased greatly as returned to our campsite and found all the boxes opened and Taj attempting to put up a tent. After watching him struggle for what felt like an hour, we took over and gave him and Damien a chance to go change. We got the tent up in 10 minutes. Taj's face was in shock when he returned and saw we were through.

Damien gave Su-Min and I the job of prepping dinner (PB&J sandwiches) and gathering firewood so he could get the fire going. Once that was done, we settled onto the ground next to the heat. The cloudy sky had darkened our day even though it wasn't quite night. The heat felt good as the shade beneath the trees turned cool. With all the moisture in the air, the mosquitos had turned up quick, but the smoke from the fire also kept them at bay.

Fireflies lazily bobbed in the distance, their lights like tiny lanterns floating in the sky. Su-Min and I sat on a large burlap sack (we didn't know what critters were crawling around that ground) and the boys had settled themselves on a large fallen log. I stared across the flames at them and knew there were no boys against girls. It was the four of us against the wild.

"What was that?" I jumped at the sound of a hoot and stared into the trees.

"An owl," Damien said rubbing his eyes. "I'd say let's go explore, but maybe we should save that for tomorrow. I'm thinking of retiring early tonight." He yawned. It wasn't late, but I agreed with him.

"Where do you think the others are?" I asked.

"How do you know its not just us?" Damien responded. He had a point.

"I can't sleep on an empty stomach," Taj said rubbing his midsection. I frowned. The boy had already had two sandwiches and I watched as he reached in the plastic bread bag for more. He pulled out four slices and I just had to say something.

"Don't you think we should save that for tomorrow?" I asked.

He paused and then lifted his eyebrows in surprise as if he hadn't thought of that. "We got fruit don't we?" he said. "And look, I'm hungry now. I can't wait 'till tomorrow." He began spreading thick clumps of peanut butter with a plastic knife over a slice of bread. Made it look like the thin slice was 'bout to break in half. "And I don't think y'all will mind if a brother gets his fill when he can. I'm not stopping y'all from eating."

Damien said nothing and Su-Min slowly took a bite out of her apple. I decided it wasn't my place to say anything more. If no one else was going to complain, well, neither would I. We did have a basket of fruit for the morning, but I sure was banking on toast the next day. I watched Taj polish off the rest of the sleeve of bread and felt my irritation rise. I thought he was finished after four sandwiches? How many did he need to eat? Didn't he notice none of us took more?

He stopped chewing and stared across at me. I didn't avert eye contact. His lips spread into a lopsided smile that deepened his dimples and made me flush with warmth. I couldn't stay mad at Taj. Not with that face, that grin, those brown eyes. I smiled back and shook my head. Beholden was making me go mad.

Soon the hidden sun sunk into the earth and the fire's warmth became more apparent. I searched the sky for stars but saw nothing but a mass of navy ink and only a blinking light that might have been an airplane. Damien put one more log on the fire and instructed us to all head into bed. I did not argue. We trickled into the tent and I tried to make myself comfortable, yet again, on a rocky ground in a sleeping bag that was just too thin. I shifted from side to side and heard someone mutter quit moving around. I froze and sighed. The ground was cold. And I wasn't the only one who couldn't sleep. Damien sat up and sighed.

"I can't sleep."

Someone rustled around and I heard Taj say, "You think they watching us?"

"Absolutely," Su-Min said.

Damien put his glasses on, brought out a small LED lantern and leaned back on his elbows. In the soft white glow I could make out everyone's face.

"I guarantee you my dad ain't watching. He's probably in the garage working," he said. Su-Min asked him why he thought that and Damien went on and talked about how much his dad loved his tools and rambled about a time he broke his daddy's belt sander and how his daddy made him pay for it and how bad he felt because his daddy's workshop is his life and on and on and on.

My attention had shifted. I watched Taj get up and leave the tent, mumbling something about using the bathroom. I squinted my eyes wishing I had X-ray vision like Superman to see through the tent walls, but all I could see was the outline of his shadow as it became smaller and smaller.

"You mean you don't want to go to college?" Su-Min asked. I looked at Damien in surprise.

"Well," Damien said. "My dad wants me to be a biochemist, but all I want to do is…"

"Is what?" Su-Min asked.

Damien shook his head and was quiet for so long, I didn't think he'd say. Finally, he whispered hesitantly, "I want to be a forest ranger."

At first, I wanted to laugh, but then I realized he was serious.

"Aren't those the people who work at campgrounds?" Su-Min asked as she sat up beside me.

"State or national parks," Damien corrected. "What's so bad about that?"

"My dad would be pissed if he found out," Damien whispered.

"When did you decide to be a forest ranger?" Taj asked stepping back into the tent. I hadn't even heard him return. I watched him settle back into his sleeping bag and couldn't help staring at his face. There was something crumbly beside his lips. Was that food? He looked at me and brushed his mouth with a smile. I forced a smile back and looked at Damien, but when Taj looked away I couldn't help but steal tiny glimpses at him.

Damien said he'd always been interested in the outdoors, but when his older brother went to college it gave him the idea. One summer he visited him at Oregon State University and they camped at some state park which inspired Damien. I could see the hope in his eyes, the spark as he talked. At first, it seemed an odd career choice, but then the more I thought about it, the more it made sense.

"That's really cool, Damien," I said.

He looked at me and pushed his glasses up the bridge of his nose. "You think?"

"Yea," I said with a smile. "You'd be a great forest ranger."

"Thanks, Nora," he said and then added. "So, what do y'all wanna do?"

"I want to own a coffee shop," Su-Min blurted. We all looked at her as she grinned shyly, then continued. "With open mic night, karaoke, local art on the walls, baked goods, even books with indie authors on stands…"

She was animated, swinging her arms through the air as if she could see her vision within reach. "Oh! And book signings! I'd love to have everything that supports our city. I'd even have it downtown in that empty store, you know the one off Clinton Avenue?"

"Yea," I said feeling her contagious excitement buzz through me like electricity. "That store's been empty for years. That's a good spot."

"You'll have lots of competition," Damien said. "And where would you get the money? And aren't there already plenty of hipster coffee shops downtown?"

"Damien, don't be a killjoy," I said. "No one downed your forest ranger dream."

Damien pinched his lips together and furrowed his brow, then let out a big breath and said, "You're right. Sometimes I just get carried away. My mouth flies off before I can stop it."

I understood that. Especially when someone had a brain like Damien's—practical and decisive. I was glad Su-Min understood that too.

"It's okay," Su-Min said dreamily. "I know it'll take a lot of work and money, but I want to do it. Just like you want to be a camp counselor, Damien."

"Forest ranger," Damien muttered. "And I like your idea Su-Min, I just want you to be successful. I can help you with some tips on how to financially make this thing happen. Have you thought of getting a small business loan? And are you still going to college? I suggest you consider some business courses from a community college. That'll give you a good start."

Damien's list grew longer, but Su-Min's face never stopped glowing. I knew Su-Min was incredibly gifted with art ever since we were kids. And she was an entrepreneur already, making her own crafty gifts and selling them to our class and teachers around the holidays. I think she even sold stuff online. And her creativity always showed in her style of clothing. There wasn't a day she didn't wear some wild earrings or outfit that no one else could ever pull off. Talia always said she looked tacky, but I secretly wished I could dress as bold as she did.

"What about you, Taj?" Su-Min asked.

"I like what my dad does," Taj said. His answer didn't surprise me. During youth group, Taj was never afraid to ask questions that we were all thinking and always gave deep answers.

"A preacher man?" Damien asked. He was silent for a moment and I waited for some critical comment, but instead, he said, "Yea, you'd make a good preacher. I'd go to your church."

"And you, Nora?" Taj asked.

I looked down at my hands and shrugged. "I don't know," I said feeling my heart beat faster. Was it just me or was the tent suddenly stuffy? I shoved the sleeping bag off my legs.

"You don't know like you don't want to say?" Su-Min asked. "Or you really don't know?"

"I really don't know," I lied.

"Come on, Nora. You've got to be interested in something."

My hands were sweaty. I didn't want to talk about this. I'd already heard it from Mrs. Hughes, our counselor, and from Abuelita and Tony. They all thought I was a ship with no captain, a train without a conductor, a nose-diving jet without a pilot. I didn't want to hear a lecture from my own friends. There was no room for dreaming of what I wanted to be. There was only bills to pay and money owed. My mama had worked hard enough. It was time for me to pay her back.

"I mean, we graduate in a few weeks," Su-Min pressed on. "How can you not have any idea what you like or what you want to do?"

I was silent, hoping her questions would stop. I didn't want to explain our financial hardship as I'm sure everybody (but Su-Min) had their own problems. Besides, it wasn't any of their business.

"Unless you need Talia to tell you what to like." Su-Min's voice dripped with sarcasm.

I stiffened beside her.

"That's low," Damien said.

"I know," Su-Min sighed and I could see the guilt in her eyes. "I'm sorry, it's just that you seem so lost Nora like you always need somebody holding your hand and giving you directions."

That hurt.

"You don't know me," I said tightly.

"But I do," she said firmly. "I know how much you like to read. You always had a comic or some fantasy book in your hand. I remember when I was reading *Where the Red Fern Grows*, you were reading Lord of the —what was that stupid book with the hobbit? And growing up all you wanted to do was write stories. You used to let me illustrate them, remember?"

Her memory astounded me. I was speechless. How could I have forgotten? Su-Min and I used to pass boring afternoons sitting on her murphy bed writing our own comic strips. I'd create the characters and she'd bring them to life. And then we'd go around selling our homemade comics to her mom, my mom, Abuelita—anybody—for a dollar (which was a lot to us back then.) I'd lost that part of myself. Or maybe I just covered it up—with school work, my job, youth group, worries about how we'd afford college and now my dad—I didn't want to think about some fantasy of one day becoming a comic book writer. I know my mom had dreams of starting her own cleaning business and that's what I really planned on doing once I graduated. I planned to help her.

"What happened to you?" Su-Min asked. "Does it have to do with your dad?"

I didn't know what to say. My tongue had suddenly gone paralyzed. I just shook my head. They wouldn't understand.

"Uh, Sonora?" Damien asked. "You there?"

"Now, that I expect from Nora," Su-Min said softly. "You were always so quiet."

Damien popped up to his knees and leaned on the bed. "But dangerous. Remember that summer at the Boys and Girls club when we went roller skating? I think we were in the third or fourth grade? Anyway, Su-Min, you 'member those fools who made fun of you? They acted like they'd never seen a Chinese person before."

"I remember that." Su-Min nodded. "I was crying and our counselors were too busy on their phones. Didn't even try to help us."

"Yup," Damien said. "'Cept Nora."

There was a tense silence. Like a wrecking ball slowly swinging toward its target. I waited for the explosion.

"Well?" Taj asked. "What did Nora do?"

"Yea, Nora," Damien said a bit too smugly. "What did you do?"

I looked down into my lap and laughed. "I went to their lockers, took their jackets and dumped them in the toilet."

"Dang, Nora!" Taj said with a chuckle. "Did they ever find out it was you?"

I shook my head. "But one of the mom's went into the bathroom and found her son's jacket. She was pissed."

"Oooo! That's right!" Damien said with a fist to his mouth. "She was cursing all the way out the door. Dragged him by the shirt with one hand and held his dripping coat with the other."

Laughter rose up around us and the sound felt good, releasing the tension in my shoulders I didn't even realize I had. I was able to lay back down and use Taj's jacket as a pillow. I breathed in his scent and sighed.

"You know Nora, I do have to say I'm surprised you're not doing whatever Talia's doing," Damien went on. "You two are always together. When she was the head, you were the caboose. If Talia said she was going to Hollywood, you'd be going right with her."

I lay still awaiting the oncoming insult.

"But now I see something I hadn't seen before," Damien went on. "You surprised me in this game, Nora. Maybe Talia's the one who needs you. The beauty needing the brain."

My cheeks got hot and I pinched my eyes closed.

"What you talking about fool?" Taj interjected. "Nora's got both brains and beauty!"

Damien sounded embarrassed. "Oh, yea—I didn't mean it like that. I meant—you know what I meant. Y'all both attractive," Damien stuttered. "I mean, she fine if you like a girl who gotta decent face and rack. Although I do love me some legs and booty—"

"And what about me?" Su-Min asked. "Everybody's talkin' 'bout Nora and Talia, but Su-Min gets no love?"

While the boys gushed about Su-Min's beauty I heard rustling outside the tent and shot up.

"What was that?"

The talking immediately stopped as we listened to the rustling outside. Loud crunches and twigs snapped and we jerked our heads in the same direction. Damien put his finger to his lips and got up slowly, grabbed the lantern and unzipped the tent. My heart was hammering against my chest. Damien peeked his head out and snapped it back in.

"It's a raccoon!" he hissed. "And a possum!" His eyes were wide as he turned back to watch the creatures. We all quickly joined him and I spotted the ugly white looking oversize rat of a possum and the furry black and brown raccoon. They were rummaging through one of our tubs. The raccoon pulled out an opened bag of chips and began loudly crunching on the snack food.

"Who left the box open?" I hissed. No one said a word, but I knew. I looked accusingly at Taj whose face did not give him away. He played possum very well.

"Well, we can't let them eat all our food," Damien said. He loudly unzipped the tent and began yelling. "Git! Git out of here!" And made himself very big by standing on the tips of his toes and bellowed in a deep voice. The possum immediately jumped up and ran, but the raccoon looked unimpressed. He just kept on crunching the chips. Taj seemed to get enough courage to join Damien and the two of them yelled and clapped their hands and shooed the creature until it skittered back into the darkness.

"Thank God they're gone," I said as Su-Min and I came out into the open.

"Thanks, boys for taking care of it," Su-Min said. "I wonder who left the lid off? I could've sworn—"

"What matters is most of the food is still there," Taj said quickly.

I stared at him and almost frowned until Su-Min grabbed my hand and said, "We'll clean it up. You boys go back to bed, you've done your duty."

Damien cleared his throat and shrugged, while Taj murmured thanks and they both returned to the tent.

We picked up the plastic wrappers and paper strewn across the ground. I found it odd Su-Min had volunteered us so easily, but then understood when she grabbed my arm and whispered, "Do you know who left the lid open?"

I looked into her eyes that were as round and big as plates and nodded. I mouthed Taj's name and she nodded back. We finished picking up the trash and I sighed deeply. I sat down on the burlap bag beside the embers left by the fire. I wasn't ready to go back inside the tent. Not yet.

"What's wrong?" Su-Min asked quietly. But there was no need. I could hear both boys snoring loud enough for all creatures high and low to hear.

I shook my head and stared into my hands. Su-Min sat down beside me and we both gazed into the darkness. How could I tell her what I was thinking? Would she listen? I decided I had to give it a shot.

"Well…" I began. "I like a—a boy—and..." I looked to see if she was amused or completely disinterested. She was neither. So I went on. "And this boy isn't what I thought he was—I mean—maybe he's not himself because of the game…" Shoot. I'd said too much.

"Or maybe you're able to see who he really is—because of the game," Su-Min said. I looked at her. She seemed so confident and carefree. Even though it was dark, I sensed the same Su-Min from back in the day. This night had reminded me of a friendship I had missed out on. I felt compelled to give her such a big hug and say I was sorry.

"You think he's always been that way?" I asked softly, pridefully stuffing down my emotions.

"I think," Su-Min began. "maybe you liked the idea of him. Like, there was this book I wanted to read so bad. The artwork on the cover was so good it spoke to me and when I finally got it and sat down to read, I was disappointed. It looked good from the outside. I'd even heard great things about it, but it just wasn't for me. I think that's how this crush might be, Nora. He looks good, you've heard great things about him, but once you get to know him, you realize he's just not for you."

She stared into the black night as the shadows closed in around us. Her words were true. Su-Min had touched a nerve that sent a pulse through my veins and straight to my heart. We got back into the tent and I snuggled into my sleeping bag, feeling my annoyance dissipate and my mind relax.

Supposed to be

We woke up to rain.

The soft pattering on the roof of our tent would've kept me asleep for a few more hours, but the chill shook me awake. I got up and stretched, feeling a crick in my neck and tried to work it loose, but failed. Taj sat up and rubbed his eyes. Damien quickly exited our shelter muttering about bathrooms and Su-Min sat up slowly, scratched her head and then plopped back down into her sleeping bag. I couldn't fall back to sleep if I tried. But I had no desire to get wet this early. So I sat in the entry of the tent, grateful for the rainfly that now had a purpose, and waited for Damien to return.

"You sleep good last night?" Taj asked from beside me.

I shook my head. "No, did you?"

"I slept aight." I stole a quick glance at him. His doleful brown eyes were heavy and his shoulders slumped. Three days ago I would've died to wake up next to Taj and be this close to him, but now the thrill was gone.

Damien sloshed across the muddy ground carrying something in his hands.

"Here," he said thrusting the bags at us. "Ponchos. But I don't think they'll help much. It's pouring."

I was grateful anyway for the protection. I slipped on the obnoxiously yellow garment, stepped out into the rain and rummaged through our food crate to see what we could scrounge up without cooking. The weather had taken away our only source of heat. I found a roll of summer sausage, a sack of apples, two bags of smoked jerky with one bag opened and a box of crackers. I left the opened bag of jerky in the bin with the rest of the food that might be needed for the next couple of days.

If I were still here in a few days.

Thinking about how much time we had left, I removed my slippers and stumbled into the tent trying not to track in mud. I handed out food to Su-Min and Taj while Damien was outside setting up some system he said would catch rainwater. When he came back, he brought water bottles and instructed us to eat as much as we could because we'd need our energy.

"But what about having enough for tomorrow?" I asked. The food bin already looked low. "And don't we only have three days left?"

Damien nodded. "If we make it three more days."

I watched as Taj inhaled his share of the camp breakfast and then said with mouth still full of summer sausage, "You don't know if they'll bring us more food tomorrow, Nora. You gotta stop worrying."

"Besides," Damien went on. "We need our strength for the hike today."

"Hike?" Su-Min asked mid-bite. "In the rain?"

"Don't y'all wanna know where we are?" Damien sat down and tied the laces on his sneakers. I wish I had chosen to wear tennis shoes on the day Beholden came. "I say we pack up and then get going."

I had no desire to go trekking in the rain on this abandoned land just to see where Beholden stuck us. But it made sense to Damien so we trusted he knew what he was talking about. He instructed us to cover our clothes with bug spray, pack a few more snacks, water bottles, a first aid kit, a poop kit (which basically consisted of tissue in a ziplock bag, that little baby shovel, and hand sanitizer.) Once we started the hike he yelled at us to stay in a straight line. The rain let up a little so even though my slippers were soaked through, at least I wasn't getting dumped on. And things got even better when the light drizzle instantly stopped as if God turned the water spigot to off. I started to smile when the sun showed its face for an instant, but it was accompanied by the buzzing of insects and muggy air. My smile left and my mood darkened. Mosquitos must've wanted a little sunshine too because now they buzzed by my ears, in my face and landed all over my sweaty body.

"Glad for that bug spray," Su-Min said sarcastically as she swatted the air.

"What?" Damien said. "I didn't say they wouldn't try to bite you."

And try they did, but I didn't feel any bites or stings despite their persistence. We kept to the shore, as Damien directed, walking along the water or as Damien put it "Find the water and follow it." He said we couldn't get lost or lose our way if we stayed near the water and he was right. The path was easy. A little rocky and muddy at times, but simple enough. We trudged along and listened as Damien pointed out different plants that I'd never heard of and even gave us tips on how to recognize poison ivy. Something about leaves of three, let it be.

"You sure know a lot about the outdoors, Damien," I said being careful not to slip on the rocks. "I didn't know this side about you."

There was a patch of silence and then he said quietly, "Not many people do." He rubbed his head and looked up at the once again cloudy sky. "Guess I don't have a lot of frien—"

"How long we walking?" Taj asked breathlessly. "Cuz this could go on forever."

"Uh, let's go a little bit further," Damien said. Was it my imagination, or did it look like he was relieved for Taj's interruption? "I'm pretty sure this is an island," he went on. "I feel like we might be halfway around. If it is, then I think I know where we are."

"You do?" I asked. "Where are—"

"Where the hell y'all come from?"

I heard Lashonda's voice before I saw her. We had come around a large rock and there she was, sitting with her toes in the dirt and wearing nothing but her bra and panties. She was scratching ravenously at her legs and ankles, and it looked like a rash had spread all over her lower body.

"Lashonda?!" Su-Min cried. "What happened? Where have—"

"Ay, y'all!" Lashonda hollered into the trees behind her. "Look who I found!"

"Well, technically we found you," Damien said. "And what is that on your legs? Poison oak?"

"Where are your clothes?" I asked.

"Damn! Will y'all quit with all the questions?" Lashonda snapped. And as she began to explain, I watched Omri, the twins and Talia emerge from the trees. Talia had creamy white patches all over her face and frowned at the sight of us, while Omri jumped with excitement. The twins didn't react at all. Apparently, they had also come to the island yesterday. They too had tubs full of supplies, but their tent got a hole in it (which they couldn't explain) and they had tried to hike through the woods last night (Talia's idea) but had to stop when Lashonda and Talia got some mysterious rash.

"It's poison oak," Damien said knowingly.

"I told y'all they were still in the game!" Omri shouted with a smile.

"Isn't that amazing," Talia said sarcastically.

She did not look happy to see us and you know what? I felt the same. I had gotten used to it being just the four of us. I was happy about competing against Taj, Su-Min, and Damien in the end. My mind hadn't missed Talia and now that she was back, I felt a sting of bitterness.

We stood awkwardly, glancing at one another as if we didn't know what to do next. I'm sure everyone's thoughts were similar. Should we join together or stay separate? And if we did unite, which camp would we go to?

"Our camp is pretty dope," Taj said without hesitation. "And we've got a tent and a fire pit already started thanks to yours truly." He put his hand on Damien's shoulder. "Y'all should come with us."

I wanted to smile at Taj's invitation. It was nice of him to offer.

Damien lowered his shoulder so that Taj's hand was no longer on it. "But, we don't know if it's us against them." He frowned and shoved his glasses up. "I don't want to join the competition."

"Who says we want to join you anyway?" Talia said with her hands on her hips. She looked a bit funny with the white patches on her arms which I noticed were starting to flake.

"What is that, calamine lotion?" Su-Min pointed at her face.

"What do you think?" Talia snapped. "It was all we had."

"I told her I ain't looking like no zebra," Lashonda said and scratched her arm.

"Yea and when you have permanent scars, don't come crying to me!" Talia shouted.

"Come on, y'all," Omri said. He looked at us with pleading eyes. "I can't stand being wet all the time. We need to get dry. I think I'm growing webbed feet."

"Yea, it's pretty messed up," Adrian said. His eyes were bloodshot. "I didn't even sleep last night."

"Okay, hold up," Taj said. "Let me talk with my team and then we'll get back with you."

We huddled together a few feet away and Taj didn't even have to convince us. Damien was the only one who begrudgingly agreed.

The trek back to our camp went quick. Talia and her team carried their two tubs and left their collapsed tent behind. When they saw our little set up there were no oohs and aahhs. There was only:

Lashonda: Where y'all poop at?

Omri: Taj, I thought you said your place was dope? This ain't dope.

Talia: This is it?

Adrian and Akeem: Silence

Su-Min: Look! Another clue!

That got everyone's attention. We all huddled around as Su-Min carefully read the card out loud. I tried to focus, but I think the bug spray had worn off. I felt a tickling sensation on my neck. I slapped at it and my hand landed on an insect larger than a mosquito. Quietly, I tried to pull the bug off, but to my horror, it was stuck.

"There—there's…my neck!" I stuttered.

Everyone looked up.

"What?" Lashonda asked huffily.

I pointed at my neck and screeched, "My neck! There's a bug stuck to my neck!"

The group surrounded me and I heard Taj first.

"That's nasty."

Damien said, "Back up people, it looks like a tick."

"A what?" I screamed.

"Calm down, Nora," Omri said and sat me down on the fallen log. "You'll be alright." He put his hand on my arm.

"Get it off!" I yelled and tried to do what any normal person would do if they had some foreign creature stuck to their skin. I tried to yank it off.

"Don't!" Damien cried. "Or its head'll get stuck in there and you could get infected."

My heart was in my throat. I wanted to faint, but couldn't. The tickling sensation now felt on fire as if my body recognized the alien presence and was subtly warning me.

"Just please get it off," I begged. I didn't notice the hot tears falling down my cheeks.

"Get oil," Adrian said. "You can choke it out."

"No, we need tweezers," Damien said.

"Dude, I saw Bear Grylls use oil."

"That could potentially release the bacteria into her skin," Damien yelled.

I'd had enough. "Just DO something!" I screamed.

Feet scurried behind me, followed by low whispers and then I felt pressure on my neck.

"What's going on?" I said.

Omri sat beside me. "Damien's going to pull it out."

Tears streaked down my face as I felt a slight pinch and then, "It's out."

I blinked and looked up and around. "It's over?" I said.

Damien held out the tiny black creature and showed it to me. "Easy," he said. And then he handed me rubbing alcohol and told me to clean the area while he destroyed the tick. With shaking hands, I wiped the back of my neck and looked up to see Talia and Lashonda staring at me. Talia whispered something to Lashonda and she snickered.

"What?" I said.

"You cried like a baby, Nora," Lashonda said. "You alright? Acted like you lost a leg or something."

Talia laughed. "Yea, you don't see us crying over poison oak, but you got stuck by a little bug and freaked the hell out."

My cheeks warmed and my chest burned with anger. I wanted to say something, anything, but this part of me never worked properly. I couldn't make a snappy comeback or sarcastic retort. So what did I do? I looked down at the ground as they laughed together and walked away.

"Don't mind them, Nora," Omri said from beside me. "They just mad 'cause nobody care about their ugly rash."

I smiled slowly and tried to stop my tears from brimming over. Why did the waterworks always choose to come at the most inopportune time?

"You should've seen Talia last night," Omri continued. "She was crying about everything. Bugs, spiders, snakes."

"Snakes?" Su-Min sat down on the burlap mat and crossed her legs.

"Yea," Omri laughed. "She saw one when she went to the bathroom. Said she wasn't going into the woods alone anymore." He shook his head. "So, when we got to start the next phase?" He was looking at Su-Min. I had no idea what they were talking about since I hadn't heard the clue.

"They said they were going to come get us," Su-Min answered.

"Who do you think your partner is going to be?"

Su-Min shrugged then glanced up at me.

"Partners?" I said. "I missed it. What do we have to do?"

"Oh yea, you were dealing with the vampire bug," Omri chuckled. "We don't know exactly, but all it said is we got to have partners. Then they'd come get us and something about a chief."

I nodded. My head felt like a spinning top. Not only was I now clueless in the game, but I looked weak. Nobody wanted a partner as a crybaby. I looked around the campsite as Su-Min picked at a scab on her foot, Lashonda and Talia were eating jerky from our tub, Damien was gone, the twins were drinking water bottles and Taj was laying inside the tent. I was sure the twins would join forces, Taj and Damien seemed like the obvious team and Su-Min had—wait a second.

"There's an odd number!" I shouted. I didn't mean to, but that's the way it came out.

"Whachu talkin' 'bout Nora?" Omri asked.

Talia and Lashonda had stopped talking and were looking my way.

"One person won't have a partner," I said lowering my voice. I had an uneasy feeling that person might be me.

"We know," Lashonda said. "you just figure that out?"

Omri got up and opened their cook tub. He brought out brown bananas, bread and a jar of peanut butter. He sat down next to me and said, "Wanna peanut butter and banana sandwich?" Grateful for the distraction, I nodded and rubbed at my dirty hands.

Su-Min piped up, "I want one too."

"Comin' right up," Omri said as he sanitized his hands and passed it around, then proceeded in making us sandwiches.

"Omri," Talia called. "Can I talk to you for a sec?"

"You can talk to me right now," Omri said as he sliced the bananas.

Talia's voice was tight and her teeth were clenched together. She walked over and hissed loud enough for me to hear, "Why are you giving them our food?"

"Theirs…ours…who cares?" Omri said and handed me a sandwich. "Here you go Señora."

With both hands, I took a huge bite and watched Talia's face grow cloudy as the sky. She stormed off and I heard her and Lashonda snapping at each other. I realized the two had surprisingly grown chummy.

"Looks like we pissed off your team," Su-Min said as she took her sandwich.

"They ain't my team," Omri said. "I'm supposed to be team Omri, ain't I?" He looked at me. "You're team Nora." He nodded at Su-Min. "And you're team Su-Min." He paused, then said, "At least that's how it's supposed to be."

Damien returned with a bunch of branches and started the fire, something I didn't even want since as it was already boiling outside. I don't know if he just felt like it was his duty, or he had nervous energy, because he went to work starting that fire like it was his last mission on earth. Talia and Lashonda continued to noisily eat out of the tub and once Taj was up he joined them. The twins replaced Taj in the tent and it seemed like they slept for an hour before we heard rustling in the trees. I looked up and heard the sound of a beating drum accompanied by a thin man.

He slid from behind the trees, so tall he could have been one of them. His brown hands lightly tapped an African drum that hung from a leather strap slung over his shoulder. He wore a red cloth that looked like a toga, with a cord tied around his waist. He had multiple bronze bracelets around his wrists and large holes in his ears plugged with fat rods. I stared at his face. Steely, yet soft. His scalp was shaved all around except at the crown where a group of tiny braids fell down his shoulders past the shells that hung around his neck.

"Jambo," he said in a soft voice and held up one hand. "I'm Josef. Please fall in line right here in front of me."

I didn't understand the first part, but I was quick to obey the rest. Everyone, including the awakened twins, stood in line. I looked at my classmates as this man probably did. We were dirty, tired and covered in scratches and bites.

"Follow me," he said. "The Chief is waiting."

We walked into the trees. Everything looked the same. It was a blur of woods, wet ground, and a cloudy sky that soon poured down rain.

"Oh, come on!" Damien yelled at the sky.

No one remembered to bring a poncho or pack snacks. We never sprayed ourselves with bug repellent before we left. There hadn't been any time. Once Beholden started, there was no waiting. You just had to go. I fell in line behind Su-Min and Talia was right behind me. She had been oddly quiet and terse since we'd gotten back together. I knew she was mad at me and that put a tiny bit of worry in my stomach. I was just about to say something, but Su-Min turned around and muttered about how we forgot our poop kit. I laughed and my worry melted away. Even though we were drenched and shivering, I was glad I was playing the game with Su-Min.

Suddenly our guide halted and spun around.

"Choose a partner," he said. "The Chief is waiting up ahead."

I was shocked by how quickly the others flew into action.

"Adrian," Akeem said.

"Taj," Omri blurted.

Su-Min said, "I choose Nor—"

"Nora!" Talia yelled and grabbed my hand.

Su-Min frowned and opened her mouth to say more, but Lashonda cut her off.

"You said you was going to be my partner!" She walked up to Talia and thumped her in the chest.

Talia stepped back, dragging me along with her and said, "Yea, well, I changed my mind. Nora's my partner." She carefully walked around the fuming Lashonda and pulled us up to the man in the red dress.

"I'll be your partner Su-Min," Damien said.

I glanced back at her face. She looked sad. Betrayed even. I felt awful. Why hadn't I spoken up? Why didn't I say anything? I didn't agree to be Talia's partner. But when I looked at my best friend she beamed down at me.

"We'll make a perfect team," she said with a grin. I smiled back and tried to hide the uncertainty inside.

"I shoulda known your shady ass was lying," Lashonda barked at Talia's back, then turned to the group. "Everybody don't trust Talia! She lie to yo' face!"

"Can we go?" Talia asked our guide. "Or do we have to sit here and listen to her whine?"

I heard Lashonda's feet pound toward us, but the man in the red dress stepped between us and the oncoming force. He held up his hands and shook his head.

"Do not fight with your fists," he said. "Fight with this." He pointed to his head.

"What the hell you talkin' bout Kunta Kinte?" Lashonda asked. "I'm from the streets and this chick right here disrespected me so I'm 'bout to disrespect her." She lunged for Talia and barely missed her hair.

"You stay here," he said to Lashonda. "I will be back for you."

He motioned us to hurry through the woods and we left Lashonda seething in the trees.

The rain drizzled down our faces as we walked toward a small hut made of straw. I wondered how long it took Beholden to build it. The guide instructed us to wait outside while he took us in two at a time. The first group was Su-Min and Damien, then Omri and Taj.

"You ready?" The guide turned to me and Talia as Omri and Taj exited. Their faces looked confused and surprisingly, Omri had nothing to say. He just seemed upset by something. Worried, I nodded and tried to be cheerful, even though inside my gut was twisting in anxiety. I got the feeling that something bad was about to happen. I just didn't know how soon it was going to be.

Avalanche

"Mind if I smoke?" A heavy man with thick coiled hair sat on the ground. His clean-shaven face smiled up at us as we joined him on the woven mats. His broad bare chest was covered with black curls and sweat beads dripped down his massive shoulders.

"Yes, I mind," Talia said.

But the Chief did not put away the pipe. The smell reminded me of my abuelo, who consistently smoked many nights after an argument with Abuelita. The sweet and spicy scent was a hypnotic memory that took me back to my six-year-old self, where my grandfather would turn to me and say, "Join me on the porch, *mija*? This old fart needs some space from his other half." And my abuelita would say, "Your ex-other half." I smiled at the memory and immediately noticed the large man smiling back at me.

"What's your name?" he murmured. His bright eyes searched my face.

"Sonora," I said feeling ashamed I'd been caught daydreaming.

"Are you enjoying yourself on my island?" he asked.

"Um, yessir," I answered politely. What should I have said? No? I mean, our night hadn't been as awful as Talia's, but it wasn't amazing either.

"Can we move on?" Talia asked. "Don't we have to answer some questions or something?"

My heart jumped. I must've missed that part of the clue. What kind of questions?

"Patience," Chief purred. "What's your name, restless one?"

"I'm not restless," Talia snapped. "And it's Talia." She folded her arms and puffed out her chest. "Now, can we get on with it?"

He laughed from his gut and it shook just as I imagined Santa Clause looked when he laughed. He smiled widely at us. His teeth were white like pearls and his wide nose flared as he snorted, "You are fire, my girl! I will call you Firecracker and you may call me Chief." He clapped his large hands and sat up straighter. "Now, on to the questions. Three riddles I will tell, you," he began. "Yes, four I will say. Answer them all and you'll receive a grand pay. The first—"

"Wait!" Talia interrupted. "Are there three or four?"

Chief ignored Talia's question and continued. "No matter where I travel, no matter where I roam, no matter where I find myself, I always am at home. What am I?"

There was a moment of silence and then Talia answered first, "A snail!"

While I followed with, "A turtle!"

She snapped her head at me and hissed, "We both can't give answers."

I shrugged.

"It's okay, Firecracker," Chief said with a chuckle and his pipe clenched between his teeth. "You're both right!" He blew out a stream of smoke. "The second riddle: How many months have 28 days?" he asked.

I knew the answer. But my words didn't come out fast enough.

Talia blurted, "February!"

"I'm sorry!" Chief said and his shoulders sagged. "You are incorrect."

Fuming, I turned to Talia and said, "All of the months have 28 days!"

"That is the correct answer," Chief said pointing to me. "next time consult with your partner Firecracker."

"My name is Talia!" she snapped.

"Next riddle!" he said calmly. "If you are running in a race and you pass the person in second place, what place are you in?"

Talia opened her mouth, but I grabbed her hand. "Wait," I said quietly.

She frowned and looked at me. "What? It's first place," she said.

"No," I said. "Let's think about this. Don't just blurt out the first thing that comes to your mind."

"I'm not—" she started to argue.

But my brain was whirling. I knew the answer. "It's second place," I said with a smile. "You just passed the person in second, not the person in first, so you're now in second place."

"Huh?" she said confused.

"That's the answer."

"Whatever," she said looking uncertain, but turned and said confidently. "Our answer is second place."

"You are correct!" Chief said and rubbed his chin. "Okay, this next one is a bit harder. Three things are never satisfied, four that never say, 'Enough!' What are they?"

Talia stared at him, scratched her head and shrugged. I knew we had to think about this one. I felt like I'd heard it before. Sounded like one of those proverbs Abuelita always quoted. In total, four things were never satisfied and I figured one of them must have been fire because fire always wanted more. What else never had enough? I thought back to my talks with Abuelita and tried to remember her words. The grass always needed water. And what about death? People always died. But that was only three. I needed one more.

"Water," Talia spoke in a rush. "And a dog? A rat?"

"No, Talia," I moaned and slapped my forehead.

"We don't have time for you to sit there, Nora!" Talia said accusingly. "One of us has to answer."

"I'm sorry, Firecracker," Chief said. "But you are incorrect." He motioned behind us and said, "Let the next group know they may come in."

"But what are we supposed to do now?" I asked as we stood up.

"Josef will let you know," Chief said.

Talia stormed out ahead of me and I followed. The twins brushed right past us as they entered the tent.

"What's with you?" Talia snapped over her shoulder. I knew she was talking to me.

"What's with you?" I asked right back.

"I basically answered all those questions for us, Nora, while you did nothing."

Uh oh. She turned to glare at me. Arms crossed, hip out to the side and red face said I-don't-even-wanna-hear-it.

"Uh, I know I answered some," was all I managed to squeak out. I was more concerned with our audience. Everyone was looking at us. Which made me want to hide behind a rock.

"You answered one," she said. "And then you didn't even try."

"I was thinking!"

"Whatever." She threw her hands up like she was done and then came back for round two. "You're always thinking, Nora, but not ever doing."

And it was like a switch went off inside my head. My thoughts suddenly clear, I knew exactly what I wanted to say. And like a freight train without brakes, I blurted, "And you never seem to think! You just go! Talia always goes! And everybody else must follow."

"Oh, so that's how you feel now?" Talia's eyes bulged in shock.

"That's exactly how I feel," I said as the adrenaline coursed through my veins. "You're bossy! You never ask me what I want to do, you just order me around. You think I like being called your tagalong? You think I want to be in your shadow? Well, you're not my only friend Talia. The world doesn't revolve around you."

The words tumbled out before I could stop them. Can you put a lid on a volcano? Or prevent an avalanche from sliding down a mountain? I had lost control. My tongue had a mind of its own and I could not stop it. So I was not surprised when Talia took a step toward me and I took a step back. I heard a low groan from Omri's direction.

Talia jabbed my shoulder. "You know what you are, Nora? You're pathetic. Too scared to lead so, somebody else has to. You can't do anything on your own." Her voice darkened as she continued. "That's why you'll never win this game. In fact, I don't even know how you got this far. I don't need you. I never did."

Talia's flaming face made me cower. Reminded me of who I was. Instead of embracing the burning heat inside, I squelched it. My eyes shifted around at the others. Damien looked away and Su-Min stared at us pitifully. My wits had returned like the sun after a cloudy day. I had been impulsive and regret the words once they hit the air. Seeing the pain and fury in Talia's face increased my grief even more. Not knowing how else to react, I did what came natural. My lip began to tremble and suddenly I knew the waterfalls would start.

"Oh great, now you're going to cry," Talia slapped her thigh and walked into the woods. "Come get me when she's done blubbering."

"I'm not crying!" I shouted, but I knew it was too late. As soon as one drop slid down my cheek, it was quickly followed by another. I turned away and wiped my face, sniffing quietly.

"You're too sensitive," Damien said.

"Shut up, Damien," I said heatedly.

"See, why don't you talk to her like that?" Damien said. "Talia ain't nobody. Just look at her like she's me and tell her what you really think."

"She did," Su-Min said with a sigh. "It sucks when people don't listen."

I walked away from the group until I could no longer hear them talking. I didn't need to know what they thought about me or what they thought I needed to do. I walked and walked until I was sure no one else was around. I plopped down on a large boulder and hugged my knees to my chest. I wanted to cry more, but I refused to let Beholden or my supposed friends get the best of me. But I couldn't stop the voices in my head.

What's the deal with Talia? Who does she think she is? Why she gotta talk to you like that? Because you act like a child. Everybody watched you cry. You're weak. You'll never win this game.

I buried my head into my knees and whispered aloud, "Stop it, Nora. You're being ridiculous." But was I? Maybe this game was too much for me. Maybe Abuelita was right. Once you played Beholden you ended up losing yourself.

"Yo! Nora!"

Omri was calling me. I slid off the rock and slowly walked back through the mushy ground. I was glad at least the rain had stopped.

"Yo! Hurry up Nora!"

"I'm coming, I'm coming," I mumbled.

"Just leave her," Talia was saying when I walked up. "She's going to—"

"She's going to what?" I snapped.

"Alright, people get at your markers," Josef yelled. And that's when I noticed everybody was standing behind a spray-painted yellow line on the ground. Omri and Su-Min were waving me over, but just as I figured out what was happening, Josef blew a whistle and the group took off into the trees.

"Run, Nora!" Su-Min yelled back. "To the beach!"

My body flew into motion before I even had time to think. My hands swung back and forth, my feet pounded the earth and I was flying. Hopping over logs and pushing my body harder than I'd ever in my life. I don't run track and I'm not on cross country, but dang I was bookin' it faster than most.

I passed Damien and then Su-Min. I flew past the twins who were crouched on the ground. I glanced back at them and saw one of them was hurt, but my legs kept pumping. I was close to Talia. Funny, I didn't really care if I won or not, I just wanted to beat her. I was close now. Close enough to reach out and touch her hair, but then I saw it before I could stop. Her hand shot out and a large stick collided with my legs. My feet jumbled and I fell. Hard. I yelled out in pain and heard people pass me by, but then somebody came running back.

I thought maybe she did it on accident. Maybe Talia came back to see if I was okay.

"You alright, Nora?" It was Omri. Of course, he would come back.

I waved him off. "Go 'head Omri," I grunted. "Don't lose for me."

"I'm not," he said standing up. "I'm just making sure you aight." Then he turned and ran.

I got up and slowly jogged the rest of the way to the finish line which wasn't much of a beach. Mostly muddy rocks with long strands of grass poking between. Everybody including Lashonda had gotten there before me. The only person left was Akeem. I looked over at Talia and wanted to shout, "What the hell was that?" I wanted to yell every curse word in my head until I had no breath. But all I managed to do was glare at her until she glanced at me and then looked away.

"Hey, where's your brother?" Taj asked.

"He twisted his ankle," Adrian answered. He rubbed his elbow and looked a little concerned.

And then I saw something I hadn't the entire game. Josef, the man in the red dress, came running out of the trees with a phone.

A real cell phone y'all. He was talking into it, all out of breath when he got to us and then put it in his back pocket (which I didn't even see on that flimsy rag) and informed us Akeem had to be taken to the medical unit. He sprained his foot and was now out of the game.

"Yes!" Talia pumped her fist into the air and then realized her mistake. "I mean, sorry." She looked at Adrian then turned her attention to Josef. "So how do you know who won? You weren't even watching."

Josef looked down into his hand as if something was written on it and said, "We are always watching. Taj came in first, then Lashonda, Talia, Damien, Su-Min, Omri, Adrian and last was Sonora."

"Dang," Lashonda grunted as she squinted into the sky. "Where y'alls cameras at?"

Josef continued. "I would like Taj, Lashonda, Talia, and Damien to stand over here." He pointed to his right. "And the rest to stand over here."

"Alright winners," Lashonda grinned as she walked over to Josef. "Let's get at 'em. What we win? Some steaks and burgers? We gonna sleep in an actual bed? We get a mosquito net? A/C? What?" I slowly joined the losers on the left.

"You four put these on," Josef said as he handed us familiar black hoods. I sighed as I yanked one angrily over my head. "Now hold onto this person's shoulders." I could feel his hands move mine onto someone's broad arms and land on either side of their neck. From the touch, it was clearly a guy and the last time I checked Adrian's skinny self didn't have many muscles. "Okay, now follow me, slowly now—slow." We gradually walked holding onto each other and as crazy as it sounds, my body began to perspire. I'm not sure if it was the heat or the fact that I suddenly realized I was touching Omri. I should've been creeped out, but instead, I felt awkward and nervous.

What was wrong with me?

I shook my head to throw off the thoughts but did not succeed. Slipping over some rocks I accidentally pulled on his shoulders and he quickly asked, "Yo, you good?"

"Yea," I said softly and my heartbeat even faster when I knew it was definitely him. I didn't understand why he was on the losers team. That boy was a fast runner. And how come he was so quiet? Omri never stopped talking.

We crunched for a while longer until Josef informed us to stop. Then I heard him one at a time, telling someone to climb down.

"Where we going?" Omri asked when it was his turn.

"Just be careful of your step," Josef answered. I was next. He told me to turn around and take my time as each foot hit the rung of the ladder. Instantly, my skin tingled.

"Are we on a cliff?" I asked. "Am I going to fall?"

But Josef did not say a word as I slowly climbed down, still unable to see. Once I hit bottom I stood there awkwardly for a moment. Then head a rustling sound and felt a rush of wind.

"Ah, hell," Omri said. "Y'all can take your hoods off now."

I slowly removed my hood and stared in shock at my surroundings.

"This ain't right," Omri muttered as he scratched his head. Then took both hands and rubbed his face and groaned. Su-Min plopped on the ground and Adrian looked up and my eyes followed.

The ladder was gone. Josef was gone. And all that was around us was red dirt and rocks. Above us was a gray sky and trees that now seemed unreachable.

I didn't know how we'd ever make it out of that pit.

When Souls Collide

We all tried climbing out of the pit, but the muddy walls were slippery. Then we tried hoisting each other up. First Omri lifted Su-Min since she was the lightest, but she only reached halfway. Then he and Adrian lifted me, but I wasn't any better. Then Omri, me and Su-Min tried lifting Adrian (who was much taller) and he still didn't make it. We gave up out of breath and plopped on the ground. Thunder rumbled in the distance and we all looked up into the sky.

"I hope it doesn't rain," I said. "What will they do then?"

"Maybe that'll be good," Adrian said. "Then we can just float out of here."

"Or drown," Su-Min muttered and crossed her arms.

I shuddered at the thought.

"Well, at least we're not out of the game," Omri said standing up and stretching. "We still gotta chance." He looked up and then began studying the muddy wall. While he tugged at roots and tried to again, climb out, I sighed and looked around. There was a long stick against the wall and a big rock beside it.

"How long do you think it took to dig this hole?" I asked.

"Who cares?" Adrian asked. "We need to get out of it." He stood up and began climbing beside Omri, but I was tired. I sat there and watched them climb and slip a little ways down, then climb higher and slip again. Omri was 3/4 of the way there but then slid all the way back down again.

"Dang!" he yelled and hit the ground with his fist.

"Give it a rest," Su-Min muttered.

"I can't!" Omri shouted. "I gotta pee!" He climbed up the side again and I couldn't help but smile. When I glanced at Su-Min she was smiling too. Omri was like a spider as he moved legs and arms up, up, up then doo-oown the wall.

I was grateful for the small distraction because my thoughts were a mess. I couldn't stop thinking about my fight with Talia. Part of me was pissed at that stunt she pulled when we raced to the beach, but another part of me felt guilty for what I'd said to her. Words I could never get back, no matter if they were true or not. I replayed our conversation over and over in my mind. I didn't know how I got this far in the game. In fact, I should've been home. And with that thought, my mind slipped into a depressive state as I worried about the phone call to my dad.

While the boys continued to try and climb out, Su-Min and I sat in silence and watched. I think exhaustion had taken every ounce of us. And when the sky turned dark and the moon gave us a bit of light, the boys plopped on the ground in a heap of fatigue.

"I'm sorry," Omri said. "Y'all gonna have to look away. I can't hold it any longer." And before I could say another word, he turned away, unzipped his pants and I whipped my head in the opposite direction, my eyes glued to the wall.

"Mayne, warn a brother next time," Adrian yelled.

"I said look away," Omri said. "And you act like you ain't ever seen one before."

"Damn, how long you gonna go?"

"I been holdin' it since the Chief's place."

"Mayne you gonna lock your bowels all up. Go find a tree next time."

"Did it look like—"

"Omri!" I yelled. "Are you done yet?" The stream was loud and strong.

"Uh—almost…aight. I'm done."

I turned around and saw Su-Min pinch her nose and walk to the opposite side of the pit beside me. "Let's make that the designated bathroom area," she said. "No one step foot over there."

"Yea, I don't wanna be here any more than you do," Omri muttered. "And don't act like ya'll don't gotta go, because at some point, you will."

Adrian and Omri moved to our side and I watched Adrian sprawl out on the ground. He asked us to wake him when we got out. Su-Min sat next to me and I soon felt her head slip onto mine. Her breathing deepened and her body grew more relaxed. I had my knees propped up with my arms dangling over them, my back leaned against the muddy wall. I swallowed the lump in my throat and looked up at the sky, startled to finally see some stars.

Suddenly, I missed home. I wanted to be with my mom, Abuelita, and Tony. I know I started Beholden in order to avoid home, but now that didn't matter. Even though I didn't want to think about my dad or the fact that I needed to return his phone call, I missed mi familia more. I missed laying on my mom's lap and feeling her fingernails as she rubbed my scalp. I missed Tony and the way he smelled like wood after work. I missed Abuelita and her floured hands after she made us a batch of buñuelos. I even missed reading the twins a goodnight story. I couldn't let my dad prevent me from wanting to be with them.

After he showed up randomly last week in front of our apartment, my mom flipped out and thought he was going to try and kidnap me again. I never realized how much fear she lived in, wondering if there'd be another day her child was taken. They verbally fought until Tony showed up which only escalated and then our neighbors called the cops. My dad had a bad temper and was swiftly arrested.

I'd never seen Tony so mad, but I guess he was more protective over me and my mom than I thought. That next night my mom talked with Pastor Jeff, Taj's dad, and she decided to bail my dad out. I asked her why she did it and she said, it's funny how we as people react. We call it survival, a natural tendency to lash out and do what's best for us. But when we can calm down and truly see things, take a deeper look, then we discover something we hadn't seen before.

She said she wanted to learn my dad's true intentions. And when they met for coffee the next day, she discovered he was trying to reconnect with me and was getting his life straight. He said he'd changed, been sober for a couple of years, and wanted to start a relationship with me and the entire family. Well, this was shocking news to her and after some encouraging advice from Pastor Jeff, she and I decided to give it a try. Well, she decided. I agreed but was internally unsure.

I didn't know this man. He'd been gone for years. He hadn't even tried to reach out or pay child support. My mother had to work her butt off to take care of me. I knew I needed to give him a chance, but a part of me wanted to say no thank you, I'm doing fine all by myself.

But I hadn't done fine by myself. There were many moments growing up I wished for a father. Many times I saw the pain in my mother's face when I asked her who my daddy was. Many times I heard the tightness in her voice when she changed the subject, a subject I grew to avoid.

And all the yearnings I had for a father to tell me 'well done,' for a dad to let me sit on his lap, for a papa to tuck me into bed and say 'goodnight.' He missed out on all those and now he all of a sudden wanted to come back when I was grown at 18 years old? That, to me, was far too late.

"What you thinking about?" Omri whispered.

I paused, feeling my thoughts ripple away like waves on the ocean.

"My dad," I answered honestly.

"The one who kidnapped you?"

"Yea."

"He still in jail?"

"No." I sighed. "My mom bailed him out."

Omri paused, then said, "She a good woman."

I rolled my eyes. "Yea, she said he's a changed man and I need to give him a chance."

"And are you?"

I shrugged but realized he couldn't see me in the dark. "I guess," I muttered.

"At least he's trying," Omri said quietly. "Most of 'em don't come back. Ever."

My chest burned with anger. "At least you got a dad," I said touchily.

He was quiet and in the silence, I realized my own hasty mistake. Yea, Omri had a dad, but everybody knew what sort of dad he was. Stone-faced, serious and always seemed to be disappointed. And Omri's mom was gone. A father was all he had. I wanted to apologize, but the moment had passed.

"You ever look up at the stars at night?" he said. "I mean, I ain't ever seen the sky so blazing."

I looked up and was in awe. Being away from the city had truly made a difference. The black sky was twinkling with tiny lights and my thoughts softened. Looking up I realized how big this world was and how little my problems felt.

"You ever think of that story," Omri began. "In the Bible when Abraham was lookin' up at the sky and God told him his purpose? Laid it all out for him. Said, your children going to be like them stars. So many you can't even count them all." He chuckled aloud and my heart warmed at the sound. "Abraham didn't even have kids at the time! Wife was barren—"

"And they were on the road," I said. "Traveling to someplace—"

"They didn't even know where," Omri finished. "And Abraham went outside and talked to God…" His voice trailed off. "You ever do that, Nora?" he asked me softly. "I do. All the time. I look up and ask him why. I ask him why things are the way they are. Why my dad so mad. Why my mama gone. Why am I…the way I am."

The silence that followed was filled with confused feelings. I wasn't supposed to care for Omri. I wasn't supposed to have this moment of connection and understanding. But I did. I felt so close to him without physically even being near him. Suddenly, I wanted to know all his thoughts, ask why he had hidden this side of him. And before I could help it, tears formed, close to brimming over and I looked through the blurry darkness and whispered, "And what does God say to you?"

No sound but the deep breathing of our two peers was between us. For a good while, I thought Omri wasn't going to answer. But then he did.

"He reminds me of that first time he laid hold of me. My heart was his. I didn't want nothing but him. And then I see what really matters, ya know? I see all 'a this is for show. It ain't what's real, Nora. It's just a shadow of what's to come."

The beating of my heart seemed to still at his answer and then he stopped and I craved for more. I clung to each word as he continued, "So I gotta press on even if my dad won't see it. If my auntie think I'm crazy. My uncle think I'm nuts. I know I ain't perfect, but even if everybody in the whole damn world think Omri out of his mind, I'm not going to stop. I'm going to do what HE says, 'cuz that's all that matters."

My heartbeat was loud. Louder than I'd ever heard it. My ears drummed with the deafening pulse and my heart wanted to soar up to the heavens and touch the stars. My collision with Omri was more than words. It was like my soul felt a familiar match. His words made me realize how similar we were and gave me the courage to speak.

"I started going to church with Abuelita," I said slowly. "And things were weird at first, but then I had this experience that's hard to explain…" I trailed off. "I mean, I've always believed in God. I know he's real, but I didn't have a personal connection, you know? It was like, I read about him in the Bible. I heard about him from Abuelita, but I didn't know him, know him."

I paused and let the words sink in. I hadn't talked about this with anyone. Not even at church.

"But one summer, when I was in Mexico, I was at the end of me. Some bad stuff happened that brought up the past and—and I just asked myself those same questions. Why God? Why did this happen to me and why did you allow it to happen?" I felt like my words came out in a sudden rush and I had to stop myself from saying more. I'd said too much.

But the quiet didn't deter Omri. I thought he'd say something stupid, but instead, he just sat there. And I needed that stillness. I needed the quiet to remember and think back to that moment. That summer, I'd laid in bed next to Abuelita. The window was open allowing a cool breeze to enter into tia abuela's stuffy house. I could see the moon from where I lay and it was so bright and beautiful. My heart ached as I cried and tried to process my life and what I was doing. Filled with regret and wishing God would just take my life away, I prayed and asked him to show me if he was real. I wanted to know if this God my abuela served was true.

"I can't explain it," I continued aloud. "But I felt something shift inside me. Like, a warm touch from the inside that told me this is what real love feels like. A feeling that says everything's going to be okay. A feeling that says every stupid mistake that I've ever done is forgotten. And Omri, the moment I realized the Creator of the world was okay with me, okay with just the way I was and every dumb thing that's happened, well…there's got to be a reason for it all… ya know?"

I didn't think my words made sense. But Omri's next words made me smile.

"I know exactly how you feel."

Suddenly, the atmosphere in the pit changed. I no longer felt the pressure of Su-Min's sleeping head on my shoulder. I could no longer hear the heavy breathing of Adrian across the pit. All I heard was Omri's footsteps as he walked over to me and sat down. The heat from his body close to mine was strange and I was more aware of it than ever before. I wanted him to reach out and touch me. I'd never seen this side of him before.

I stole a peek at him and could only see the outline of his face. He wasn't looking at me. Part of me thought I was going crazy. This was Omri Jones. Ridiculous and risky. But what if he wasn't the problem? I used to think his silliness was endearing. He always made me laugh, that's why I went with him to the Beautillion ball when he asked me. It wasn't until Talia said something that made me change my mind. What was it? Oh, yea. She said he was a terrible kisser.

The heat returned to my cheeks as I recalled that conversation. I was getting ready for the ball and Talia had come over to help me with my hair. She was good at that sort of thing and while she was styling my up-do, out of nowhere she told me I better avoid kissing Omri because she said it was not a good experience. I wasn't mad about the kissing. I was mad that he had already kissed my best friend. The whole night I was in a foul mood. And all he kept wondering was why I wasn't happy and what had he done?

I never told him.

"Omri," I began. "I always wanted to know…" But the words wouldn't come. Like slipping on ice, I couldn't get a grip on how I wanted to say it. But there was no time like now. I'd never get another chance once Beholden had its way. "Omri," I tried again. "Talia said y'all kissed. When did that happen?"

Omri sighed deeply. I expected a quick joke, not a straight answer. That was the Omri I was used to. But he took his time answering. Like he was weighing the situation.

"I figured she told you," he said in a big breath. "I shoulda known to mess with her. That girl crazy." He cleared his throat. "I, uh, was at Theo's party. It was stupid. I was stupid. Shouldn't have been there, but you know, didn't want to be home. I drank too much, smoked too much and Talia—well…she was just there."

I swallowed hard, tried to get the lump out of my throat.

"I shouldn't have been there, Nora," he said. "I don't do that stuff no more. That's not me."

I nodded, knowing he couldn't see. But I didn't have words at the moment. I just looked up at the sky and thought about Omri's words from earlier. My heart settled, as if at peace with what I'd just heard. What was I thinking? Talia was irresistible and I didn't blame Omri for falling. And at that moment, I felt like exactly where I was.

In a pit.

"I was mad at you," I finally confessed. "I'd been mad at you for that. I'm sorry I treated you so bad at the Beautillion. I shouldn't have done that—"

"Nora, she didn't mean nothing—"

"No, lemme talk. I just need to say I've made a lot of assumptions." And it was as if God sent lightning to strike my mind at that exact moment because my words came out precisely how I wanted them to. "I've been looking at people all wrong, believing they one way, when really they're not that way at all." I thought about Su-Min and the pain of our friendship. Damien and his aspirations. Talia and her betrayal. Even my former crush on Taj. I looked at Omri and asked, "Does that make sense?"

"Oh yea," Omri chuckled. "I get it. I'm always flying off at the mouth. My dad says I don't think before I talk and he's right. I always move before I even know where I'm going. That's why my uncle wants me to join the army. He think I'll make a good soldier."

"What do you wanna do?"

"I don't know," he sighed. "Guess I'll have to wait and see..." He looked up at the sky. "Guess I'll have to wait on HIM to see."

I nodded knowingly. The silence gave way to the sounds of crickets, frogs and other rustlings from up above. I thought I felt something wiggling beneath my back, but I was too tired to see what it was. My head began to slowly nod and then before I knew it the feeling that everything was right with the world drew me into a heavy sleep.

Like a Lemon

My body was cold and damp when I woke up and something was crawling up my arm. I jumped to my feet and knocked the critter off, hearing a soft thump as it hit the ground. The sky was still dark and I saw the silhouette of someone crawling up the wall of the hole and then sliding back down. It was Omri.

"Get it off!" Su-Min screamed as she hopped around and began slapping her own body. Adrian slowly got up and shook off his arms. Then started to climb the wall right beside Omri.

My legs felt like they were on fire and to my horror when I reached down to feel them, my hand ran across tiny little bumps all over my skin.

"I'm almost there!" Omri yelled from the very top. "I can see a fire! Oh sh—" A hand shot out and pulled Omri up.

It was Josef.

"Jambo!" he yelled.

"What the hell…" Omri stopped to catch his breath. "…you doin' up here?" I heard a mumbled reply and then Omri's head poked over. The sky had gradually turned from black to soft blue. The sun had risen and it was turning day. Omri reached his hand down and waved us up. "Come on y'all. I'll help you up. Hand me that stick."

Adrian grabbed the stick, climbed a bit and threw it to Omri then hopped down and motioned to Su-Min. "You first," he said. "I'll stay down here and make sure y'all get up."

Su-Min climbed with Adrian's and my help from beneath. Once she was most of the way up, Omri held down the stick and she was easily pulled up and out of the hole. Next came me. I wasn't as light as Su-Min, but I was a better climber. My hands grabbed the roots and I easily hoisted myself up. Yesterday my body felt like it wanted to quit, but today it wanted to get home. Producing energy I didn't know I even had, I climbed until Omri's stick came down and I held on as Su and Omri pulled me the rest of the way. Adrian came last, bursting with his own excited energy and before I knew it we were all sitting around a fire with Josef, eating fried plantain, dumplings, and cold orange juice.

"Got any water?" Adrian asked.

Josef handed him a water bottle from a straw sack. My thoughts were a blur. I wondered where the others were and if we were still in the game.

And as I glanced around the campfire, my eyes met with Omri's and I wondered about our moment last night. Feeling my stomach jolt as our eyes connected, I lowered my gaze and kept eating. The questions would soon get their answers. I just needed to be patient and wait.

"Eat until you're full," Josef said. "You won't eat for a while after."

Adrian took thirds and Omri took seconds. Both boys inhaled their food off the paper plates and I queasily looked at another batch of fried bananas and warm biscuit and shook my head. I'd eaten too quickly and now I felt sick.

"Dang, I ain't never had anything that good," Adrian said rubbing his stomach. He sighed and sat back on his elbows.

"Last year," Omri began. "My auntie took me on a cruise to Jamaica and we had a dish like this. Was better there, but it's still good."

"I ain't ever been on no cruise either," Adrian said and stared into the fire. I looked at him as if seeing him for the first time. He looked sad. His small eyes drooped and he wiped his arm across his pointy nose. If his brother had been here I wouldn't be able to tell them apart.

"Are you and Akeem fraternal or identical twins?" I asked. I don't think I ever knew or never took the time to ask.

"Fraternal," Adrian said. His long brown fingers drew lines in the dirt and I thought that was the end of the conversation until he said, "But everybody still can't tell us apart. My mama still call me Akeem sometimes."

I smiled.

"I can tell the difference," Su-Min said. "But only when you talk. Your brother has a lower voice...I think."

Adrian didn't say anything and I figured at that moment he was thinking of Akeem. So, I said, "I'm sure your brother will be okay."

"Oh yea," Adrian said. "He'll be aight." He brushed his hands together. "Akeem don't ever cry when he get hurt. I tell him, he like a brick."

I nodded and thought back to the moment I passed him while running to the beach. The whole thing seemed like a distant memory, even though it had just happened yesterday. I felt a twang of guilt. I didn't even stop to help him or see if he was okay.

"The sprain didn't look too bad," Su-Min said.

"Yea," Adrian replied. "He been through much worse. Broke his ribcage, his arms—" Adrian shook his head and muttered something under his breath.

"How'd he do that?" I asked, interested in this mysterious accidental prone twin. I was pretty sure Akeem must've been into wrestling or some crazy sport I'd never heard of.

"Uh..." Adrian began. He seemed to be thinking hard and then shrugged as if he made up his mind. "He got into it with my pops. Man got a temper like a hornet." He shook his head.

My heart plunged into the ground. And before I could say another word, Omri said, "I hear that."

Adrian looked up and as if encouraged by the support, then continued, "Akeem strong, but got too much heart, too much passion. He always got in my pop's way. And don't nobody get in his way. Especially not my moms."

I was silent. This wasn't my time to talk. I could sense it. There was no unnecessary blurting. There were no rash words to smooth over the conversation. This was a talk that needed to happen. I could see it on Adrian's face.

"Is that how Akeem went to the hospital with two broken arms?" Omri asked. I'd forgotten about that little secret from the mystery brunch phase during the two truths and a lie game.

"Yea, my moms had enough that night," Adrian seemed to go on as if not even hearing Omri. "And when she tried to fight pops—" He pounded one fist against his palm. "Akeem stepped in to make. Him. Stop." His fists were balled tight and he slowly shook his head. "I shoulda done something." He looked down.

And like mud wiped away from my eyes, the view was clear before me. Adrian and Akeem, twins born into a rough home, with no money and no good family, was not fair. I always spoke of how unfair my life had been, with no father, but Adrian and Akeem didn't seem to have anyone on their side. Not even people from school. When was the last time I saw them with anyone other than themselves?

"What are you going to do after graduation?" Su-Min asked. "Leave home?"

"What?" Adrian laughed. "Go to college? I don't got no college money."

"If you win you could," Omri said in a serious tone.

Adrian rolled his eyes. "Yea, if I win."

Just then, Josef stood up and wiped his bare legs. "Okay, let's get going. Your penalty time is up." He pulled out plastic, square packages and threw them at each of us. Inside was a bathing suit. "Put these on and then meet me back here so we can get started." We must've looked stupefied, because he clapped his hands and yelled, "Hurry up!"

And then we were sprinting. Su-Min and I found a well-covered bush where we changed into our bathing suits. They were simple: one-piece and white. How Beholden knew our sizes, I still don't know. But questions weren't asked as we followed Josef through the trees all the way to the shoreline, where we heard voices shouting through the bushes.

"You can't handle, this!" Lashonda yelled and thumping her own bikini-clad chest. "Yea, you stand there looking mad, but you won't do nothing, 'cause you know I'll whip yo' ass!"

"Lashonda, you all talk!" Talia yelled back wearing a similar bathing suit.

Taj was wearing white trunks and stood beside them looking annoyed. Damien sat on a rock in the same attire.

"Yo' face so ugly, lookin' like a cow and a horse had a baby," Lashonda shouted. "Don't nobody wanna be with that fat face—"

"Yo mama," Talia spat.

"—Grill look like an ugly pig snout. Don't know how you keep a boyfriend. Don't nobody wanna sleep with yo—"

"Lashonda!" Taj hit her arm.

"Boy! Don't touch me like you know me," she fumed and clenched her fists like she was 'bout to fight Taj. "I ain't your girlfriend. Them eyes don't hypnotize me. Damn. Yea, I see them walking up, don't you think I know?" She looked at us and rolled her eyes. "They behind anyway. I got this."

"Well," Omri smiled and folded his arms. "It's good to see y'all too. I just love a good catfight."

"Shut the hell up Omri," Talia said cutting her eyes.

"She don't want none of this," Lashonda still glared at Talia. She was rabid, practically foaming at the mouth, possessed with beating her target no matter how long it took.

"Let's move on with the game," Josef said. "Everyone pay attention to the instructions because I'll only give them once and then I'll start with the penalty team once you get started."

"Wait," Damien said. "Why do they get to start with us? Aren't they penalized?"

Oh, how I missed Damien.

"Yes, they have to complete their penalty first, then they can continue in the phase." Damien sighed in relief as Josef continued. He walked toward the water where there were two piles of sacks. In each bag was a puzzle piece and whichever team put the puzzle together first—won. The task seemed simple, except when Josef said we had to do it in the water.

"In the water?" I groaned and let my head drop into my hands like a rock.

"What?" Su-Min asked.

"I can't swim!" I whined.

"Like, stuck in the shallow end, can't swim?" Omri asked.

I nodded.

"Dang, that sucks for y'all," Lashonda said, not looking at all like she cared. "Yo, Josef? Can we begin or what?"

"We can help you," Omri said to me. "We're a team, right?" He looked around our group of four until his marble, dark eyes found mine and my heart seemed to grow bigger.

"You guys do realize we have to also complete the penalty," Su-Min said. She turned to Josef. "Can you explain our thing now?" Josef was talking to the other group in a low voice and then blew a whistle. They had already started.

Josef explained our game to us as quickly as he could. Our task seemed pretty basic. There were styrofoam puzzle pieces hidden in the water. Someone had to run and dive for them, then bring them back and put the entire thing together. Seemed easy enough, but I could feel my muscles tightening in my shoulders as we decided who would do each part. Omri had taken swim classes since he was a baby. Said his mama always thought it was important. Su-Min had also learned a couple of years ago and even Adrian had learned to doggy paddle during the summer whenever he went to the community pool.

I rubbed my neck again, feeling the pain now move to a throbbing ache behind my right eye. I'd never learned. After one incident when I was four, my mama never put me back in swim class and I had a deathly fear of water.

"It's going to be okay," Su-Min said as she grabbed my hand. "You'll be fine."

"Yea, Nora," Omri said. "You stay on the beach and help Adrian put the puzzle together and Su-Min and I will look for the pieces."

I looked at them both with fear in my eyes and nervously smiled, but that didn't decrease the throbbing behind my eye.

The other team was screaming and splashing as they quickly assembled their puzzle. Omri and Su-Min raced down to the water and began bringing back netted bags that held about three puzzle pieces the size of my palm.

This wasn't too hard. Adrian and I quickly began organizing the pieces by color and once we found any edge pieces, I began lining those up in a straight line. Our system worked. I had most of the outside of the puzzle completed by the time Omri brought up the last bag and Su-Min began dumping it. Omri plopped down on the ground for a second, breathing like his lungs were about to collapse, and then jumped up to help Adrian and I complete the puzzle. We finished in little time and as I stood back to admire our handiwork, Josef came over and blew the whistle.

"Good job. Head over to the next phase and get started."

I looked back at our picture. One word was written across it in bold blue letters: ABNORMAL. Swirling red and green fish framed the word and I wondered what it all meant and how it connected with Beholden.

"It's about time y'all showed up," Lashonda yelled as we approached.

"I knew you missed this body," Omri said and slapped his bare chest.

Lashonda walked up to him and shoved him into the water. "Shut up, fool!"

Omri laughed. "Shonda, you better watch out before I sick my señorita on you."

My heart stopped and I looked around in fear. Was Omri going to really talk about that right now?

"Don't nobody like you," Lashonda said rolling her eyes. I sighed in relief when she didn't pick up on the joke. I held my face as the pain in my right eye slowly spread to my left.

"Lashonda, we don't got time to talk to them!" Talia yelled.

"Don't tell me what to do!" Lashonda snapped.

"Will y'all quit fighting and help?" Taj whined.

As my team began laying out the puzzle pieces, I saw the other team had still not gotten their puzzle in place. In fact, their pieces were randomly floating all over the water. And then I noticed something else. The puzzle pieces looked familiar.

"Hey," I said as Su-Min started laying out our pieces.

"We should put them together on the beach first," she was saying.

"Hey!" I said again.

"And then we can take them into the water so Nora doesn't have to swim far."

"Yea," Omri said. "I like that. And the pieces won't go floating everywhere."

"HEY!" I yelled between the two. Frowning, I pinched the bridge of my nose right between my eyes, hoping to assuage the discomfort that had built up like a volcano. "These pieces are the same as the last puzzle."

Su-Min and Omri looked at each other, then back at me.

"You mean you already put this one together?" Su-Min asked.

I nodded. "The pieces are exactly the same, just bigger."

"Yea," Adrian added. "We know where everything goes."

Su-Min squealed. "We're going to win!" She raced around and began shoving foam puzzle pieces in my face. "Let's get started!"

We realized the pieces locked into place once put together. It reminded me of one of those large colorful alphabet foam mats the kids played on in my daycare. The pieces were easy enough to snap together and once the other team saw what we were doing, they changed their tactic. Then we were all on the beach, running and bumping into each other.

"Over here!" Omri yelled. "Nora, that piece goes there!"

My head was pounding and the yelling and running didn't help. Now the sun was baking my skin and I felt sick. There was no time to complain though. Our puzzle was completed and I was dragged into the water. Holding onto the edge of the large mat, I figured all we had to do was let it sit on the water, but Josef insisted we go further out.

My anxiety increased as I sputtered and coughed when water flew into my mouth. My toes bounced on the bottom, but my head still wasn't high enough.

"Close your mouth," Su-Min yelled as she tread water across from me. "Put your arms out like this and just float. Relax your body!"

Didn't she know yelling 'relax' doesn't relax anybody? I wanted to strangle Su, but instead, I concentrated on not getting water in my lungs, even though my body felt like it was sinking. Thankfully, Josef blew the whistle and said we were done. Huffing, I walked out and plopped onto the muddy grass, dripping wet and shivering.

"You alright, Nora?" Omri asked as he playfully punched my shoulder.

"She'll live," Su-Min said with a wet smile. "We did it! We finished first."

I tried to catch my breath and revel in the moment, but my head pounded, holding my emotions captive and it seemed the only way to release the pressure was to appease it. I ran into the trees behind me and ignored the distant calls as I retched into the grass.

My stomach heaved up the fried bananas and something that was probably water mixed with stomach acids. And as disgusting as the act was, it was what my body needed. The tension behind my eye receded and it left me exhausted. I wiped my mouth before leaning on an oversized rock and slumped to the ground.

"I told you she wasn't okay," Omri said as he walked up with Su-Min beside him. "You want me to get you some water?" he asked. And before I could answer he was gone. Su-Min sat down beside me and touched my hand, then took it away.

"You okay?" she asked quietly.

I just moaned and held my head in my hands.

"It's the game, huh," she said. "I know I feel dehydrated and tired. Feels like I haven't pooped in forever."

I laughed, then winced as the pain punched my head. My body couldn't even handle a giggle.

"You know, I remember you used to get them headaches every time we did anything outside," Su-Min said. "My mom would give you a cold towel and you'd be in bed for hours."

"Yea," I said and sighed. "And I can't believe you would wait around to play with me. You know none of my other friends ever did that? Candice even told me she wouldn't be my friend anymore because I always got sick."

"Candice who? Candice Brant?"

"Yea," I said. "Her and T--" I almost said Talia, but stopped myself. Thank God, Su-Min didn't even notice.

"Well, she probably didn't understand."

I picked at the tiny bumps that covered my bare legs and said, "I couldn't control when those migraines came."

I remembered the embarrassing moments when I'd suffer from those unbearable headaches. They always seemed to happen at the most important events. Sleepovers, playdates, school dances or even worse, my birthday.

"I always tried to prevent them," I continued. "but nothing ever worked."

"You couldn't help it," Su-Min said understandingly. I looked up at her.

"Thank you," I said.

She looked at me and shrugged. "It's no big deal." Then her eyes flickered away. "Here comes Omri."

He shoved a cold bottle of water under my nose and I gratefully took it. The wet condensation dripped between my fingers as I gulped the liquid down. It was well needed. My head still throbbed annoyingly behind my eye, but at least most of the pain had lessened.

"We better join the others," Omri said. "Somethings going down."

The other team had completed their phase and now sat out of breath on the shore. Josef was leaning on his large staff and speaking with Adrian. Adrian had his head down and was nodding. I wonder if he told him something about his brother.

"Because you won," Josef announced when we walked up. "Your team must choose one who is safe and one who is terminated."

"Terminated?" Lashonda blurted. "You mean they get to decide which of us is out of the game?"

"That is correct," Josef answered.

"Damn!" Lashonda slapped her thigh. The bottom of her bathing suit was riding up on one side, exposing more of her behind than she intended. "Don't do me like this, Josef," she pleaded. Then looked at our group. "Omri, Nora, Su! Su! You know I love y'all." She paused. "Yea, and, uh, you too uh —" She snapped her fingers.

"Adrian," Damien muttered.

"Adrian!" Lashonda yelled. "Come on y'all. Don't let a sister go out like that."

"Her?" Talia yelled. "Don't save her. Save me! I can help you in the next phase. I know what it is! We'd make a great team, y'all!" Talia looked directly at me with pleading eyes. Her curls frizzed around her round face. "Sonora, we said we'd have each other's back! We said we'd make it to the end together."

Damien muttered something else under his breath and Talia shot him a cold look. "Shut up," she sneered.

"I didn't say nothing." Damien lifted his hands.

"Damien said, Talia didn't have Nora's back last night," Lashonda announced.

"I don't know what you're talking about," Talia said. "Don't listen to her Nora."

"Uh-uh," Lashonda shouted. "You said that Nora wouldn't be in this game without you. You said that Nora was scared of her own shadow and that's why she never told Taj she liked him—"

"Shut up Lashonda!" Talia screeched. "I wasn't even talking to you last night. I was talking to Taj! And that was a private conversation!"

"I don't give a damn who you were talking to," Lashonda rolled her neck as she spoke. "Your ass was so loud everybody could hear. You might as well put up a damn billboard. And look-ee here. You can tell Nora know I ain't lying, 'cuz she mad as hell."

And I was. If anger had a name it would be Sonora Ramirez, because at that moment, my latino fire and ghetto blackness wanted to jump Talia and beat her to the ground. I couldn't believe she talked about me behind my back. And told Taj I liked him. Well, used to like him. Things had changed since Beholden started, but she didn't know that. And she had the nerve to say I was scared of everything?

"I can't believe you," I began taking a step forward. My fists were like rocks at my side, balled and hard as stone.

"Nora, let it go," Omri said warningly from beside me.

"Yea, remember this when you make your decision," Lashonda said gleefully.

"Nora, don't listen to her," Talia said. "I didn't say any of that."

But the truth was out there and it would never be hidden again. Her face told me everything. Taj's face did too. He looked pitifully at the ground without words.

My team huddled further away and began the discussion without me. I couldn't speak. My head was swimming like a hurricane of fiery darts. Darts I wanted to direct right at Talia.

"You good with that decision Nora?" Omri asked.

I blinked and looked down at the ground. They had written names on cards. One said SAFE and had Taj's name on it. The other said TERMINATED and had Talia. I nodded. I didn't care. In fact, I was done playing this game. Embarrassed by my best friend's confession, I didn't need $250,000 to make myself look like an idiot.

I did just fine doing that all on my own.

Omri handed our cards to Josef who read the names aloud. Taj smiled and nodded, Lashonda was just glad she wasn't out of the game. Talia was silent and pinched her lips shut. Josef told her she had to follow him. The air was thick and I thought she would leave peacefully, but I should've known better.

"You know he doesn't like you, right?" She turned around and smiled condescendingly at me. My skin prickled as Talia's smooth voice persevered. "Ain't that right, Taj? You told me so last night."

"Talia, stop," Taj said.

"Well, I don't like him either," I blurted and Taj's face looked shocked. Instinctively I followed with, "I mean, only as a friend."

"That's not what you told me," she shot back.

"Well, things change Talia," I said firmly.

"Things change?" Talia laughed airily. "What about all those messages you wrote him but never sent?" she went on. "And how every day you checked his status, read his posts, tweets—"

"Dang, Nora, you stalked him?" Lashonda asked.

My cheeks burned and I shook my head violently in protest, but there was no denying what was clearly true. I do not have a good poker face. My shame was bare for everyone to see.

"You're speechless," Talia said. "No surprise there from Nora who always thinks, but never speaks up."

"Girl, will you go?" Omri yelled.

Josef took Talia's arm and lead her into the trees and I was painfully aware of the awkward silence that rose amongst us.

"So…" Damien began and cleared his throat. "Is Taj safe till the end of the game—or?"

"I think he's safe for the next phase," Omri said. Damien nodded and I could see the wheels turning in his head. He was already planning his next move.

But the little competitiveness that I had left was gone. Sucked out of me like a milkshake through a straw. I was done. Squeezed like a lemon. I was ready to go home.

"You just have to make it one more day," Su-Min said to me. "We have till tomorrow and then its all over."

"Yea," Omri said as we walked back to our tent. "Don't give up now, Nora. Don't let Talia get to you."

But it was too late. I had been broken within a week. I had been peeled back and every layer torn off. I had been exposed and everybody saw what was truly inside me. And you could call it Talia, you could call it my talks with Omri or my heart to heart with Su-Min, but it wasn't really any of those things.

It was Beholden.

Something Else

The familiar, southern humidity made my skin instantly perspire and the darkness forced my eyes to search frantically for my sleeping bag.

My legs were still freshly slathered with calamine lotion, not to mention the bandaids laid across my ankles and thighs. I'd found new cuts and scratches since the last time I'd looked at them. The eerie squeaks and croaks drew my attention to the crescent white moon that hung like a fingernail in the blue-black sky. Su-Min had removed the rainfly and unzipped a large window in the back. There was no breeze, but at least I could breathe fresh air and look up through the canopy of trees.

Everyone else had gathered around the fire. They offered me food, but I wasn't fond of chili from a can or Josef's homemade cornbread. Omri told me it was delicious and I should eat, but my gurgling stomach did not agree. Instead, I retreated to the tent and intended to sleep my cares away.

But the bugs did not allow that. I heard buzzing and immediately my hands whizzed, chopping through the air. I was in no mood to get bit up.

The flap opened just as I found my sleeping bag.

"I thought you'd be asleep by now," Su-Min said as she carried in a cup with a spoon. She took a bite of the steamy stew and sat down beside me. "We're going to have to make some room." She looked around. "It's supposed to rain tonight and I don't think anyone wants to sleep outside."

I looked at her and lifted my eyebrows curiously.

"Josef told us," she said and slurped another bite. She sat quietly and looked into her cup and then said, "You okay, Nora?"

"Yea," I said throwing my voice a little too high. I was trying to sound convincing, even though I was breaking down inside.

I scratched at a lump growing on my leg beneath the sleeping bag, then had to stop myself before I accidentally opened up a mosquito bite.

"You know, friendships can be complicated," Su-Min said and laughed. "Just like boys."

"Oh, don't I know," I said and sighed. My legs felt tingly like a spider danced lightly across my thighs. I scratched again, wanting the itching to stop.

"You know, nobody believes anything Talia says," Su-Min said. "Don't let it get to you, Nora."

I nodded and jumped when the group around the fire erupt in laughter.

"Guess someone said something funny," Su-Min said. The noise felt good though. I needed something to lift my spirits. I needed to think about someone other than me. I looked up at Su-Min and bit my bottom lip. She'd been there with me from the beginning without even a promise. Her actions had spoken much louder than words. I needed to get something off my chest.

"Su-Min, I'm sorry," I blurted out. "I'm sorry about your sleepover. I'm sorry I stopped being your friend. I'm sorry I've been such an ass." Like a broken dam, the words flew out strong and hard and there was no holding them back. "I tried to make it up to you this year. I pushed for you to be Most Likely to Succeed, even though Damien thought the superlative was redundant."

Su-Min smiled. "Its alright, Nora. I haven't been the nicest to you lately." She took another spoonful of chili and swallowed before speaking. "So, are you going to win this game or what?"

"Me?" I said. "No, to be honest, I don't even care about this game anymore."

"You better not let Lashonda hear you say that," Su-Min said.

But I didn't care. Things had changed since I started this game. And now I was wondering why in the world I was still in it. "I'm no longer about winning the money," I continued. "I started this game because…"

"Your dad," Su-Min said. "You don't wanna see him?"

"Yea…" I said slowly. "And I thought I could be somebody different. You know, prove that I wasn't just the same ol' quiet Sonora."

"But I like that you're quiet," Su-Min said. "And you proved that quiet people can get ahead in the game too. Look how far you made it."

I nodded. "Yea, and look what a fool I made out of myself. I don't know how I even got this far."

"Maybe you were supposed to make it this far for a reason," Su-Min said. "You know money's not everything...I should know." Her words sent my mind a-spinning. I always thought Su-Min had everything I wanted, but did she really? I looked at her, then laid back with my hands behind my head. The stars were fading and the moon was almost covered. I wondered if Abuelita was looking up at the moon tonight. She wouldn't watch Beholden even if I was on it. I wondered what Tony and my mom thought and if they were crowded around our little flat-screen TV or putting the twins to bed. My heart ached inside with nostalgic longing. "Well, all I feel like doing is going home."

"Then go home then!" Lashonda yelled as she threw back the tent flap and stepped inside. "I'm about to win me some money while Nora cries like a baby."

"Lashonda, don't even start," I groaned.

"Girl, you go cry a river and I'mma be spendin' that cash, na mean?" She bounced her shoulders and stuck her arm out like she held a wheel in her hand. "Driving my Bentley. Y'all wish you could touch this."

"Shonda you ain't win the money yet," Su-Min said. "The game's not over."

"But I'm closer to it than the both of you. If there's one thing Talia was right about, Lord may she rest in peace, is that y'all are weak."

I turned over on my side and tried to ignore the sound, like an incessant yapping dog, I had to tune her out. While Lashonda kept mouthing off, I looked up once more into the pepper sky and thought I saw something twinkling before I felt tiny drops hit my head.

"It's raining!" Su-Min cried and shot out of the tent. The boys helped put the rainfly back on, zipped up the windows and just as we all huddled inside, the rain began to fall. The drumming on the roof should have sent me straight to sleep, but my mind was alert. Unlike the pit, I was keenly aware of the rocks beneath my back, the scratching of limbs against the tent walls, and every shadow that moved outside sent me further into my sleeping bag.

I still couldn't believe Talia. I'm pretty sure every secret I'd told her would be out before the week was over. Now everyone in school, no everyone who watched Beholden, knew about my ancient crush on Taj. Including Taj. I looked over in the direction where he laid. His head was turned the other way and his body was still but lifted softly and steadily as he breathed. I was such a fool to think he would even like me, and then questions began to whir through my mind, like why didn't he like me? And what was wrong with me?

And before I even considered answering those questions, my heart reminded me of something else. I didn't even like Taj anymore. If there was one thing Beholden had shown me, it was that. In fact, through this game, I realized I liked someone else.

I turned over and poked my head up to see if I could get a good look at Omri. He laid on his back and stared up at the ceiling, his eyes wide open. I ducked back down and pretended to roll over, hoping he hadn't seen me looking at him. What was my problem? Omri? Talia would've thought I'd gone crazy.

But Talia didn't know me. For so long I had been following and trying to be like someone I wasn't. I liked Omri 'cuz he made me laugh. I liked his craziness, in fact I wish I was more like it. And despite Talia's insistence that Omri was stupid, he wasn't. He was actually really smart. Maybe he just came off that way because no one gave him a chance.

I hadn't given him a chance.

I sighed deeply and thought about our conversation from the night before. Omri was deeper than I thought. And the way he talked about God was really confident like he didn't care what anybody else thought. I liked that.

I looked up at the ceiling too and began to pray. I prayed about Talia, about my friendship with Su-Min, about this game and then I prayed about my dad.

Maybe I needed to treat my dad like Omri. Stop assuming he's one way, and wait to see if he's something else.

My heart began to relax into a slow and steady rhythm and I thanked God that I no longer had a headache. Tired and finally drowsy, I drifted off to sleep, hoping I would be in bed longer than everyone else.

But that didn't happen.

I awoke to a baby crying. At least it sounded like a baby. I sat up, along with Omri and Taj. The air was damp and heavy, like a pair of wet jeans taken too early out of the dryer.

"Nora," Lashonda mumbled. "Quit crying."

"That's not me," I snapped. It was too early for this. Still dark outside, I shoved the sleeping bag off and watched Taj open the flap and squint outside.

"Josef? That you?"

The crying began again. I shivered. What type of creature was that?

"Shut up!" Lashonda yelled. "I'm trying to sleep!"

But the crying continued and got louder. Taj got up and stepped out of the tent. Omri joined him.

"Uh, y'all?" Omri called. "You better come look at this."

We all scrambled out of the tent and my mouth dropped in shock. Furry little goats stood around our campsite chewing grass and bleating like little kids. Lashonda finally crawled out and started yelling.

"What the hell are these?" she asked. "I ain't touching no animal."

"It says we have to lead them to their pens on the other side of the island," Taj said shining a flashlight on a blue card. "And it says we should start now."

"Now?!" Su-Min shrieked.

"But I didn't even have breakfast yet!" Lashonda whined.

"It's still dark out," Damien yawned. "You sure we got to start now?"

But Taj and Omri had already begun pulling their goat into the trees and I grabbed the first one that came to me. It looked friendly enough. With grass still between its teeth. I pulled on the rope that hung around its neck.

"Come on, goat," I urged. "Let's go. Move." But no matter how hard I tugged, it planted its feet and wouldn't budge.

"But how do we know where we're going?" Damien asked as he struggled with his own pet.

No one answered. Finally, after seeing how much it enjoyed the grass, I pulled a fistful and held it out in front of its face. That got the animal moving. I don't know why I wanted to stay in the game, but suddenly the excitement pulled me back in. I figured I should keep fighting until the very end. I followed Taj and Omri into the trees and noticed the blue flags hanging on branches.

"Where's Adrian?" Su-Min asked as she pulled her goat along. She was using the same method, holding the grass out in front of the little goat. The sky had turned pink with the sunrise and I laughed as I thought about that morning.

"I bet Adrian woke up first and started without us," I said. "Good for him."

"Well, if there's anyone I want to win this game," Su-Min said with a grunt as she pulled. "It's him."

I nodded in agreement.

We both dragged our goat along and I could hear Lashonda cursing at her kid behind us. Now that the sun had risen, I could see my goat was brown with a large white patch on its belly. Its name tag said, Eli.

"Come on Eli," I said coaxing the goat gently. "You can do it. A little further."

"I think mine is pooping," Su-Min said and wrinkled her nose. She glanced at it and stopped. "Ew! Its definitely taking a dump right now." She stood a few feet from it and held her nose. I passed her and kept going. I could hear Taj and Omri a few feet ahead of me. Both of them were talking to their goats.

Taj was serious and monotone as he said, "Come on, goat. Giddy yup. Come on, faster." He yanked on its neck and the little creature dug its hooves in. It swung its antlers up and almost caught Taj by the shirt.

Omri, on the other hand, was dancing and singing to his goat. "Come on little goatee, you look like old bologna, your hair is so revolting, I see somehow you're molting." Despite looking ridiculous, his little song worked and the fact that he was holding lots of grass over the animal's head. The goat baa'd and trot merrily along behind Omri as if it lived for his terrible singing.

"Yo, Sonora!" Omri saw me coming. "I got a new girlfriend. Her name is Anna." And then he broke out into another song as he sang to the beast. "Anna Anna, bo-banna, banana-fana, fo-fanna, fee fi, mo-manna, Anna." He swung his hips and I couldn't help laughing. I glanced at Taj who didn't think it was a bit funny.

He let out a frustrated breath and said, "Come on goat! Let's go!"

Eli and I soon passed Taj as his goat sat like a rock. Omri was still ahead of me, but I could hear Su-Min coming from behind.

"Phil and I are coming!" Su-Min yelled from behind. "His bladder is empty and we are on a roll!" And she was running too. Her goat was practically pulling her along. She passed Taj and then passed me. But Omri's song had paid off because Anna seemed like she would follow that boy anywhere. He picked up speed and then the two of them were off.

I could see Adrian standing with his goat in the pen and Josef stood at the gate. Omri made it in next, then Su-Min and me. I expected to see Taj follow, but Damien emerged from the trees after me, panting and out of breath. His glasses were crookedly hanging off his nose and sweat poured down his head. Finally, Taj came out, dragging his goat and last Lashonda. I wanted to giggle. She'd carried the animal all the way and dumped it into the pen.

As she plopped down on the ground and let her braids hang all over her face. She roared, "I hate that damn goat! Stupid thang. Don't listen to nobody."

"Sounds like somebody else I know," Omri said and Lashonda shot him a violent look.

Josef cleared his throat and clapped his hands. "It looks like we have two who will leave us this phase."

The group got real quiet.

"Two?" Damien asked and pushed his glasses up his nose. "I thought it was only one." He looked nervously around.

"Did you not read the card?" Josef asked. I shook my head. I don't think anybody did.

Taj removed his card from the goat's neck and read it aloud. "This is the last phase. There are three rounds. In the first round, you must take your goat to its pen. Warning, there will be two eliminations."

Lashonda shook her head. "I ain't leaving."

"I'm sorry," Josef said. "But you and Damien must follow me."

"Me?!" Damien shot to his feet and pointed at Taj. "But I beat him! He should be eliminated!"

Josef shook his head. "He is safe for this round."

"You've got to be kidding me!" Damien yelled and threw his hands up. "I can't believe this!" He looked at us and shouted. "Why'd you have to vote him as safe? Why couldn't you vote me?" I knew who he was talking to. I could feel his eyes stare like fiery lasers into mine and Su-Min's faces. We had had a connection and he thought that meant something.

"It's just a game, Damien," I said. "No hard feelings."

"Yea, whatever," he muttered as Lashonda and Josef walked away.

"Damien we're still friends!" Su-Min yelled.

But Damien didn't answer.

"Well, he's pissed," Su-Min whispered. "Think he'll talk to us once this is all over?"

I sighed and watched as he stomped over the rocks. "I think he'll get over it."

At least I hoped he did.

We sat down around the crackling fire and Adrian walked over with a plate of food. It was piled with a hamburger, chips, coleslaw and watermelon. My mouth watered at the sight.

"Where'd you get all that food!" Omri asked.

Adrian pointed behind him as he shoved more into his mouth.

We rushed to the tables and each person, starting with Taj, began piling their plates. I noticed there were two tables. I walked up to the other table and peered down at the plates. Each one was labeled. One was a plate of banana leaves piled with what looked like bugs. I read the label. It said fried crickets. Another plate had fried frog legs and another said chocolate flies. I covered my mouth.

"Did you guys see this over here?" I pointed to the table.

"Who would eat that?" Su-Min asked as she started to take a bite of her hot dog.

"Wait!" I shouted taking a step back and looking at both tables. And that's when I saw the two signs. The table with the insects had a large white poster that said EAT. And the table with the hot dogs and hamburgers and fruit had a large sign that said DON'T EAT. I pointed. "Did you see the sign?"

Omri dropped his food onto his plate and stood up. He looked at one sign and then looked at the other. Then took his plate and dumped his food back onto the table that said DON'T EAT.

"Yo, you serious man?" Adrian said.

"If the table say don't eat, I ain't eating," Omri said as he piled his plate with flies and fried frog legs. "And I've had frog legs before. They ain't bad."

I swallowed hard and took a plate from the same table.

"Josef never said we couldn't eat this food," Adrian went on. "So, I'm eating." He kept chewing, but Taj and Su-Min looked uncertainly down at their plates.

"But what if it's poisoned?" Su-Min whispered as Taj started to take a bite.

He shook his head. "They wouldn't do that."

I sat down beside Omri and looked at my frog-leg, chocolate flies and burnt crickets.

"Bon appétit!" Omri said and took a big bite. "Mmmm," he said. "Soooo good. Señora, you've got to try them."

I made a face and put a fly on my tongue, then crunched it around my mouth. The chocolate masked the obvious texture of a bug, but I tried to pretend like they were chocolate covered raisins.

"I can't believe you're eating that," Su-Min said with disgust. "That's so gross." She got up and put her plate back on the table.

"You're not going to eat?" Taj asked as he put some chips in his mouth. "I'm starving." It was probably mid-morning, but it felt like we had been up already half the day.

Su-Min shook her head. "If the table says don't eat, I'm not eating. I'd rather starve." She crossed her arms.

I took a bite of each item on my plate and choked the entire thing down. Then gulped from a water bottle and waited.

It seemed like we had been waiting for a few hours before Josef returned. He walked slowly with his staff and this time lead a cow behind him.

"Oh, Lord," I said. "Don't tell me we gotta push that thing now."

Josef chuckled and then rubbed the side of the creature. "No, my friends, you do not. I have come to inform you that Round two is complete and unfortunately three of you have been eliminated."

My eyes widened.

"Sonora and Omri may stay, but the rest of you must come with me."

"You're kidding," Su-Min said.

"I knew it!" Omri pumped his fist into the air.

"How could I have missed it?" Su-Min shook her head. "I should've seen the sign and—wait a minute! I never ate from the table!"

Josef nodded. "But you also didn't eat from the other table."

"You mean I had to eat that stuff?" Su-Min shivered and thew up her hands. "Fine, I'm out."

Taj put his plate on the ground. "Guess I should've known."

Adrian stuffed his face with a little bit more and muttered something with his mouth full before he stood up.

"Before I return," Josef said as he walked back the way he had come. "Milk Issa for me, will you?" I noticed the bucket he had placed beneath the cow. "And," Josef said. "Expect to see two wild cards. One from your past and one from recent. They will compete in the final round with you."

Finish Line

Josef's words resounded in my head. Wild Cards. I vaguely remembered them from watching the show. Any person could be a Wild Card if they competed in a penalty phase, but the Wild Card was usually very difficult to win. As I worried who the Wild Cards would be, Omri got right to work.

"Now's the time to focus," he said as he quickly got the bucket and placed it beneath the cow. "You can do this, Nora. Don't think about who's coming back." He began pulling on the teats of the cow. "Give me a hand," he called out.

But I was in a daze and my fear paralyzed me. I knew in my gut who was coming back and I couldn't bear to see her again.

"Don't think about it," Omri said again. "Come over and help!"

I moved slowly toward him and sat down. I'd never done this before and neither had Omri. But at least he was persistent. His hands maneuvered up and down, but nothing came out. Even though there was no result, that didn't stop him. Omri's jaw was clenched tight and his brow furrowed in concentration with every pull. His muscles stood out with every jerk and I thought how much I liked the way his thick eyebrows met when he frowned. I didn't realize I was staring until he glanced back at me and grinned. "I don't know what the hell I'm doing," he said. "You wanna try?"

I gave it a go, but my mind was no longer focused on the cow. My eyes floated and connected with his. I shyly looked away. And even though we were both so totally dirty, I wanted more than anything to stay in that moment. I wanted to say so much more, but that didn't happen. My eyes flitted up and saw two figures walking toward us. I knew instantly who the first person was.

"Aw, am I interrupting?" Talia asked with one hand on her hip. She was still in her bathing suit but wore her white slippers.

I stood as Omri cleared his throat and continued to (unsuccessfully) milk the cow. I crossed my arms and frowned, then dropped my hands to my side as I saw the person who stood behind Talia.

Akeem hobbled slowly beside her. His ankle was bandaged and he hopped along gingerly with one crutch. Talia glanced at him and rolled her eyes.

"Don't know how he is a Wild Card."

"I won jus' like you," Akeem said breathlessly. He passed her until he reached us and nodded at me and Omri.

"You alright?" Omri asked as he stood and brushed off his swim trunks.

"Yea, just a sprain," he said. "Ain't nothing. Thought I'd see my brother here though." He looked around.

I shook my head. "He got eliminated."

Akeem nodded.

Talia stood by herself as the three of us recounted what went down since we'd last seen Akeem. He laughed at our story in the pit and I caught Omri staring at me which made me flush with heat.

"We had some fun, hey Nora?" Omri said and hit my arm. "And this is it, folks! Last day!"

The thought reminded me that once this was all over, I had to face reality. Even though we were all going our separate ways once we graduated, we still had to see each other in school on Monday. I glanced over at Talia who sat on the ground and pulled at strings of grass. She actually looked sad.

The orange sun behind her cast a long shadow over her face. And I don't know what came over me. I guess maybe I am overly sensitive. Or maybe I'm naive. Either way, I believe sometimes what folks see as a weakness, can actually be a strength. Because right then, my heart went out to Talia and I imagined how she might've felt. So I walked over, truly wanting to make things right.

"Talia," I began.

She held up her hand. "Don't."

I sat down and bit my lip. I wasn't scared anymore and I wasn't even angry. It was like a cloud of peace settled over me and I knew what I had to do. Didn't matter what anyone else said or who was around, I felt a strong urge to say what was on my heart.

But Talia beat me to it.

"You act like you so innocent and sweet," Talia sneered as she looked up at me. "But I know you Sonora. Ain't nobody that nice. Don't come over here and try to apologize and tell me we can still be friends, 'cuz I've already decided I'm through with you." She yanked a few more strands up. "You know I've always dragged yo ass everywhere…" She shook her head. "Never again."

I swallowed hard and took a deep breath. The tension made my heart race, but my will was like steel and my face refused to turn from the heat. Abuelita's words wove through my mind. I refused to lose myself. And it was like time stood still for just a moment. I noticed everything. The leaves on the trees shook in the gentle breeze. A line of ants marched across the ground by my foot. The white puffs of fuzzy dandelions twirled up in the wind. I understood what mattered and chose my next words very carefully.

"Talia, I'm sorry you felt like you had to carry me," I said. "I never meant for you to do that. I get we've grown apart, but I want you to know I'll always be here for you." I put my hand on her shoulder and was surprised she didn't move. "You're right about one thing." She looked up at me. "I have changed. We both have and that's okay."

I stood up and walked away feeling like a large weight had been removed from my shoulders and when I joined Omri and Akeem, Josef appeared.

He told us to follow him and when Omri asked about the cow, he just shrugged and said he didn't want us sitting idle. I was sort of annoyed by the little trick but understood it did keep us busy until the next phase began. We walked for a while in silence until we reached a part of the island I hadn't seen. There was a flat, grassy meadow that was stretched out wide and far, and at the end stood two flaming torches with a ribbon strung between the two.

"Your next round is simple," Josef said. "A footrace."

We stared at him and then I looked at Akeem.

"You can't be serious," Akeem said. "I can't run!"

Josef brought his whistle to his lips and said, "Get ready."

Quickly we lined up behind the spray-painted line on the ground. The sun broke through the trees and displayed patterns of light across the grass. I was between Talia and Omri. This footrace was going to be easy. And I knew I wasn't the one to win. A smile spread across my face.

"You're clearly the winner here, Omri," I whispered out of the side of my mouth.

"Am I?" he said and winked.

I couldn't tell if he was serious. Talia bounced up and down on her toes and shook out her arms, then squat down in a runners lunge, butt in the air and hands on the ground, lookin' like she'd done this before. I just stood with my arms relaxed at my sides and waited for the whistle. What was the point of even trying? Omri was the fastest runner.

"Get set!" Josef yelled out.

Akeem stood with one crutch and appeared absolutely miserable. The look on his face made my heart sink. I reflected on the conversation with his brother earlier. The thought of him returning home to a dysfunctional home and abusive daddy made me sick. All I had to do was make a stupid phone call, but what he endured was far worse.

"Go!"

Talia shot off down the soft grass, her feet padding as she ran and I followed. I expected to see Omri burst past me at any moment, but instead, I heard huffing from behind and an outcry of, "Mayne, what you doin?!"

I looked back to my delight and saw Omri lifting Akeem upon his shoulders.

"Come on dude," Omri said gasping. "I'm getting you across that finish line."

"Mayne, naw, I don't need your help," Akeem shoved Omri away.

He's crazy, I thought. Why help Akeem? And then I thought, but why not? Wasn't it Su-Min who had said that if anyone were to win it should be the twins? Didn't I already admit I wasn't in it for the money?

So I turned back and lifted Akeem's other arm.

"I don't need y'all's help," he said.

"I know," I replied as we half-walked, half-jogged down that field. I could see Talia's bouncing hair almost make it to the ribbon and I didn't care. After this was all over, I wanted to finish knowing I'd helped someone else. Knowing that I'd made an effort to bring some joy to the twins even if they didn't win the money in the end.

But then the unexpected happened.

Talia fell.

I saw her tumble and not get up. Gaining speed, Omri and I helped Akeem along until we reached Talia where she sat on the ground moaning and holding her ankle.

"Oh my God!" she screamed. "I think I broke it! Damn rocks everywhere!"

I looked at the grassy meadow as we passed her and didn't see any rocks. Her moans turned to sobs as we got further away.

I couldn't believe this was happening. We were actually doing it. Akeem was going to win.

"You got this," Omri said as he let go of Akeem. I did the same and we stopped as he hopped over the finish line and won the game of Beholden.

The midday sun blazed directly overhead. I watched as Josef approached Akeem and shook his hand and handed him an envelope. Omri stood beside me with his arms crossed and shook his head.

"There goes $250,000."

"Yep," I said and looked at him. "You wish you had it?"

He shook his head and said, "Nah. I got something better."

"Oh yea?" I asked. "What's that?"

"A date."

"With who?"

"This girl. You don't know her. We spent the whole week together. Camped in a tent, stayed in a cabin…I even took her to this island and guess what we did?"

I smiled. "What?"

"We star gazed."

"Sounds fun."

"Was the best night of my life."

What Happened After

Home was like warm, lemon tea on a scratchy sore throat—so soothing and satisfying.

After the world's longest shower, I crashed into my twin size bed and slept for too long, straight through the twins' standard pandemonium and Abuelita's incessant check-ups. She said she just wanted to confirm I was still breathing. The smell of cinnamon and fried dough woke me from hibernation early on Monday morning and lured me into the kitchen where Abuelita's floury, wrinkled hands were hard at work pressing, kneading and flattening that dough.

"Mmm. Buñuelos," I said as my mouth watered.

"I thought that would get your lazy bones up," Abuelita said with a smile. The flat pancake-like dough fizzled as she laid it gently in the oil, flipped it with tongs like a professional and landed the warm crispy fritter on a platter where she sprinkled it with cinnamon sugar.

Then it ended up on my plate and in my mouth.

The bubbled crispy texture broke like a crunchy, sweet tortilla and I greedily licked my fingers and ate two more before I said another word.

"I didn't win the game," I sighed.

Abuelita dusted off a few more buñuelos before she said anything. She sat down beside me at the half bar in our apartment and took a bite. "Ah, *mija*," she said and licked her own fingers. "But you did."

I looked at her and she smiled. "I'm proud of you. Because you didn't lose yourself."

My chest burst with warmth, like a field, ignited in flames.

"You made some hard decisions," Abuelita continued. "Decisions that most would've said were stupid. 'If we are out of our mind, as some say, it is for God,' and what you did looked crazy, but it was right." She held my hands and squeezed them. "You and Omri blessed the Madaki boys and I know they'll never forget it." She let my hands go and went back to nibbling on her buñuelo.

"So," she sighed. "what are you going to do about your father?"

The warmth I'd felt froze, cold and hard. I let the buñuelo slide out of my hands. "I've decided to call him…tomorrow," I said and absently drummed my sticky fingers on the kitchen counter. "But first, I wanna go back to school." I wiped my hands on a napkin and stood.

"Well, I think you're making the right decision." She paused. "But this school…I don't understand how they think you can do that game all week and then be back in class the next day. Don't you get some time to rest up?"

I shook my head. "No. We don't get a pass. Plus, I think the teachers are more ready for their vacation than we are…I mean, I guess its not really a vacation —more of a termination." I frowned at the reminder of my school's decision and suddenly felt filled with an urgency to return to the familiar hallways before I could no longer walk them.

She stood next to me and touched my shoulder, "And Nora, I think your choice to talk to your dad will be good. You never know what might happen."

I nodded and tried to bury my emotions. I wanted to say I was afraid. I wanted to say I didn't trust him. I wanted to list the what ifs.

Like what if he was lying? What if he started using again? What if he dragged us into some tragic nightmare filled with worry?

"Nora…" Abuelita said softly and touched my hair. "What's on your mind?" She pulled me into a tight squeeze and I hugged her close and breathed in her sweet vanilla scent. I felt her soft silver hair and pressed my cheek into the curve of her cushiony neck. I didn't even have to say it. My grandmother was like that. She read my face and spoke to my fears.

"We can't judge him, *mija*. God says we must give everyone another chance, just as he's given us." She pulled me away at arm's length and frowned. "And if he turns out to be an ass," she whispered. "We'll let Uncle Dee take care of him. He's got a shotgun somewhere, right?"

I laughed.

"Kidding," she said and let me go.

I quickly got ready for school and thought about what my grandmother had said. I hadn't lost myself and I was proud of that. I don't know how I did it. Thinking back, I definitely felt the subtle change in me, but had Beholden done that? I didn't think the game deserved credit. The change had been happening for some time, way back from my summer in Mexico. It was only now when it finally came to light.

Abuelita offered me a ride to school, but being it was my last week, I actually looked forward to my walk. And as expected, folks wanted to talk to me about how I played the game. Jerome and his little homies kept asking me how I could give up $250,000 and Shanice said she would've jacked Talia up if she'd made it to the end. And you know what I did? I just nodded my head and smiled.

When I walked into Oliver James High the atmosphere was a mixture of excitement and depression. The news that the school was still closing put everyone in a mood. But Beholden's results made the gossip run wild.

"Can you believe Akeem won?"

"Naw, I thought Talia'd get it."

"I heard she moving to Hollywood."

"She good. She good."

"That's not what I heard. Her mama divorced her daddy."

"She finally found out he was cheating?"

"How you know?"

"I got ears, don't I?"

"Well, I heard her mama moving to an island somewhere in the Pacific."

"You don't even know where the Pacific is, fool."

"Yea I do."

"Show me on a map."

And even though Beholden gave our school $250,000 (and another went to the community), they still decided to close it down and use the money toward rebuilding it in another location. Yea, they also added some nonsense about cleaning up our streets by turning our old school into a neighborhood park. I don't know how much cleaning up that would do. But I guess it was better than nothing.

Speaking of money, Akeem and Adrian were at school and they looked good. They must've gone shopping the minute they got home because they showed up to school wearing some fresh outfits. And they weren't strangers. I was uncertain how they'd treat me, but during lunch, I was surprised when they sat down at my table, then Damien joined us, next Su-Min and last came Lashonda.

We chatted about our plans after graduation. Su-Min was going to UAH and Damien planned to take forest and ecology at AAMU. Lashonda couldn't stop herself from calling me weak for giving up that money, 'cuz if it had been her she would've beat all us in a footrace. Then she told us she was headed down to FSU and said she didn't want to see the rest of us ever again. I asked Adrian and Akeem were they were going and they said they didn't know. I had an itching question I'd wanted to ask them and so got up the nerve to do so.

"Hey, I've been wanting to know—how'd y'all figure out the mystery at the brunch so fast?"

"Watchu mean how we solve it?" Adrian said. "Mayne, folks don't think we capable?"

"Yea," Akeem added. "we can't be interested in chemical compounds or microbiology?"

"Damn!" Lashonda laughed. "Y'all don't ever talk to nobody. How we supposed to know?"

"Y'all didn't ever talk to us," Adrian said. "Why we gotta put ourselves out there?"

He had a good point. When was the last time I ever showed interest in them? My mind was usually wrapped up in me or Talia. I glanced around the cafeteria at the thought of her, but I hadn't seen her all day. She'd missed homeroom and I didn't see her in first period.

"Gimme y'alls yearbooks," Damien said. "Before the bell rings."

We switched yearbooks and I began writing a message in Lashonda's.

"And don't write have a good summer, Nora, or I'll slap you," Lashonda said. "I already know my summer gonna be off the chain."

I smiled and started to write something when Taj sat down at the end of our table. He didn't say hi to me in homeroom and when we walked into class together he'd only nodded at me, but avoided eye contact. I'd been a coward. Too scared to talk about what happened in the game. We'd been awkward the whole day and I didn't know if I should or shouldn't try to fix things.

"Ay Taj!" Lashonda yelled. "Come 'ere boy and stop acting like you don't know me!" He sheepishly grinned, picked up his tray and walked over to us.

"Hey Shonda." He looked at me and then everybody else. "Hey everybody."

"Sit down," Lashonda said. "Where your yearbook at? I haven't signed it yet." She grabbed the book from his hands when he extended it and began scribbling like mad. "Where you say you was going to school?"

"Uh, I got into Liberty," he said as he sat down next to her. I was staring at him and his eyes fluttered up at me, then away.

"Liberty's a good school," I said.

"I never heard of it," Lashonda said. "Where's it at?"

"Virginia," Taj said and cleared his throat. After Lashonda got done she handed him back his book and he quickly got up like he wanted to escape, but she grabbed his backpack and demanded he sign hers. She took her book from me and shoved it at him. Mine traveled around the table and then back to me and just as I started to put it away, I heard a commotion at the front of the cafeteria.

Omri walked in wearing his all-white pajamas from Beholden. Everybody was laughing and pointing, but that boy didn't care. He loved the attention. I could tell he lived for it. Shouting hello and slapping hands, he walked over to our table and plopped down beside me.

"Sup Nora."

I smiled, feeling my heart soar into the sky. Where anxiety lay, now sat endearing thrill. Every other care seemed to disappear and it was like the room around me was a blur. But even though my world seemed to stop, it kept going for others.

Shonda told Omri she didn't understand how a fool got so far in the game. And as they went back and forth in jabs, Omri's arm bumped mine and I felt a static touch.

"Where your yearbook, Nora?" Omri asked.

I handed it to him and as he talked and laughed with the group, he began to write something in the back. He glanced up at me as I watched him and said, "No peeking."

I looked away and smiled.

Lashonda squinted at me. "Damn, Nora, you smiling so hard yo' face look like it's 'bout to break."

I covered my mouth with my hand as the table roared in laughter. Dang, Lashonda always had to say exactly what I didn't want.

Omri handed me back my yearbook and got up. "I'm gonna bounce. Check y'all later." He handed me his yearbook and added, "I'll get it back in fifth period."

I nodded and before anyone could say another word, got up myself and dumped my tray, then headed to my locker so I could read in privacy. I said hey to Chloe B. and Theo as I passed by their usual make-out spot, then opened my locker and searched for the page Omri had written on. In tiny, neat print, he'd written a simple question.

Second date Friday night?
-Omri

Butterflies in the stomach couldn't begin to describe the feeling I had. It was more like hummingbirds flitting around the ribcage in my chest. I quickly scribbled in his yearbook.

Si. Let's go stargazing.
~Nora

After our first day back, the rest of the week went by like any other. Seniors had already completed most of their final exams and our week was free with Senior skip day and other nonsensical activities. Receiving our cap and gown was just the cherry on top.

Talia finally showed up and acted like her usual self, except she still didn't talk to me. I mean, she was cordial enough, but I knew things would never be the same. Friday, Su-Min came over and helped me get ready for my date with Omri. We'd hung out more since Beholden. We'd both decided to take some classes at the local community college during the summer together. Plus, Su-Min got a job at a coffee shop downtown.

Things were changing fast. My friends. My love interests. And now my life. I planned to meet my dad for breakfast the next morning and he was coming to my graduation in the afternoon. And I'm not going to lie and say I wasn't scared, because I was. But now, it was like I had more control. Everything was within my grasp. Beholden had shown me that I didn't need to fear what was in front of me. That I needed to look deeper than the surface. I couldn't assume folks were one way, just because everybody put a label on them.

I heard a car door slam outside and Su-Min looked out the window. "It's Omri and oh my gosh, he's wearing his African outfit."

"No, he isn't," I gasped jumping up.

She smiled at me. "Just kidding. He looks good."

And as I went to the window and looked down, I felt solid being exactly who I was. I didn't need to be the Rockefeller Christmas tree. Getting to the end of Beholden had been all me, not anybody else. I might cringe at attention or shy away from crowds or sometimes be overly sensitive, but that's okay. I didn't lose myself in Beholden.

I'd found it.

About the Author

Mia Amalia Snowley was born in Huntsville, Alabama and grew up on southern fried chicken and her abuela's enchiladas. She is a graduate of Life Pacific University and desires to create fiction that displays diverse characters, tells engaging stories and more importantly, tugs on the heart. She currently resides in the Midwest with her husband Ryan and their four children.

Made in the USA
Columbia, SC
15 August 2019